The Trail to Ogallala

**Center Point
Large Print**

In Memory of

Gladys Gilman

2002

**This Large Print Book carries the
Seal of Approval of N.A.V.H.**

ॐ श्री गणेशाय नमः

BENJAMIN CAPPS

The Trail to Ogallala

With a new Introduction by BENJAMIN CAPPS *and
an Afterword by* DON GRAHAM

CENTER POINT PUBLISHING

THORNDIKE, MAINE

To Dr. Mody C. Boatright
In appreciation of the instruction and
encouragement he gave me many years ago

This Center Point Large Print edition
is published in the year 2002 by arrangement with
Golden West Literary Agency.

The text of this Large Print edition is unabridged.
In other aspects, this book may vary from the original
edition. Printed in Thailand. Set in 16-point
Times New Roman type by Bill Coskrey.

ISBN 1-58547-109-7

Library of Congress Cataloging-in-Publication Data

Capps, Benjamin, 1922-
   The trail to Ogallala / Benjamin Capps.-- Center Point Large Print ed.
      p. cm.
   ISBN 1-58547-109-7 (lib. bdg. : alk. paper)
      1. Cattle drives--Fiction. 2. Cowboys--Fiction. 3. Texas--Fiction. 4. Large type books.
   I. Title.

PS3553.A59 T7 2002
813'.54--dc21

2001047768

CONTENTS

INTRODUCTION

L ate one night near the last of December, 1961, I sat at our modest red dining table and began writing in longhand what might turn out to be the introduction to a novel about trailing cattle in the nineteenth century. Since I was doing various other writing chores at the time, the introduction was not finished until two or three weeks later. Vaguely I knew that the writing was not at all suitable for publication, but rather was a guide to myself, a censor to my imagination, a decoy to my muse. It started off about like this:

"Come along with me, ungentle reader of today. We are going on an adventure of epic proportions, driving half-wild cattle up the long trail north through the plains wilderness." Then I proposed that we examine some of these cattle, called "longhorns." We find one on the open prairie with two mounted cowhands in hot pursuit, swinging their lariat ropes. The "critter" has a wound in his flank which needs to be doctored. He breaks one lariat rope while they are trying to subdue him. (A lariat rope with a knot in it is no good for roping anymore.) But they get the heaving, white-eyed beast flat on his side and, with a stick, rake the blow-fly screwworms out of the wound. Then they paint the bare, raw flesh with creosote. They take the rope off the horns first. (A cow rises back end first.) Then loosen the rope on the back legs and run for their saddles. The critter gets up, wheels around, and, seeing nothing to take revenge on, hightails it toward the creek bottoms.

Whereupon I proposed this to the reader: We will have a

crew of ten to sixteen workers to drive these animals north; how many longhorns do you think we should drive? How big a herd? One to each man? Fourteen? Well, we are going to drive three-thousand! Do you think we can do it?

I orated to the reader about the variety of cattle workers who will drive the herd north. Most will be young, but some older. None of them own much in the way of property. Most of them take pride in being the skilled laborers which they are. Most of them have learned that a cowhand sometimes has the choice of laughing or crying, and it's probably better to laugh.

I warned the reader that we might lose some sleep, that we might run into danger, that the long trail in the wilderness demands backbreaking work, that we would not see signs of civilization for weeks at a time.

This grandiose introduction or prologue was never a part of my manuscript, but it served as a guide during planning and research and writing. I wanted to find realistic characters, situations, events, avoid easy romantic elements, yet keep hold on the epic.

Themes in fiction are not absolute truths. Jack London wrote a great story, "To Build a Fire," in which a man foolishly tries to make a day-long journey on foot during an extremely cold Alaskan winter. He demonstrates the frailty of man as he struggles against, and is defeated by, a vast, overwhelming, uncaring, amoral Nature. His dog companion, whose "instinct told it a truer tale than was told to the man," survives. It is a powerful story with a truthful theme. But the theme is only one side of a coin. In my trail-driving novel I wanted to demonstrate the other side of the coin. This intention on the part of the writer makes the story a rather positive or affirmative statement about the human condition.

Some kind critic wrote that no one could have written *Trail to Ogallala* unless he had spent all his life around cattle. Well . . .? I was born and reared in northwest Texas about halfway between the Chisholm Trail and the Western Cattle Trail, but the long trails had been closed probably forty years before I saw daylight. Ranchers, when I was a kid, drove their cattle to loading pens on the Fort Worth and Denver Railroad, or the Wichita Valley, or the Wichita Falls and Southern. Many of the older men must have been on long drives, but it was not especially discussed; it was taken for granted.

I lived on a ranch from about the age of eight to the age of sixteen. Range cows in the 1920s and '30s were mostly Herefords; they were bred up through several generations, using Hereford bulls on the original longhorn stock. Many of the cows were probably one-sixteenth longhorn, and a few were "throwbacks" that seemed to have little if any Hereford blood. Those throwbacks and that sixteenth seem like a symbol of the many strings of the past which always remain in contemporary life, clues to the way things used to be.

Anyway, as a youth I handed a few red-hot branding irons through a plank fence, cold end first, and threw a few bundles of Red-top cane off the wagon to hungry cows in January blizzards, and cut a few ice holes for stock to water; by the age of fourteen or fifteen I had even earned the responsibility of holding the struggling, kicking back legs of a stretched-out bull calf while his manhood was compromised, his hide was burned briefly, his ears were notched, and he got a shot of blackleg vaccine.

However, contrary to the words of the kind critic, it seems doubtful that anyone would learn to write a passable historical novel if he spent more time around cattle than he did in a library. *The Trail Drivers of Texas,* edited by J. Marvin Hunter, along with literally dozens of other volumes, provided much authentic data, as well as ideas for characters and incidents. It was the author's first hope in *The Trail to Ogallala* to echo the real facts, to be authentic, at the same time that he sought the true epic in what men did here in this part of the earth not so long ago.

Benjamin Capps
Grand Prairie, Texas

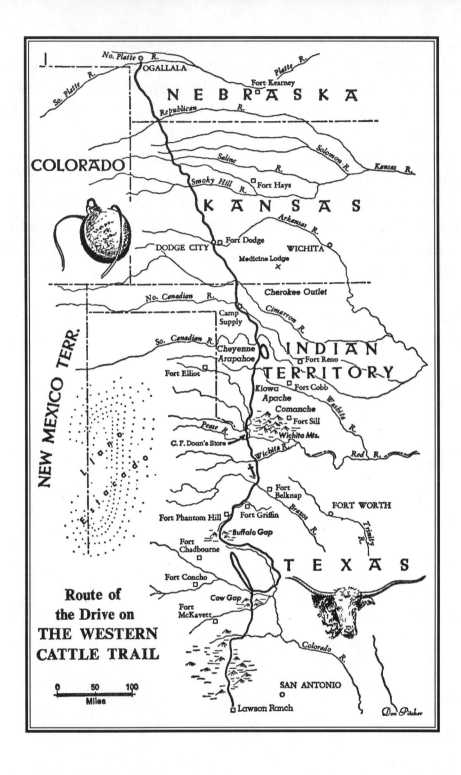

Route of
the Drive on
THE WESTERN
CATTLE TRAIL

0   50   100
Miles

Don Pitcher

Of a Broken Promise

Come along, boys, and listen to my tale;
I'll tell you of my troubles on the old Chisholm Trail.
Come-a ti yi yippi, yippi yea, yippi yea,
Come-a ti yi yippi, yippi yea.

T he three riders were driving the herd of she-stuff, just over three hundred head, up the long gentle rise south of the Lawson headquarters buildings. Billy Scott, on the left flank, could see the dust of the larger herd, which was being held ahead, and now and then a rider circling.

Scott and his two companions were six driving days from the south, from the heart of the brasada, the wilderness of thorns. No more than a week earlier the dead hand of winter had lain across the semiarid wastes. Thickets of thick-leaved prickly pear and finger trees of catclaw had appeared dusty gray and lifeless; mesquite and huisache had stood barren, waiting, interspersed with dark clumps of secretive chaparral; the center stems of the Spanish dagger had tilted or already fallen to decay on the ground. The brasada had waited, a miscellany of harsh plant life characterized by drab color and flinty thorns, for a signal that would turn it from a desert into a low-growing jungle. The signal had been subtly given, light late-winter showers and a few sunny afternoons, and its effect was as yet small but sure. New grass was thrusting up in bright patches

11

through the long, dead grass which lay on its side. Bare mesquite limbs showed the knots of swelling buds. A thicket of hog plums already had covered itself with blossoms, startlingly white. Here in the hilly country near the Lawson ranch, the brush was thinner, but the first magic of the growing season was here. It could be felt more than seen. It was something that might cause a lone rider, especially if he were young, to laugh out loud when there was nothing funny to laugh at.

Billy Scott felt good. It wasn't just fresh air and spring coming; it was that big herd ahead, probably nearly three thousand head by now. He had been waiting a long time for this drive. He was twenty-eight years old and had been punching cows for fifteen, trailing them north for more than ten. But this spring was it. He was making the big jump, from a thirty-a-month trail hand to the highest notch a cowboy can reach: trail boss. He would draw down a hundred a month, but the money itself wasn't as important as what the money meant. He felt like an officer with his first independent command or a new captain with his first ship. It was good, real good, to be twenty-eight and smell the early spring, to face a big, tough job and know for sure that you can handle it. He felt as sure that he could handle it as he was that the horse Blackjack he was riding was the best all-around cowhorse in the world.

He caught the eye of Cory, the slender rider behind the herd of cows, and motioned for him to take the pressure off, let them drift in more slowly. A minute later the slender, dark-complexioned rider had come up beside him.

"Let's take them in real easy, Cory. We don't want to spook the big bunch with these strangers."

As they trailed them in, letting them graze along, the rider who was leading their pack horse, an older man called Shorty, rode around to them. Scott was a few paces ahead of them, and the other two talked in voices louder than necessary.

"Cory, I been thinking about this here drive," Shorty said. "We know the boss, me and you, and I don't figure we'll have to work very hard."

"I wouldn't think so, being good buddies with the boss."

"We probably won't have to stand night guard, do you reckon?"

"Shoot no! being good buddies with the boss like we are, me and you. We won't have to stand no night guard."

"And no falling out early in the morning neither, Cory. We'll just rise up and shine whenever we happen to get ready. We'll catch up on all the sleep we lost during the winter."

"Hell yes! We got it made on this drive, Shorty, me and you."

Scott finally turned and said, "I'm going to work you two lazy bastards harder than anybody else. You can just get ready to ride drag and eat dust clear to Nebraska."

They whooped and crowed like roosters. The two seemed like princes to him; he knew that they weren't actually just kidding him, but reminding him of the position he had earned, glorying in it with him, as freehearted as two children. He had about made up his mind—he would need to look over the outfit Lawson had got together first—but he would probably put Shorty on the left point, which would make him segundo, or straw boss. Cory, who was a top hand but hot-tempered, he would probably put on right point.

He noted with satisfaction that the big herd was being held loosely. The critters looked fairly quiet for a mixed herd, just made up. A chute full at a time was being cut out and hazed into the branding chute. The rich smell of burning hair was in the wind. The freshly road-branded cattle were drifting away on the other side down toward the creek, loose herded.

Scott waved one of the circling herders back, and the bunch of young cows began to melt into the larger herd. From near the pens, a rider on a big black horse came toward them in a long lope, a man so thin that his gray shirt drooped from the points of his shoulders like the wings of a sitting buzzard. Man and big horse moved as a single living creature. As the rider came nearer, Scott saw that it was an old man with a pointed beard and thin face, a stranger. He looked angry.

He pulled up in front of them, near enough to speak in a normal voice, though somewhat shrill. "What are you men doing?"

"Howdy, mister," Scott said. "I'm Scott."

"That means nothing to me, sir. Can't you see you've let your cows mix in with this trail herd?"

Scott studied him a moment and said, "Well, I hope so, mister." From toward the house he could see another rider coming fast, a chubby form that bounced in the saddle. He knew this one. It was the rancher Brown.

He eyed the stiff old man and was glared back at in return, each of them too proud to offer explanation. Scott built a cigarette, waiting, while the old man's eyes burned into him.

Brown yelled and waved, joggling violently as his horse broke from its run into a fast rough trot. He seemed about to lose his saddle at every step. "Hi, Scott boy! Glad to see you." To the old man, the stranger, he said, "Well, there's some more cows for the road brand, Colonel. How many head, Scott? Three hundred?"

"Three hundred and six." He waited for some more explanation.

"Come on up to the house, Scott," Brown said.

"Mr. Brown," the old man said, "please tell Mr. Greer I need to know what's going on around here. I need to know in advance. They might have started a stampede driving a bunch of heifers like that into a big herd."

"Well, that's the last of them, Colonel. I'm sorry if you didn't know they were coming, but that's the last bunch." Whoever the "Colonel" was, Brown was trying to get along with him. "Come on up to the house, Scott." He motioned to Cory and Shorty. "Come on, boys."

The Colonel wheeled his horse and headed back toward the herd. When they had separated some distance from the old man, Scott asked, "Who in the hell is he? This Colonel?"

"Colonel Kittredge. Horace Kittredge. Well, how is everything with you, Scott boy?"

"What's he doing here? Is he a cattle inspector of some kind, or what?"

"I'll let Greer explain, Scott boy." The chubby rancher appeared embarrassed and he asked, to change the subject, "Are many of the cows you brought carrying calves?"

Scott figured he could be patient, if Brown were determined not to explain. "I don't think so. We cut out the ones that showed to be very heavy. Most of these dropped calves in the fall, and some are young stuff—never bred."

They tied their horses at the side of the big house, which had a gallery running around three sides, and drank from a gourd dipper at a washstand. To Cory and Shorty, Brown said, "You boys want to wait out here? Or why don't you go in yonder and tell the cook I said to give you some coffee."

Scott went with him into the front room, where they found the rancher Greer. He arose and shook hands with Scott, then sat back down. Scott began to feel that he was going to have some explanation now or know the reason why. "Where's Mr. Lawson?" he asked abruptly.

Greer propped one fine-tooled boot up across his other leg and frowned. "Scott, Mr. Lawson is dead."

"Dead?"

"He died in his sleep two weeks ago. We buried him a week ago last Sunday. I believe he wrote you; I guess he died the night after the letter was mailed."

It was hard to imagine Lawson dead. "I'm sure sorry to hear it," he said. "He was a grand old man."

"He was the best," Brown said. "He was a grand old man. Have a chair, Scott boy; sit down."

Scott asked, "How's Mrs. Lawson taking it?"

"As well as could be expected, I guess," Greer said. "She's a very impractical woman. That fact, and then the fact that she is grief-stricken, of course, has caused . . . uh . . . some confusion."

"We still want you to go on the drive, Scott boy," Brown said. "We're counting on you. We have big hopes for you in the future."

There was something screwy about it that he hadn't dug out yet. Surely the drive was going and he thought he had already been hired. Then he realized that Brown's embarrassment and Greer's "confusion" had something to do with the angry old man he had met out there beside the herd. "Who is this Colonel? What's his name, Kittredge?"

Greer frowned some more. He was tapping the finger tips of his two hands together, carefully matching them up. "Colonel Kittredge will be in charge of the herd, Scott. He will be trail boss."

"How come? I don't get it. What's the matter with me?"

"Well, the first thing I'd like to say, Scott; we certainly don't think there's anything the matter with you. We have perfect confidence in your ability—that you could handle the job."

"You're the best, Scott boy. We trust you all the way. We know we can count on you."

"Well, you trust me, but you give Kittredge my job."

Greer said, still speaking slowly, "Mrs. Lawson hired Colonel Kittredge, and without our knowledge. We certainly would have honored Lawson's promise to you."

"Did she know about the promise?"

"I don't know, Scott. I honestly don't know. She's a hard woman to talk to right now. I mean, really talk to, you know. One day she leaves everything to me; the next, she hires a trail boss, just because she knew his family back in Georgia."

Scott rose. "Well, looks to me like that's it. If she's running the show, and she's hired someone else, I may as well get lost, pronto."

"Now wait a minute, Scott. She's not running the

show, I am."

"Then what kind of runaround are you giving me? This isn't the only outfit going north this spring. I can get on a dozen places between here and San Antonio. I might even accidentally find one I can boss. Plenty of drovers know I can handle the job besides Lawson."

"Wait a minute, Scott. Sit down. Sit down, please."

"Yes, Scott boy, sit down. Don't get sore."

"I'm not sore," he protested, though he was.

"I think anyone could understand your point of view," Greer said, "but we'd like you to understand ours. In the first place, did I make a promise to you? Did Brown? No. We are caught in circumstances beyond our control, just as you are."

"You were in the drive with Lawson."

"Not this drive. I was to be paid Texas prices for my cattle. I think if you understand our situation you'll be willing to go along with us. I'm actually in charge of the Lawson estate, legally, but we have problems with Mrs. Lawson. You know what she said that Sunday morning before the funeral? That the drive would be canceled; it wouldn't go. She was going to shut this place down and go into mourning for six months. Never realizing that calves have got to be worked, and hands have got to be paid, and a contract has got to be filled in Nebraska for two thousand beeves and a thousand cows. That's what I mean by her being impractical. The value of her property will allow her to move to San Antonio—she has a daughter there—and live in comfort the rest of her life, but only if her interests are handled intelligently. And I swear, Scott, if it's left to her, she'll be dead broke in less than a year. Lawson lost

18

money the last two years. So did I, for that matter. And I have not been paid for my steers out there in the herd. Brown has been paid, but the money will have to go to finance this drive. Now, Mrs. Lawson refuses to understand these matters. She's lost somewhere in the past. Don't get me wrong; she's a fine woman."

"She's the best, Scott boy. She's a fine woman."

"What I don't understand," Scott said, "is what you want with me."

"We want you to go along as a regular hand. The Colonel will organize the outfit as he thinks best, but I'm sure he will recognize your ability. If you will make this drive as a regular hand, Scott, you have our firm promise that you will be in charge of the drive next season. In fact, we'll use you as a foreman the year around if you are willing. Mr. Brown and myself will be associated together in the cattle business, and we can certainly use you as a man who knows stock and one whom we can trust."

Scott was interested, but uncertain. "If Mrs. Lawson can make a decision about a drive this year, how do I know she won't do it next year?"

"Oh, she'll have nothing to say about it. In fact, we have to get all her affairs straightened out in the next month or so. I'll have to go north to meet the herd. Scott, I mean it when I say we are being frank with you. Brown is buying all the Lawson interests, and he and I will be partners. Now, that may sound as if we were taking advantage of the widow. Do you think Lawson trusted me?"

"I'm sure he did."

"All right. Do you believe I would cheat his widow?"

"No, sir."

"Well, I just want you to know we're laying all our cards on the table."

"We've got nothing to hide, Scott boy."

"Now, we need Mrs. Lawson's trust and cooperation right now, I wouldn't offend her for anything. But I want you to see her; she speaks of you very kindly. I want you to see her, and if you believe you should tell her to dismiss Colonel Kittredge and honor the promise to you—go ahead. But don't be too hard on her, Scott. Don't judge her quickly. In fact, I think her present condition is very sad, considering the woman she's been. And I wouldn't want you to get the wrong idea about the Colonel. He has been a top-notch trail boss. In fact, he has been in charge of herds probably as long as you have been trailing. And, as well as I can determine, he has never lost a herd. He knows the work from A to Z."

"He's the best, Scott boy."

"I wonder who he trailed for last year?" Scott asked.

"King, I think."

"Well, I wonder why he isn't taking a herd for King this year, then?"

Greer began tapping together the tips of his fingers again. He had some idea that he seemed not so much reluctant to express as concerned that he express in the right words. "Any number of things may have caused Colonel Kittredge to be uncommitted this spring. I certainly have no doubt that he knows cattle."

Scott was beginning to place the man in question, from rumors he had heard one time or another. "I've heard something about him. He's had trouble with hands quitting. He's known as a very religious man, and strict." He

repeated this hearsay to see whether it would be con-
firmed.

"I can't say about that, Scott. I do have reliable information that he has never lost a herd; I think that fact pretty
well . . . uh . . . indicates that he can handle all the problems."

"He knows cattle, Scott boy. He knows the work from A
to Z."

"Well, Mr. Greer, what's wrong with me just drifting on
and finding another job for now? You're not short on regular trail hands. Then next winter I could contact you, and
if you still had a job for me, I would be interested."

"It's not that simple, Scott. We actually are short on good
trail hands. We need you and the two men you brought
with you. And the plain fact is that Colonel Kittredge is too
old." Greer evidently had placed all his cards on the table
at last. "I know a foreman doesn't need to go around
busting steers and other hard physical work. And you've
seen the Colonel; he appears to be completely capable. But
who knows when he might go, like Lawson did. We can't
afford to lose this herd—for any reason."

Scott shook his head. "I don't like it. Seems to me you're
asking me to take on responsibility without giving me any
authority."

"No, it's just that we will feel much more confident if
you are along, Scott. As I said, we are caught in circumstances beyond our control, but the only thing we expect of
you is that you make a good employee, as you always
have."

"We know we can trust you, Scott boy. We know you'll
get the herd through."

"Well, that's just the thing, Mr. Brown. You needn't count on me to get the herd through unless you put me in charge. I need to think this whole thing over. When does Kittredge plan to leave?"

"He'll throw them out north of the creek tomorrow and start the day after. But I want you to see Mrs. Lawson, Scott, before you make up your mind. If you're sore about the broken promise, you decide yourself whether you should tell her about it. Come to dinner tonight. Don't worry; I have the right to invite you. Brown or myself has been here every day and night since Lawson died. We've had to more or less make ourselves at home here to keep things running. But Mrs. Lawson will be glad to see you."

He actually didn't care about the dinner, would have preferred to go on out to the chuck wagon which was camped beside the creek. But he agreed. He thought he ought to see Mrs. Lawson, and maybe that would be the best way.

Shorty and Cory were sprawled on the gallery. They made some remarks about now nice it was to be good friends with the boss and be allowed to lay around while other poor peons road-branded the cattle.

"What did you find out about that old goat that got smart with us out there?" Shorty asked.

"Yeah," Cory said. "First thing you ought to do, Billy, is go out there and fire that old man. He can't get smart with you, can he?"

Scott laughed wryly. "It's beginning to look like maybe he can. Fellers, if we trail north with this outfit, I think we're all three going to work." They dumped their saddles and gear in the near-empty bunkhouse and staked their horses in some good grass by the creek while Scott told them all about it.

"Hell's fire!" Cory exploded. "If that ain't a raw deal, I never saw one. Say, Billy, why don't you pick a fight with him? Me and Shorty will stand behind you if you want to start something."

Scott and Shorty laughed at the idea.

"I mean it! I ain't kidding! Leastways *I'll* stand behind you—all the way." His hand was on the wooden handle of the .44 revolver at his hip.

"Simmer down," Scott told him. "The old man just took a job that was offered him. That's no reason to pick a fight with him."

"Well, I sure don't see how you can be undercut like that and it not be nobody's fault."

In the late afternoon Scott went back to the house. He had cleaned up, shaved, put on his Sunday shirt. Greer and Brown were there, and Colonel Kittredge and Mrs. Lawson.

The woman, in black, looked frail. Her hair was white, her face colorless, making a contrast with her dark sunken eyes. She spoke slowly, calling Scott "William" and "dear boy." She seemed not to hear any talk except her own. When they sat down to eat, she said, "In the old days, we had very lovely candlesticks, very tall with four candles. The darkies would set the table, but my mother would always place the candlesticks just right. You remember my mother, Colonel. She always placed the candlesticks and lighted the candles." They listened to her when she spoke, and nodded.

"Colonel," she said in her slow voice, "you must teach William all about the Chisholm Trail. He's such a dear boy."

"Well, we'll be going up the Western Trail this time, mam," the Colonel said. He seemed rather stiff but at home in the awkward atmosphere. His gray beard was neatly pointed, making his thin face look still more angular. Though his dark coat, white shirt, and black string tie were wrinkled, he wore them as if he were the best-dressed person present.

"And you must learn all you can about the Chisholm Trail, William. Colonel Kittredge will teach you. He has a brilliant record in the war." She toyed with the food on her plate and ate nothing. Between occasional slow remarks she looked with soft reproach at her guests, and past them, through them at nothing, her dark eyes perhaps searching for misty objects lost in the years.

Scott had not intended asking her anything about the promised job, in spite of Greer's suggestion. He had never felt completely at ease with her, though he did remember her when she was more active and knew what was going on. He had respected her, felt some awe of her, and felt some obligation, at least enough that he thought he should say that he was sorry about Mr. Lawson. But now he could see that it was impossible to say anything to her at all, even any kind of condolence.

He ate in silence and felt a twinge of bitterness at the idea that Kittredge would teach him "all about the Chisholm Trail." But how could he hold it against the poor old woman, who did not even know that the old trail was all but closed by the tick quarantine, that now the myriad thousands of steers were trailed to Dodge instead, and that she herself had a contract far beyond in Nebraska. His bitterness was not lessened by the realization that the Colonel might, in reality, be able to teach him some things about trailing cattle.

Greer asked, "Do you expect any trouble on account of the mixed herd, Colonel?"

"No, sir. I had rather drive a mixed herd after they are trail broken. They do better than steers alone if you don't let them get into bad habits. I don't care about those young Spanish heifers, but we'll settle them down."

Brown chuckled at this, though it wasn't meant to be funny.

"I'm interested in your methods, Colonel," Greer said. "Do you believe in driving as hard as possible the first week or so?"

The Colonel bowed slightly at Mrs. Lawson. "If Mrs. Lawson will forgive me for talking business . . . I believe in three rules to start them: one, get them away from their home range as fast as possible; two, bed them down tired; three, bed them down full of grass and water. That's the ideal. But you must compromise with the terrain. I expect to go north out of here, holding west of the main trail till I hit the Llano. Then I'll follow down it to near Mason; by that time I expect the herd to be easy to manage."

Scott was thinking that if the Colonel was going to teach him ideas such as that, he was several years too late. Even so, in the curt explanation of the Colonel was the ring of a kind of authentic understanding that goes with long competence.

Finally, they began to push their chairs back, and Mrs.

Lawson rose. Scott was ready to get away from them. He made some brief excuses. Then Mrs. Lawson came toward him with her hand outstretched. He took it to shake hands, and she, not quickly but unexpectedly, kissed him on the cheek. Then she turned away, and he got out. He had already been conscious of his relative youth, and she had kissed him as if he were a young boy. He thought: Damn her, she wouldn't take such a liberty with one of the other three men.

Greer caught him on the front veranda. "You didn't ask her about the job."

"No, I didn't mean to."

"Well, have you made up your mind? You can see our problems. And we need you, Scott. We'll take it as a favor if you'll go. I don't want to rush you, but . . ."

"I'll let you know first thing in the morning."

Cory and Shorty weren't at the bunkhouse. He knew they were probably still out sitting around a fire at the chuck wagon, shooting the bull. He selected a bunk that had no gear around it, undressed, and lay staring up into the blackness. The facts upon which he had to make a decision ran through his mind, but, as is often the case when a man is undecided, he seethed with a clash of forces, not facts, but nebulous shapers of facts to their own illogical ends.

A drive was going north and it had the same lure that it had always had. The same pull that had drawn him as a green kid drew him still. The desire was burning now in the breasts of a thousand young men, kids, who thought if they could just go up the trail it would be the most glorious adventure possible in life. Their attitudes were based on romantic ignorance, as his had been many thousands of miles of cattle trailing ago. But strangely, when the ignorance was exchanged for hard experience, something of the romance remained. He had heard them, various ones, when the going was rough, say, "I swear to God I'll never do it again. I'll take up farming. Hell, I'd rather be a sheepherder." But when winter had softened their memories, when spring came around again, they would sign up for another drive. And now the herd was out there, restless under a heavy guard, some cows refusing to lie down, bawling mournfully for newly weaned calves. And the trail was out there, nine hundred long country miles, a thousand hills and countless unnamed creeks, mighty rivers, the great plains.

And a stronger force than the romantic call of the trail was influencing Billy Scott's decision, a kind of stubborn determination. He had that which in a horse is called "bottom," which will cause the horse, after carrying a rider for a hard day's work, to go ahead and do his best at whatever is required of him. He had the quality that Shorty had, too. Shorty had been a bronc rider too long and had got his insides all shaken up, but would still climb on board a bronc he didn't have to ride, especially if someone insinuated he was too old, would rake him from neck to flank, and would allow himself to be thrown before he would claw leather. But Scott's stubbornness went further. He thought he had found the secret of trailing cattle; it required in a man hardihood, endurance, infinite patience, and confidence that a man is smarter than a cow. With strength and physical skill you could throw a big steer, tie him, and prevent him from doing what he wanted to do;

but with physical strengths and skills alone you could never make him walk the long hundreds of miles where you wanted him to go. There was no grand final action a man could take; if he had responsibility, he must have endurance and patience and knowledge. He could not bluff. The trail was too long, too full of possibilities for error. If the Colonel believed he had a pupil to teach, he would know better in the months ahead. If the Colonel were himself bluffing, he would find it necessary to show his cards to everyone who had a right to see.

Scott was half asleep when he heard the voices of Shorty and Cory. They were at the bunkhouse door, fumbling with a lantern. He heard the scraping noise as the globe of the lantern was levered up. Shorty asked, "You got a match?"

"Yeah. My ass and yore face." Cory thought it was very funny.

"Shut up, and give me that match. You're going to wake somebody up." They came toward him, holding the lantern up, peering. "Is that you, Billy?"

"Yeah. What kind of an outfit they got out there?"

"Pretty good, I guess," Shorty said. "Old man Ostler is going to cook."

"And say, Billy, old Blackie is out there. Remember old big Blackie? Looks like he's going to be segundo. Ain't that something?"

"Yeah, that's something, if it's so. With him segundo we won't ever get as far as Indian Territory."

"You decided to go along, then?"

"Yeah, I'm going," he said.

One Good Horse

*On a ten-dollar hoss and a forty-dollar saddle
I'm going up the trail with them longhorn cattle.
Come-a ti yi yippi, yippi yea, yippi yea,
Come-a ti yi yippi, yippi yea.*

The next morning Scott caught Greer before sunrise and told him his decision. "We'll go, Mr. Greer. But, like I said last night, don't count on me to do anything but make a hand. I'll take orders and do my best."

"That's all right, Scott. We appreciate it."

Brown came out onto the gallery where they stood in the cool morning air, stretching and yawning. He had no shirt on and his belly bulged under his long underwear. "We appreciate it, Scott boy. You're the best. We know we can count on you."

A rider had come from toward the chuck wagon on the creek. He dismounted and tied at the rail in front of the house, moving deliberately. Greer called to him, "Can I do something for you?"

The lanky cowpuncher appeared defiant. A big chew of tobacco bulged his jaw. He came halfway toward them, stopped, spat on the hard bare ground of the front yard, and said, "I come after my time."

"What's the trouble?"

"Ain't no trouble. I just made up my mind not to go."

Greer frowned. He seemed reluctant to press the man

and yet unwilling to accept such abrupt action. He smiled suavely and spoke with condescension. "Well, that's your privilege. Of course, most men would think they owed some kind of explanation, quitting at the last minute."

The cowboy folded his arms, spat again, finally said, "I've rode for that Colonel before, and he ain't changed none."

Neither of them spoke for a minute; then Greer said, "That's a Lawson horse."

"Yep."

"You go into town or somewhere and get some transportation, and when you bring the horse back, I'll have your time figured."

The man left without another word. "I don't think he's much of a hand anyway," Greer said. "His attitude certainly leaves something to be desired."

"Not much of a hand," Brown agreed, scratching himself luxuriously on both sides at once. "Afraid of a little work."

Scott suspected that they were criticizing the man for his, Scott's, benefit, trying to reassure him, but he didn't need it. His only concern now was to make some arrangements for the four horses he had brought from the south. They belonged to him personally.

"Whatever you say," Greer told him. "We'll take care of them for you, or we'll pay you fair prices for them, whatever you want to do."

"I wouldn't want to sell Blackjack."

"I'll take them up to my place," Brown offered. "You put them in the corral, Scott boy. I've got to go up to my place today and I'll take them. I'll watch them and they'll be fat as butter in the fall."

They wanted him to eat breakfast with them, but he refused. "I better just get on out yonder where I belong," he said.

Scott, Shorty, and Cory joined the outfit that morning. Several regular hands of the Lawson spread were working with those signed on for the trail; even so all of them kept busy. Besides the work of burning on the road brand, an I-D Connected on the left hip, the two bunches, branded and unbranded, had to be held under control. Since they had been in the area a week, some of them, the sparse new grass had been cropped over two or three times, and they had to be allowed plenty of room for grazing. The branded bunch lay strung out two miles up the creek. Then, too, holding them was work because of the fact that many of the wild critters considered their being a part of a big herd merely a temporary accident, which they were willing and eager to remedy.

The hands were tired and sore. It was the first hard riding of the year for most of them, but, worse, they had stayed up more than necessary the last few nights telling long lies about drives in years past. Amid this bunch of weary but good-natured men, one man stood out, colorful, flamboyant—big Blackie Blackburn.

Blackie was tall and heavy and appeared clumsy. His black hair stuck down out of the front of his hat, almost meeting with his heavy eyebrows. His cheeks were apple red and his voice was loud. Kittredge was busy elsewhere much of the day, and Blackie rode around yelling, "Give 'em hell!" without meaning anything by it. He was like a big overgrown boy in school, overbearing, dominating the games of his smaller schoolmates. But most of them appreciated the show he put on.

Blackie loved to give a hoolihan exhibition. When a big steer with independent ideas broke from the herd, the big man would pound after it, yelling at the top of his lungs. He would come directly in behind the steer, lean over and grab its tail, dally it around the saddle horn, then spur his horse to lurch ahead and send the steer clattering head over heels. The steer would rise, dazed, shaking his head, and trot back meekly to the herd.

They talked about it even though most of them had seen it before or done it themselves. "Learn him some manners, Blackie!" "That Blackie is strong as a bull." "Ain't he though?" And someone added, "Dumb as a bull, too." They laughed at the big man as much as with him, but it was clear that he had gained the job of segundo, at least for the time being.

Scott, determined not to show any jealousy, said nothing against the big man, though he noted a fact that he would have taken action about had he been the boss. When Blackie tailed down a steer, for one second there under the weight and the strain his pony's legs would almost buckle. His horses were putting in a hard day's work in an hour's time. Scott said nothing, but the matter did not go unnoticed. Someone else asked, "How fur up the trail do you reckon his string of horses will last?"

The remuda for the drive was made up of eighty-five horses, but these varied greatly in value. Twenty of them were big geldings of thoroughbred breeding on Spanish stock, well shod; most of these were solid colors, black or bay or sorrel, some with a white blaze in the forehead or white stocking feet. The other sixty-five of the band were mustangs, unshod, half broke, of all colors, dun or buckskin, blue and red roan, grullo, palomino, paint or pinto, gray, white, brown. Some of the mustangs were beautiful ponies with flying manes; others were flea-bitten nags with necks like goats. Many a good, tough cowhorse was among them, but they were generally untrained and untried. Some of them had seen as few as three saddles.

Of the horses with thoroughbred blood Kittredge had chosen seven for himself. The thirteen others were apportioned one to a man for use as night horses. Each trail hand's string of six horses was filled out with mustangs, and the choices of these had already been made when Scott, Shorty, and Cory joined the outfit.

Scott was assigned to the loose holding of the branded herd, and he determined to use the day to find out as much about his string of horses as he could. One listless gray he estimated without putting a rope on him; the big bay which was his night horse he saved to try out at night. One coyote dun was so skittish that he was difficult to catch in the trees near the creek, and he let him go rather than disturb the remuda too much. Each of the three he rode that day pitched. The grullo unseated him; he got up and dusted his pants to the accompaniment of laughter from the two riders with the horse band.

Blackie, who had just ridden up, yelled, "You want me to cool that bronc down for you, cowboy?"

Scott grinned and said nothing, climbed back on the horse, and stuck. He believed the grullo would make a good mount but would probably pitch every time he was ridden.

Branding was completed in the middle of the afternoon, and the three thousand head of cattle were thrown across the creek, where they were allowed to drift among the low hills until sundown. Then they were brought together a quarter of a mile above the chuck wagon and bedded down. Some of them milled about, bawling restlessly, until after dark. The first guard was posted of Lawson hands who were to stay behind, for Colonel Kittredge wanted to talk to the trail outfit all together on this last night.

Greer and Brown came with the Colonel and chatted good-naturedly with the men as they squatted about the cook's fire. When the Colonel rose to speak, Ostler was scraping at an iron pot.

"Mr. Ostler, stop that noise," he said abruptly, "and give me your attention, please."

Everyone stared at the Colonel, surprised at the sudden sharpness of his voice. The chatter stopped; for a minute a hush fell on them, and they could hear a grunt and a bawl away up at the herd and a cowboy singing slowly in time to the walking of his horse and, down on the creek, the preaching of small frogs. The Colonel stood in the edge of the firelight, his slight body erect. He paused for an almost painful length of time before he went on.

"Men, I did not hire you, and I think it necessary that we have complete understanding before we set out north. The success of this drive is of utmost importance to the owners of these cattle and to myself as foreman. I expect every man of you to accept it as important and serious. We're going to take this herd through, every last one of them, and they're going to be fat when we get there." His voice was not so loud and sharp as it had been when he spoke to

Ostler, but it tended to be high-pitched and there was no kind of apology in it.

"The work is hard, especially the first week or two. Replacing trail hands on the road is difficult. If any man rides north with me tomorrow and then quits before we get to Ogallala, Nebraska, he not only forfeits any pay, but I personally promise you that he will never trail another cow, if I can help it, as long as he lives.

"Every man is expected to do the job he is assigned without complaint. If I tell you to swim a river, I expect you to get in there and try. Every man will wear a side gun at all times when he is away from the wagon. But no gun will be fired near the herd, or at any time for any reason except in emergency or under orders."

The Colonel paused at times as if to let his words sink in. The men waited without a sound.

"There will be no liquor in camp. Mr. Ostler, I expect to hold you responsible to see that there is no liquor of any kind carried in the wagon."

"You mean you aim for me to search the bedrolls every morning before I load them?" Ostler was inclined to be grumpy and it showed in his voice.

"I mean I intend for you to follow my orders to the best of your knowledge. If there's any bedroll searching, I'll take care of it.

"No man will be excused from any hard duty because he is too old or too young." Here the Colonel's eyes were on the boy they called Kid, who was not over sixteen years old. He had applied for a job with the outfit twice from Lawson and once from Greer, had been turned down because it was obvious to anyone except himself that he was too young, and now, by some miracle, he had been hired at the last minute to take the place of the hand who had quit that morning. The boy watched the Colonel with his mouth open, hanging on every word as if he would memorize it all.

"No gambling of any kind will be tolerated in camp. If you have cards, get rid of them.

"The cook will have grub ready on time so that the work will not be held up. He will leave hot coffee ready for every man when he goes on guard.

"I will read a passage from the Holy Bible every morning before breakfast when it's convenient to do so. I expect every man to go about his business when I am reading but to be quiet and pay reverent attention.

"Are there any questions?"

The men shifted about, making themselves more comfortable and glancing at one another. Finally the one called Dandy asked, "We going to get to go into Dodge or any place like that?"

The Colonel's face could not be seen clearly, but he was frowning. "You will probably be allowed to go into Dodge if it doesn't interfere with the work. We're not making the drive for a good time."

"Can we draw some of our wages at Dodge?"

"Within reason," the Colonel said abruptly.

No more questions seemed to be forthcoming, so the Colonel read from a paper the guard assignments and the assignments about the herd. Their own names sounded strange to them. Instead of Blackie and Johnny and Shorty and Billy and Dandy and Professor and Baldy and Kid their names were Charles Blackburn and Juan Martinez and Henry Snow and William Scott and Alexander Rice and Robert Woodberry and George Neil and Paul Henry Rogers. Each of them heard his own name with a little start of recognition. From the Colonel's lips it was like a roster of casualties of some battle fought long ago.

It seemed to Scott as if some chance fate were conspiring against himself and his two friends; after having last choice at the horses, they were assigned to the third guard from one to three-thirty in the morning, and in the daytime they were assigned to the drag. He was sure that it was purely a matter of luck, for the Colonel didn't seem to know any of the men well, and Scott was determined not to complain. He figured there would be some changes in the months ahead anyway; even if it only amounted to a rotation of assignments. It was nice to get the drag duty over before hot weather.

As for the Colonel's speech, Scott found it hard to quarrel with it, but thought more than anything else that it was unnecessary. The rules against gambling and liquor were not a bad idea; they could cause trouble, especially liquor. He would have tried to be equally strict himself without sounding so hard to get along with. The agreement that the hands might be allowed to go into Dodge was probably a compromise on the Colonel's part. Scott would have bet money that the old man was against any visit to the sinful city. As for the business about reading the Bible, he couldn't make it out.

When Kittredge was finished, he asked Greer if he had anything to say. Greer spoke briefly in a friendly voice, as if to soften any antagonism the Colonel might have roused.

37

"Boys, if you'll bring this herd through with enough cows to meet the contract and put some weight on these big skinny steers, there'll be a bonus in it for every one of you at the end of the trail. That's all I have to say. Good luck to you. And I'll see you in Nebraska."

Colonel Kittredge rode back to the Lawson house with Greer and Brown, leaving the fourteen men about the fire. Ostler went back to scraping loudly at the iron pot, mumbling under his breath, and the rest of them made observations about the Colonel. Some of them didn't like the rules, but no one talked of quitting.

Baldy Neil paraded out to the edge of the firelight about where Kittredge had stood and addressed them in a shrill, exaggerated parody. "Men! I don't want no drinking in this outfit! Maybe a little water, but that's all. And don't think no wicked thoughts. I won't stand for it. I don't aim to put up with it."

He was rared back on his heels, standing stiffly with his rounding shoulders pushed back. They laughed and encouraged him. Big Blackie laughed at first. Then suddenly, as if he had just realized that it amounted to an insult to the Colonel, he said, "What's so funny about that? You better stop making fun of Colonel Kittredge! Before this drive's over he's liable to crack down on you."

"And before this drive is over he's liable to crack down on you, too," Baldy said. "Because you're too hard on your horses."

"And before this drive is over, I think I'm liable to punch you in the nose," Blackie said.

Baldy laughed it off. It was too obvious that if Blackie decided to punch him in the nose, he would be able to do it and make an effective job of it.

That night, in the small hours past midnight, Scott rode the big bay gelding. The horse accepted the bit readily and stood still while he was saddled. He was gentle enough. But when Scott was on top of him he seemed sluggish. "I'll see you up at the herd in a minute," Scott told Shorty.

He headed west across a clearing, not wanting to make any disturbance in the vicinity of the sleeping cattle, and lined out the long-legged bay. It took some urging with the quirt. A deep honking noise came from the chest of the horse each time his front feet pounded the turf. When Scott let him slow to a trot, the horse was wheezing. He was wind-broken. Scott laughed at himself as he walked the horse up toward the herd. His luck was holding steady, such as it was.

He had one more in his string that was worth giving a fair trial, the coyote dun that he had had trouble catching the day before. The dun had seemed skittish, which didn't necessarily mean anything. He might be gentle enough under the saddle for a night horse, or proper treatment might make him gentle enough.

The herd was restless. Here and there one of the steers would rise, stretch himself, bawl; then perhaps lie back down on the other side or wander among the scattered animal bodies to the edge of the herd and try to head back to his home range. Scott, Cory, and Shorty kept on their toes, circling, singing, turning back sleepwalkers, and checking on the band of horses, many of which were hobbled.

The next morning in the dim cool light an hour before sunrise they were awakened by Ostler's pounding with an iron spoon against a Dutch oven which hung below the rear of the wagon box. They fell out, stretching, building cigarettes, pulling on boots, jibing good-naturedly at one another. Then one or two of them suddenly became quiet, looking toward the chuck wagon, and the rest followed their eyes, and all of them became quiet.

Kittredge stood beside the wagon, as stiff as he had been the night before, in his hand a book bound in soft brown leather. The book seemed to fall open of itself in his spread hand, and he read in a rather harsh voice without much expression:

"Behold, happy is the man whom God correcteth: therefore despise not thou the chastening of the Almighty:

"For he maketh sore, and bindeth up: he woundeth, and his hands make whole.

"He shall deliver thee in six troubles: yea, in seven there shall no evil touch thee.

"In famine he shall redeem thee from death: and in war from the power of the sword.

"Thou shalt be hid from the scourge of the tongue; neither shalt thou be afraid of destruction when it cometh.

"At destruction and famine thou shalt laugh: neither shalt thou be afraid of the beasts of the earth.

"For thou shalt be in league with the stones of the field: and the beasts of the field shall be at peace with thee."

The old man looked at them out of his slitted eyes when

he had finished reading, and they hurriedly went back to dressing or rolling their beds, as if they had been caught watching something that was none of their business. They were not religious men, but they were cowed by it. It was just a jumble of words to most of them, yet it left them in a mood of quiet until they were half through breakfast. Two of them gave thought to the words that had been read, Scott and Professor. Professor mused over the words "thou shalt be in league with the stones of the field. . . ." Scott wondered about the whole matter of the reading, whether Kittredge considered himself obliged to give religious instruction or whether he read for some ulterior motive. ". . . despise not thou the chastening of the Almighty!" Did the old man think he was preparing them for a rough trip?

They drove part of the remuda into a rope corral by the wagon, and confusion reigned while they caught the morning's mounts, caused mostly by Blackie's loud voice and wildly flung rope. Scott finally caught out the nervous coyote dun. The horse didn't want to be saddled and he didn't want to be ridden, but he wouldn't pitch it out. All he would do was shy sideways and jerk his head in the air; he was a stargazer. Scott thought that the Almighty was chastening him pretty thoroughly in the matter of horses.

As the sun came up they were stringing them out north. Blackie was on the left point and the Mexican Juan Martinez on the right. The herd milled and was squeezed out into the line. By the time Scott and the other drag riders had started the last of them moving, the leaders had disappeared over the hill.

Five men rode the drag, and the work kept them busy. They couldn't keep a knot of cattle from forming at the rear, because the drag consisted not only of the lazier and weaker stock, but of the stubborn ones, the ones that fully intended to go but just didn't intend to go north. The flank riders would squeeze them out into a line, only to have them break away in bunches of a dozen at a time, which the drag riders would have to chase. Some of the heifers would run wildly from the riders, ducking their heads and crowding in among the moving herd as if for safety, then would stop, perhaps turning sideways like a boulder in a stream of water. They unlimbered quirts and the knotted ends of lariat ropes to urge the cattle along and keep out the gaps. Kittredge was letting the leaders set a fast pace.

Scott found that the dun would respond to rein pressure on his neck, but he wouldn't chase a cow and bring her back. The horse wasn't looking at the cows; he was looking at the sky and expecting a booger behind every bush or perhaps expecting to be pounded in the ears with the loaded end of a quirt.

Scott couldn't keep from thinking about Blackjack, back there enjoying an easy spring and summer at Brown's place. Brown had said he would take the four horses to his place yesterday. Here he was with the sorriest string of horses he had ever tried to trail cattle with, and the best cow horse in the world was kicking up his heels and grazing, staying at home. And there were the rivers ahead. Any one of them could be up and dangerous. What if the Red was out of its banks, as he had seen it? What if the cold Arkansas was up with those heavy logs driving along in the current? A man would be a fool to go in a river like that on a bronc.

As the morning wore on, in the midst of the noise and

work, his mind returned and returned to his big black saddle horse. He thought of the nights ahead, the stormy nights. And this herd was going to run; he could feel it already. Sooner or later they would run, probably sooner. They could have trouble with Indians; they could have trouble with rustlers. He could imagine a hundred predicaments where it would make all the difference to have a good horse under you.

He didn't spell it out to himself but he had a deep confidence that, regardless of what his reputation was with the outfit to begin with, by the end of the trail he could be Kittredge's most valuable hand. He believed that the job before them was that hard. Kittredge would come to know it, if he had any sense. But a man had to have one good horse; any other handicap he could accept, but not to have one good mount was unfair. As he sweated at the work, the miles they made north were not progress, but more distance from Blackjack.

It was the middle of the morning and Ostler was driving the chuck wagon past the drag a quarter of a mile to the side. Scott saw the Colonel ride to meet the wagon, sitting proud and straight on one of his seven picked horses. This sight triggered something inside him, the sight of the Colonel's erect seat on a good horse. Dammit! he had a good horse himself, a better damn cow horse than anything in the remuda, including the seven that the old man had picked first by his right as trail boss; and he had a right to a decent mount as much as any high-and-mighty Colonel. He yelled at Shorty, "I'll see you later," and headed out to intercept Kittredge.

The Colonel saw him and pulled up, eying him without

expression, while the heavy wagon went ahead. Scott felt determined and he didn't see any easy way to work up to what he had to say. "Mr. Kittredge, I've got a good saddle horse back at Brown's place. He belongs to me personally. I'm going back to get him."

Kittredge didn't change expressions. He looked down from the height of his big horse and spoke in a dry slow voice. "Young man, you don't have to call me 'Colonel' if you don't want to. I earned the title the hard way, and most southern people call me 'Colonel' out of respect. But you do have to obey me. My trail hands don't just ride up and tell me what they're going to do."

Scott didn't want to argue the point. He could see that he had approached the old man wrong, but he meant to have Blackjack.

"My trail hands don't just ride up and tell me they are going to leave their positions and go off somewhere. You are about twelve hours late to tell me anything, young man. I thought we had this matter settled when I spoke to you all last night."

Scott was afraid it was going to come to a matter of having his way or quitting; he didn't want it to come to that, but he meant to press it. He would bring Greer into it if he had to—they were not more than eight miles from Lawson's place now. He said, "Mr. Kittredge, I've got an old flea-bitten nag that's too old, and I've got four broncs, and I've got a big bay that's wind-broke. I think maybe the remuda is all right, but I didn't get any choice at all, and I've got to have one good horse. All I want to do is go back and get one good horse."

"Young man, I thought I said last night I don't want complaints, and here we're not ten miles up the road, and you're already complaining. What's the matter with broncs? Are you too good to ride a bronc? What makes you think you're any better than any of the other hands?"

These questions raised a flush of bitterness in Scott. He was thinking: Damn you, old man, you've got my string of horses yourself; they're mine by promise and by right.

He wasn't going to say anything about the broken promise—he was too proud—but he couldn't keep it out of his feelings. Actually, the Colonel's choice string had nothing to do with it. If the old man were going to be boss, he had a need and a right for the best horses. But any hand had a right to one good horse. He said in a tone of voice as reasonable as he could muster, "I don't mind the broncs, Mr. Kittredge. I'll ride my share. But I haven't got time to train a horse and get my other work done. I think you meant every man to have a good horse, and mine's wind-broke. If you don't believe me, you can check him. I've got to have one good horse to ride at night when the herd might run, and to swim with."

The Colonel pursed his lips and said with disdain, as if he were having trouble explaining something simple, "I don't believe you understand the issue. You tell me you're going to do this and that, for certain reasons that may or may not be good. I'm the one who decides what is done, and I don't mean to deal with you on any other basis."

Scott knew that he had approached the old man wrong. He had already accepted that Kittredge was the boss, and if the old man was so jealous of his authority, let him have his way. If the old man said "no," then he would see; he wasn't going up the trail without one good horse. "Well,

I'm sorry, Mr. Kittredge," he said. "I guess I was just disappointed about my horses. I would like your permission to go back after my horse at Brown's place."

"What's your interest in furnishing a horse for this drive? Do you have any financial interest in this herd?"

"No sir. All I want to do is make a good hand. I know the work and I don't intend to complain. All I want is a decent chance to make a good hand."

"Let me make two things clear to you," the old man said. "First, you know the owners, but that doesn't cut any ice with me. I've got a job to do and I don't mean to be hampered by some kind of supercargo who thinks he has influence with the owners. I'm the last word out here. This is my herd. Do you understand? My herd. You're just another trail hand, no better, no worse.

"Second, Mr. Greer tells me that you're a top hand. Well, if you've got it in you I'll know it. We've got a long way to go, and I'll know what you can do and can't do before we cross the Brazos. I'll know what every man can do, and every horse, too. Let me tell you something about trailing cattle, young man: the whole job is too big for a trail boss who cannot estimate men. If this Kid who is wrangling horses proves to be my best trail hand, I'll put him on the point and he'll be segundo. If you're the man Greer says you are, show me. I need good men. There's not a reason in the world why you can't be a responsible man in my outfit. And I can use you next year, too. All you have to do is show me."

The reference to "next year" was hard to take in silence. "Well, what about my horse?" he asked. "Do I have your permission to go back?"

"How do you propose to get your horse back to Texas? Your contract includes train fare for yourself but not for a horse."

Scott was thinking that, when the problem came up, Greer would be there and he wouldn't be dealing with this man. "I'll take care of it some way, Mr. Kittredge."

"Do you have a bill of sale for the horse?"

"Yes, sir."

"Let me see it."

He took out his pocketbook. He had the bill of sale stuck inside the envelope with the letter Lawson had written him two weeks ago—he didn't know exactly why he was saving the letter; maybe he would show it to Kittredge at the end of the drive. The coyote dun had decided to begin skewing around and would not come up beside Kittredge's horse. Scott had to dismount, while the old man waited impassively, and hand the bill of sale up to him.

The old man glanced at it and handed it back. "All right. Go ahead." His voice had become somewhat natural for a minute but it became harsh again as he said, "And get back in time for dinner if you mean to eat. I won't have the cook hold any grub for you."

Scott wheeled his horse and left without a "thank you." He was getting off on the wrong foot with the old man—he knew that—but he didn't think it was his own fault. All this malarky about Make sure you know who's boss! You don't *have* to call me "Colonel"! What did the old goat want to do? Show how important he was or take these damn cows to Nebraska?

He opened up the coyote dun and let him pour his nervous energy into running. The horse could run. Somebody had almost ruined a horse that could have been real good. He felt anger at the unknown bronc rider and at Kittredge, but the wild pounding of the hoofs and the muscles under him drew out his anger as it drew the nervous energy from the dun.

Brown's place was west up the creek, a mile nearer than Lawson's. He got there a little before eleven o'clock.

No activity was apparent around the place, but he found his black horse grazing with a dozen others along the creek. He caught him and switched saddles, then rode down to the house, leading the dun. He looked in his pockets for some kind of paper, after he had knocked at the door, thinking to leave a note. But after a moment, Mrs. Brown, a short, dumpy woman, opened the door and peeped up at him with small bright eyes.

He tipped his hat. "I don't know if you remember me, mam. I'm Billy Scott. Mr. Brown was going to keep four of my horses. . . ."

"Oh, law yes! I didn't know you for a minute there. Pa . . . er, Mr. Brown just thinks you're the best. But I thought . . ."

"I just came back after one of my horses, Blackjack. If you would just tell Mr. Brown I got him. . . ."

"My law yes! I'm sure proud you're going with the trail outfit. Mr. Brown is afraid of that Colonel. But he knows he can count on you. I said to him yesterday, I said . . ."

"Well, I have to hurry, mam. I sure do thank you." He went back and mounted hurriedly and waved. "Tell Mr. Brown I sure appreciate it."

He left in a lope, but after a mile pulled Blackjack down into his fast pacing gait. He would risk missing dinner rather than wear the black horse down.

When he got back to the herd his watch said one o'clock. He could see Ostler loading the chuck wagon. The herd was strung out, making tracks. He caught the old flea-bitten gray out of the remuda, turned the dun and Black-jack loose, and rejoined the drag. The other riders jeered at him good-naturedly for leaving them with all the work. They were sweating and dusty. His stomach was growling from hunger, but he figured he would make up for it at supper.

He fell into the work, yelling and prodding the stubborn drags, trying to make them come up to the pace Kittredge was allowing the leaders to set. It was clear that the old man meant to bed them down tired that night, both cows and riders.

Longhorn Critters

3

I'm up in the morning before daylight,
And when I go to bed the moon is always shining bright.
Come-a ti yi yippi, yippi yea, yippi yea,
Come-a ti yi yippi, yippi yea.

The herd was not typical. The contract called for one thousand cows, old enough and suitable for breeding but not older than six years, with no cripples or otherwise undesirable animals. These females were wanted by the Nebraska buyer to fulfill his own contractual obligation to the Great White Father, who was trying with uncertain success to make ranchers of the Indians of the northern plains. The same buyer had added to the contract two thousand steers to make the herd about the maximum size that could be safely handled. These steers were to be grown animals, no more than ten years old, not crippled, in good flesh, suitable for beef, to be paid for by the pound at the estimated dressed weight. The steers might go to one or more of several destinations: west to miners in the mountains, east on the new iron rails, north to the pony soldiers or obedient reservation Indians.

So the herd was mixed. Some trail bosses might have said, as Kittredge did, that they had rather trail a mixed herd. Some bosses would have differed. None of them would have appreciated the young Spanish heifers. And the precise mixture, the unpredictable mixture, that the herd turned out to be would have been appreciated by no one. It was mixed with more than females and castrated males. Some of them were hill cattle out of the Balcones Escarpment; others had been born in brush much farther south. Some of them, frightened by loboes or a panther, would have run for cover in the brush; others would have headed for open ground. And their blood was mixed, in the individual and in the herd. Some of them were obviously Spanish or Moorish, some even pure black of the strain that makes fighting bulls; these were fierce, with keen horns. Others were Mexican cattle, identified farther north as "Texas Longhorns," themselves a mixture of big oxen and the smaller fighting cattle from the old world, but a mixture that had grown wild and primitive in the new world, a reversion to ancestors so ancient that they did not admit the dominion of man. The cattle were of all ages within the limits of the contract. The young heifers were flighty and unpredictable, and of these the Spanish heifers were also fierce and quick, with bright suspicious eyes.

Many of them were still shedding their winter hair, so that they looked not merely shaggy but rough, patchy, coarse. Their colors were myriad, not like the rainbow, but like the earth, like a red clay bank or a gray clay bank or a blue clay bank. And more of them were motley than pure in color, like earth marked with patches of dry grass and grass shadows, or the shadows of limbs and leaves. They were the color of sandstone and limestone with highlights and shadows or spotted with moss and lichen. Some few were shiny black, some few clean white; but most were mixtures, brindled, brockled, of pointed colors, difficult to be seen. Characteristic were the line-backs, with a line of different hue covering the backbone from tail to ears, seen also in mustang horses, seen also in lobo wolves, the mark of reversion to ancient wild blood.

The beasts were equal to the distance ahead of them. They had the strength and stamina, if they could be controlled. Neither they nor their ancestors for over a hundred generations had been fed in a feed lot. They had roamed over vast areas for their food, grazing twenty miles away from water and walking back to drink three or four times a week. Their trails were a solid network north and south of the Rio Grande.

But they had walked, and run, for their own purposes, following instincts bred into them and uncovered from out of the past, on account of an environment that would excuse no weaklings. They would walk, wanted to walk, when the whisper came to them, "It's time to walk," as much from their muscles as from anywhere else, if everything looked right and everything smelled right, and if their leaders were plodding along in front of them. But leaders had to be all through the long string of cattle. What was a leader to one was a stranger to another, and more of them followed followers than followed the strong steers at the northern point.

Some of them had left their leaders or walking partners back on the southern range. They were forever searching, milling, unsettled, trying to find their places in the herd; or, failing in that, to go back. They had not been in such a large herd in the normal routine of their lives, only in times of calamity, of extreme cold or drouth; so that they carried a constant nervous expectancy.

Cattle in a bunch observe a hierarchy based on strength, vigor, aggressiveness, and set of horn. The matter of superiority rarely leads to a fight, except between bulls, but is constantly observed in the course of their activities. An old cow, many times a grandmother, comes up behind a less-favored sister and says in some silent language, "Move over; I want to try the grass here," or, "Move on downstream; I don't want to drink your slobbers," or, "Get along; I want to walk in your position"; and if the weaker sister is slow in obeying she will get a horn in her flank. These petty differences in the vast herd of strangers added to the confusion, made it hard for them to lose their fear.

The drag riders had their bandannas pulled up over their noses. Cory pulled his down to yell at Shorty, "I don't think that damn Colonel has got me working in the right place."

"You just don't appreciate a good deal," Shorty replied.

"All this fresh cowshit is good for your horse's feet."

Scott was continually observing the herd, estimating them. He was thinking: If the Colonel has got this crazy bunch road broke by the time we pass Mason, I'll be mighty surprised.

By the second day on the road, the riders were able to distinguish individuals among the cattle. Here and there animals stood out because of their appearance or action. An old black wrinklehorn steer in the lead appeared to be mostly bones. His big head sagged far out ahead of his narrow hump. His knobby knees almost knocked together, but his back legs were spread to maintain his balance. His tail bone was a peak in the rear. A deep hollow showed between his ribs and hipbone. He was crowding the ten-year limit, but looked older because he had passed a hard winter. He would weigh a thousand pounds and at the end of the trail he should weigh sixteen hundred. His massive outswept horns would need to be tilted to pass through the door of a cattle car. His walk was a swinging stride that caused his dewlap to sway like the pendulum of a clock. He seemed calm enough to make a good lead steer, but he was stubborn. To turn his course Blackie or Juan Martinez on the points had to press so close as to spook the other leaders.

One white and red roan steer had long keen horns winding to the sides. The light red on his back changed to speckles, then to white in his face and under his belly. His big head was topped by a frizzle of white hair between his horns, and streams of white hair flowed out of his ears. He had already been named by Dandy, who yelled at him,

"Get back in there, Cotton, God damn your hide!"

One cow was big and crowding the age limit, so that it would have taken an expert to tell whether she were over six years old. She was a dun with big horns and had a pile of wrinkles over and between her eyes; these wrinkles, together with her knobby nose, made her look tired. She was always stopping to stand and bawl mournfully. Baldy had christened her Old Lonesome.

One steer was a dirty black except for face and belly, and the dark color of his sides came up on his cheeks and around his eyes like blinders. He had a low brisket and a high thin hump, giving him the appearance of great depth of chest, but his hindquarters were smaller, staglike. He held his head erect, looking, smelling, and his horns curved up high with black rings under their polished surface. He always seemed to be waiting for something. When he broke away from the herd, he ran in a fast trot with head up, jerking this way and that, as if he were a bull entering an arena. None of the herders had named him, but if one had said, "that spooky steer with the blinders," they would have known which one was meant.

On one of the swing positions was Robert Woodberry, the Professor, a thin man with a shock of black hair and heavy black eyebrows. He was a thoughtful, cynical, casual man, not inclined to work as hard as the skittish herd and the trail boss required. But if he was not inclined to work hard, neither was he inclined to rebel. He had found out during his ten years in the West that, before conditions became intolerable, someone would rebel and conditions would change. He observed the world with somewhat lazy sarcasm.

He had been a schoolteacher before the war in his home state of Tennessee. He had volunteered when it became all but necessary to take violent sides in the war and had found soldiering an interesting experience—until they began to expect him to scream like a wild Indian and shoot people. He had not been a good soldier, had been quiet about this fact in public, but inside himself had been both ashamed of it and stoutly defensive of it. He had abandoned the people at home, kinsmen and friends, after the war. They expected him, an educated man, to marry and help rebuild the shattered country; so he had run, partly to get away from well-meaning friends, partly to escape from the memories of the war, partly to see the West, a land as big in extent as the North and South put together.

In those first years he had thought he would make pictures and write poetry about the country. He was impressed with it. But laziness and severe self-criticism of his efforts had caused his artistic ambitions to fade. So now he kept quiet about his past, accepted the nickname of Professor without comment, read as many books as he could without getting fired, and was generally pleased that he was accepted by the men he worked with.

He rode beside the string of cattle as it wound about among the hills and occupied his mind with a whimsy. He had read Melville's *Moby Dick* several times, and it pleased him to compare man's mastery of whales with man's mastery of longhorn cattle. He was trying to make mental calculations of the relative beast-weight involved.

Some of the steers they drove would come up to a thousand pounds right now. The tally was a little over three thousand. That would be three million pounds. But some of the heifers, especially the skinny ones, would fall far below a thousand pounds. Six hundred pounds apiece would make one million, eight hundred thousand. Seven hundred pounds apiece would make two million, one hundred thousand. Two million was a good estimate; they were driving two million pounds of beef, of rawhide and horns and bones and muscles and sinews. No blubber to it, all hard stuff.

Melville had recorded that a Greenland whale of the largest magnitude would come up to seventy tons, which would be one hundred and forty thousand pounds; and that a sperm whale of the largest magnitude would come up to ninety tons, which would be one hundred and eighty thousand pounds. Professor then made a mental calculation, dividing whale pounds into cow pounds. The calculation was difficult because the cow pounds, besides being abstractions, were living entities, some of whom stubbornly desired to break away and go home, and because his mustang pony noticed a dead limb that looked exactly like a rattlesnake. When he finally finished figuring he came up with eleven whales or fourteen whales, depending on whether one figured Greenland or sperm. They were driving the animal-weight of say twelve whales of the greatest magnitude, one for each trail hand, not counting the boss, cook, or wrangler.

But, ah, Ishmael! he thought, what if it had been your duty, not merely to go out and catch those huge animals, kill them, cut them up, boil them down; but what if it had been your duty to drive them to port, one for each member of your crew, not one for each boat full of whalers, but one for each man, drive them, force them, guide them, persuade them to come into New Bedford under their own power?

But you say that you had to sail great distances, Ishmael? So you did. Well, they say it measures nine hundred miles to Ogallala on a map, straight through as the crow flies. But we can't go straight through any more than you could go from a Pacific whaling ground straight through to a New England port. Look where the sun is; we're going more east than north right now, but we have to go around that mountain. It will be more like eighteen hundred miles before we get there—that's if we don't get lost and they don't run, and this mixed-up mess of cows is going to run! But that's not all; for the last five miles the herd made I've ridden fifteen myself, chasing bunch quitters. Then, too, we don't travel our miles by just sitting and letting the wind blow us. I'm not trying to belittle your adventures, you understand, Ishmael, but . . .

Well, you say that these animals are broken up into small sizes convenient to handle. I wouldn't say convenient. It is true that a skilled man with a good horse and a good rope can handle one of them. But if this wild animal-weight comes in smaller than whale packages, it also comes with three thousand stubborn individual wills. Unless they start to stampede or drift, then they're one beast, like twelve of your whales of the greatest magnitude tied together. And note, Ishmael, no blubber. It's all horn and rawhide, lean muscle, sinew, bone. No, you soft fellows can go whaling, Ishmael, but we who are tough, who love hard work and a hard life . . . God! What am I saying? If that damn old goat Kittredge doesn't let up on us pretty soon, I'm going to quit this outfit when we pass Fort Griffin.

They made twenty winding miles a day for the first three days, and all of it was uphill. They could see the blue foothills rising all around them, and sometimes with the herd strung out for a mile the point and the drag were no more than a quarter of a mile apart. They grazed them and pushed them and grazed them and pushed them; and Kittredge wanted them grazed fast. There was no room for them to graze unherded without scattering up the draws.

To keep the cattle moving, the Colonel had the men eat their noon meal in two bunches, half of them at a time. Ostler grumbled about the extra trouble. Because of the unsettled condition of the herd, they doubled up on night guard and each man got four hours of sleep. All of them grumbled about this, but they knew, or thought they knew, that it would not last longer than a few days.

In the dim morning light when the first steer rose and bowed his back, stretching himself, the Colonel wanted all the animals prodded up and strung out north. On the morning of the fourth day Kittredge woke the men before daylight. The neck-yoke on the end of the wagon tongue was propped straight up, and from its top hook hung the cook's kerosene lantern. The Colonel stood in this flickering light and read to the sleepy men of the first guard while they dressed to begin another day.

When he had replaced the Bible in his saddlebags, which hung behind the saddle on his already saddled and waiting horse, he said loudly enough for everyone to hear, "Mr. Ostler, why isn't breakfast ready? You've been at it half an hour. Put on some more bacon. I want everybody to eat a good breakfast, but don't waste any time at it. We're going to put the herd on the creek and let them drink, and then we're going to make a hard drive."

To Dandy, he said, "Rice, when the chuck wagon goes around the herd this morning, I want you to gather the canteens of the front six men and refill them."

To Ed Murphy, one of the drag riders, he said, "Murphy, you do the same for the rear six men. I want the canteens full when the wagon goes ahead." Then the Colonel mounted and rode out toward the bedded herd to prod up the other half of his outfit.

According to their orders, they wasted no time at breakfast, nor did they waste any time watering the cattle and pushing them north up the small valley. When the herders came near each other, they speculated together concerning the order about filling canteens.

At the drag, Scott, Shorty, Cory, and Murphy had their say about it. Scott pointed out, "There's no water in that creek we're following now. If you all noticed, those springs and seeps above camp were the last of the water. I think we've got a hard dry drive over the hump before we strike water again."

"That don't explain it," Shorty said. "Ostler's got the keg of water in the wagon. Who needs two canteens of water before dinnertime?"

Cory was suspicious. "That damn Colonel's got something dirty up his sleeve. Here we been in the saddle eight hours and we ain't but just getting the day started. I never been so tired in my life."

Scott and Shorty laughed at him. Shorty said, "Yes, you have. You've seen trail bosses start out pushing their outfit this way about four times that I know of, and every time you claimed it was killing you."

"I ain't never seen a trail boss that enjoyed it before. Most bosses will apologize for it, but this damn Kittredge enjoys it."

When, in the middle of the morning, the wagon came even with the drag, Murphy started gathering the canteens. "Hell, I don't need no water," Cory said. "I got half a canteen full. What's he trying to do, waterlog us all?"

Murphy was a serious little man with three teeth missing in front. "I got to have it," he said. "I got to have it. Ain't no telling what the Colonel will do to me if I don't do like he said."

Cory gave it to him. " 'Pears to me some of you boys are scared of the Colonel, ain't you, Murph? He sure ain't got me buffaloed."

"Me neither," Shorty said. "But I want my canteen full to be on the safe side. A canteen full of water ain't very heavy."

Scott could see that Shorty had the same suspicions that he had. The truth of the matter could be that it was going to be a long time till dinner.

The draw became more shallow as they pushed up it, and then they came up on a brush-covered tableland that stretched out ahead of them in gentle undulations farther than they could see. When Scott's pocket watch said twelve o'clock and the sun was at its highest point in the sky, Cory began to complain that his belly said dinnertime. "I don't even see the wagon up there anywheres. What's the matter with that Colonel? Don't he have a watch?"

"Maybe it's in a draw up there some place," Murphy suggested.

"How come he would hide it in a draw? I'd like to know

what's going on."

They wound across the rough tableland, skirting arroyos that led off to the east. They had come up from the fringe of the coastal plains and were crossing the southeastern finger of Edwards Plateau, which is the southeastern finger of the high plains. To the west in their line of sight, but obscured by the haze of distance, were some of the roughest mountains and most barren wastes in the United States and Mexico.

By three o'clock in the afternoon the truth had sunk in to the men. Colonel Kittredge did not mean to graze the herd, or to stop for dinner at all. Sometimes a mile out ahead of the mile-long string of cattle, they could see faintly in the bright spring sunlight the slight figure on the big horse; and so faintly as to be uncertain a movement ahead of him that might be the chuck wagon.

Scott thought the old man was making a mistake. It wasn't the route, nor even the daylong push. He, himself, probably would have chosen the same route. And it wasn't the lack of apology, which Cory had mentioned, but it would not have cost the old man a single thing to have told the men what he was doing and why.

The herd became stubborn in the middle of the afternoon. The men drank the last of their water, cursing and sweating at their work. Their horses' sides became lathered. Then finally the lead steers began to disappear into a draw ahead, and they wound down off of the tableland. The valley widened as they went down, and Kittredge led them away from the tiny stream in the middle until it had grown, fed by a dozen springs, to a creek big enough to water the cattle. He had figured the push pretty close; the cattle were sinking their noses into the cold spring water just as the sun went down.

The last half of the double night guard went to the wagon. Cory said bitterly to Ostler, who was still cooking, "Did that god-damned son-of-a-bitch that calls hisself a Colonel eat any dinner today?"

The cook shoveled a load of hot coals on top of a Dutch oven. "He never et anything out of this wagon." He looked up grinning, "But I did. I had me a nice can of tomaters."

"Well, how come you eat, when can't nobody else eat?"

"Oh, I wasn't the only one. When the Kid come up with the horses, I give him a can of tomaters too." Ostler was the only man present who could see the humor in the situation.

Cory asked, "Well, who told you that you could eat and the Kid could eat, and the rest of us out there starving?"

"Don't nobody have to tell me. I'm in charge of this wagon, and I'm in charge of this grub, and if I get ready to eat a can of tomaters, I'll eat a can of tomaters."

"Well, maybe if somebody was to tell the Colonel, you might just change your tune about that."

"Well, maybe if you want to eat a little sand in your grub the next two or three months, you just go right ahead and tell the Colonel." These words finished the argument.

The last half of the double night guard did not hunt long for a good spot to spread their rolls that night. They had been in the saddle nineteen hours, on a night horse and on a day horse, with a few minutes off for breakfast. They did not even pick the pebbles off the spots where they spread their pallets. They lay down without any conversation, and the earth felt soft.

Human Critters

4

Now, I've punched cattle from Texas to Maine,
And I know a few cowboys by their right name.
Come-a ti yi yippi, yippi yea, yippi yea,
Come-a ti yi yippi, yippi yea.

O n the right point of the herd, opposite big Blackie, rode Juan Martinez, a man who seemed to be covered with wrinkled brown leather, whose hair and stringy mustache seemed to be made out of coarse hair from the mane of a black horse. He wore the clothes of a gringo but on his bridle bit and on his spur straps he had fastened small silver chains, which made faint jingling, a sound a Mexican rider loves.

He had lived as a boy on a rancho in the disputed territory between the Nueces and the Rio Grande. He had learned to speak English as well as Spanish, and his people had got on well enough with the settlers from the north. But the land where he was born turned into a raiding ground for vengeful thieves from north and south, or rather for men who wanted to steal and kill and used vengeance for an excuse. So the family retreated south of the big river, abandoning their hacienda, taking with them the boy Juan, who was still a child but already an accomplished horseman and worker with cattle.

But the fact which came to dominate the adult life of Juan was that he was wanted in the province of Coahuila—

for murder. It happened because of a woman, an unmarried woman two or three years older than himself. She had given him every cause that a señorita can give a man to believe that she loved him with all her heart. She was passionate when out from under the eyes of *la tia,* her aunt, a suspicious old woman. One evening Juan came to the señorita's window, playing and singing tenderly, thinking about her, his soul, his heart, the light of his life. Since she did not respond, he walked around a bit and found her in the patio in the arms of some brute dressed in fine clothing. He knew it was against her will. Didn't she love him? He attacked the brute with the keen dagger which he had always carried only for show, cutting him deep in the groin and the crotch, in the belly, and then in the heart. When he had made his escape from the immediate vicinity, he hid and waited, keeping his ears open. To his great sadness the señorita named him as the murderer, and he was sought, not only in Coahuila, but throughout Mexico.

He had then come back across the Rio Grande and made his peace with the gringos. It was not difficult to find work; he could not be beaten with *la rieta.* He could put his loop, even the stiff loop of the gringos, on both front legs or both back legs or on any one leg, you name it, of a running horse or a running cow. His loop seemed to obey him, as if he sent it loving messages by the movements of his hands on the end of the rope. But he was not able to escape completely from the crime he had left; whispers of it followed him. It turned out that the beast in fine clothing he had knifed had been the son of a federal official.

As the years rolled away, he had become used to his exile and used to the whisper of the crime that followed him. He took refuge and satisfaction in his ability as a worker. He was pleased when someone he worked with called him Johnny, but he kept his distance, judging them, his black eyes darting unobtrusively.

The old trail boss, the Colonel, Juan thought of as somewhat like a priest, one who should not be judged. For Blackie he had gained quick contempt and now after having made some exploratory remarks to make certain that the big segundo could not understand Spanish, Juan would make vulgar, filthy statements to the big man, all in Spanish. "Cabrón," Juan would call him, "hijuela chingada," smiling and nodding as he spoke. The gringos altogether were a peculiar bunch of men. Of them all, Juan thought that none came near him in the understanding of cattle handling, unless it were the unimportant drag man, Billy Scott, who seemed to know what he was doing but spent too much time and care currying the back of his horse before he put on the saddle blanket.

When the herd was strung out, behind big Blackie rode Scratchy Wilson. His swing position was of some importance, for at times Blackie was required to ride ahead and drive local range cattle from the trail. At these times Scratchy advanced to Blackie's position, guiding the herd.

Scratchy looked like a middle-aged sheepherder who has not seen civilization in six months. His hair and beard grew straight out from his head and face; they appeared to have been cut at some remote time with a butcher knife. His clothes were dirty, even in these early days of the drive. Often he found the critical, cold eye of the Colonel upon him; he responded with a look of injured innocence and did no more work than he had to. He said to himself, "Can I help it if I ain't got no good clothes? He don't like my looks, I'll quit him. I ain't no nigger slave!"

Opposite Scratchy, and behind Martinez, rode Alexander "Dandy" Rice, a younger man, somewhat handsome, who wore his hair slicked straight back, plastered down with water and dabs of pomade from a jar he kept hidden in his warbag. He rode a full-stamped Texas saddle with hand-tooled saddlebags and saddle strings made by himself from plaited calfskin. All the leather of his gear he kept clean and protected with saddle soap. The band of his broad stetson hat was a tanned rattlesnake skin. The tops of his boots were inlaid with big stars of red leather, and his spurs were nickel inlaid with silver.

He was a competent cowhand, well liked, self-assured, but always broke. Every cent he had earned for the past ten years had been spent mostly for clothes and gear. Also, when he sparked a gal, he believed in spending some money on her. Also, he had the misfortune of loving to yell, when he came into a saloon, "Set 'em up to the house! Give these boys something to drink!" He loved yelling such an invitation much more than he loved drinking rotgut himself. It was a pity that Dandy's vocation paid so poorly, for he was a young man who honestly appreciated what money will buy.

He had been up the trail to Kansas four times. One time he had lain in jail two weeks in Abilene for riding horseback inside a local retail store, roping a sign on the top of a local retail store, discharging a firearm within a local retail store, and otherwise illegally creating a disturbance. But the following year he had wreaked his revenge on Kansas when, along with five like-minded comrades, he had successfully treed a small southern Kansas town. The townspeople, disagreeing on whether the trail drivers were reckless kids out for a good time or dangerous devils, and suspicious with memories of raiders during the war as well as Indians who had been deadly serious, had retreated behind barred doors and left the town to the cowboys for two glorious hours, at the end of which time their trail boss had appeared and made them holster their guns. The boss had left a sum of money in token payment for a dozen window glasses and had quickly herded his men south to the safety of Indian Territory. It had been a magnificent experience and had become even finer as it was garnished in memory and telling.

Now he was wondering if he should press the question of going into Mason. "I may get me some of them good gloves," he said to himself, "with a big cuff and maybe some fringe and a fancy pattern on the back. And when we get to Dodge, I'm going to get me another pearl-handled Colt to match mine and another holster and maybe a big silver belt-buckle set with red jewels. Boy, them pretty gals in old Dodge will open their eyes when they see me come walking down the street!"

In one rear swing position, opposite Professor, rode Art Howard, a quiet slender man with a huge walrus mustache. He hunched his shoulders as he rode, resting both hands on the saddle horn. He seldom spoke to any man of the outfit except "Booger Red" Baker, his bedmate.

Booger Red rode on the left flank. He was a squat, pugnacious young man, whose pugnacity had little opportunity of showing itself in the same outfit with big Blackie. Beside Blackie, he looked like a bantam rooster. Booger Red's fair skin would not tan; it was always sunburned. His red beard stubble gave a dirty appearance to his red face.

On the right flank rode George "Baldy" Neil, the clown. Of all the men he was nearest being fat, but was not; his build was dumpy, ungraceful, but no one could have cared less. He had a tiny fringe of hair left about his round head, but when he removed his hat and the fringe had been plastered down by the wet sweatband, he seemed to have no hair at all. His small eyes sparkled out of the wrinkles around them. No one could tell whether the hard driving of the trail boss bothered him, for he laughed about the sore muscles and the lack of sleep as he did about everything else.

Baldy was a good hand with plenty of energy but inclined to gang up with someone else and talk instead of work. Whenever another rider came near him about the herd he would yell whatever was in his mind, or rather in the muscles of his throat. "Shortning bread!" he would yell; those who did not know him didn't know what to make of it. Or, "Put up or shut up!" Or, "Hit him again; he's still wiggling!" Sometimes he would yell words that had more, but not much more, sense to them: "Ain't these cows a bunch of beauties?" When he was out of earshot of anyone else, in his saner moments he would say to himself, "This looks like a good outfit. A pretty durned good outfit! But that Corporal Kittredge is a card! I wonder what he would do if I called him 'Corporal' to his face? He! He! I wonder what he would do if somebody was to put a cucklebur under his saddle blanket!"

. . .

On the drag with Scott were Henry "Shorty" Snow and Jim Cory and little Ed Murphy. Scott had known Shorty and Cory several years. Cory was a wiry, dark-complexioned man in his early twenties. He was quick to anger and ready for rash action, but quick to lose his anger and loyal to his friends. More than once, when they were drinking, Scott or Shorty had taken his gun away from him.

His friendship with Shorty, who was middle-aged, had been important to Scott. Shorty was a veteran of the war, from Virginia. He had been in the thick of it but never boasted or even talked of it much. But Scott, a native Texan, had been one of those who was old enough to see the glamour of war from afar but too young to go. He had waited with innocent impatience, disgusted that he would not grow faster. He thought that it was all victories; Galveston was retaken from the Yankees; seven thousand, five hundred Yankees were beaten and disgraced at Sabine Pass by forty-seven Texans under a kid named Dowling; a huge Yankee force with three-to-one superiority in numbers was turned away from the Texas border at the Battle of Mansfield. At the news of this last battle, the boy did his best to convince his father that he could pass for seventeen, but was unsuccessful. Finally, the boy ran away from home to enlist. He was turned down for two good reasons: he was only thirteen years old—and the Confederate States of America was no more.

He had worshiped the returning soldiers and felt sad. He would never know what the boys five years older than he had known. Later as he worked with some of them he recovered from the sense of loss he had felt.

He had been somewhat in awe 'Shorty at first, but the awe changed to the mere pleasure of friendship. He found that the ex-soldier was a good cov and, not too ambitious, more reasonable than Cory, but no d of a god. And as they rode together, it had been Scott, with the greater ambition and patience, who had becom the acknowledged leader.

Shorty was not in good physical condition. Several years after the war he had ridden broncs for a living. He refused to admit that anything much was wrong, but now sometimes he would ride a particularly jarring bronc, one that would pitch stiff-legged, and he would get off and sit down a minute and his face would be pale, and even though the day were cool, sweat would stand out in drops on his forehead. But he still never hesitated to climb on a bronc whose back was humped. If Cory said, "Let me take a little of that meanness out of him," Shorty would say, "Let you? Hell, I was riding horses when you was still in didies!"

Shorty had learned that you could live with such a thing if you never let it worry you. Sometimes he almost believed that it was the way everyone felt. When he worked hard enough for sore muscles he would also have a sore belly, not much worse than the muscles. It would feel like he was carrying iron weights inside. But if he lay pretty still at night it would go away by morning.

The oldest man on the drive next to the Colonel was Ostler, the cook. The cook was gray-haired and squint-eyed. He appeared slow and clumsy but knew how to get his work done. When he fussed about the work to the others and to himself, his main purpose was merely to assert the importance of his position.

Some cooks drew five dollars a month more than a regular hand and assumed some kind of authority in the area of camp. Ostler had been hired at the same wages as everyone else. He didn't fuss about this to the other men, because he didn't want them to know it. He said to himself, "That's fine with me. Fine. But that blamed Colonel might as well not ask my advice about things, because I ain't going to tell him nothing. And that dumb Blackie better not get uppity and go to giving me orders, neither." Actually, it was fine with him, about the money. He could maintain his petty position in camp by diplomatic fussing and bullying, yet feel that if anything went wrong, he wasn't to blame; he was just another hand. He had a peculiar kind of soured conscience that made him prefer to feel mistreated rather than feel inadequate. But he did his demanding job well.

Every morning he rose before daylight, pulled the ashes from the coals of his fire, perhaps removing a kettle of red beans he had left simmering through the night, added wood, ground a pound of Arbuckle coffee and started it brewing, cut thick slices of salt bacon and set them frying, along with pancakes made of flour and meal and water and a dab of sourdough. He awoke the men by pounding on a pot or tin plate and shouting, "Fall out! Rise and shine! Another day, another dollar! What you want to do? Sleep all day?" Having already gulped a cup of coffee, he felt good enough to enjoy their discomfort at being awakened.

After breakfast he had to wash the dishes and load the wagon carefully. He had a big load, and everything had to be placed so as to bear the jolts and careening of the miles ahead. The bulk of the load was eight bedrolls, one for the Colonel and one for each pair of men, a half-dozen warbags containing the men's personal belongings, the Colonel's suitcase, his own saddle, the wagon tarp, a big roll of heavy three-quarter rope. Of these items he always fashioned himself a seat at the front. Most of the grub and eating utensils were carried in the grub box, a tall cabinet tied down with iron straps in the rear of the wagon box. After loading he harnessed his four mules, filled his water keg if the camp were near water, and set out to pass the herd.

He had a noon camp to make, dinner to fix, more dishes to wash, another drive to night camp. Sometimes, if the country were smooth and open, he would doze, letting the mules pick their way. He would come awake at some jolt and whip up the team and say, "Get up, you lop-eared bastards! Don't you know that crazy Colonel aims for us to go in a run from one camp to another? Blame, I don't know how he expects me to keep up with him. I got a hundred things to worry about. Here we ain't been gone a week, and I'm just about out of coal oil. What will it be when we get up yonder and not a stick of wood for a hundred miles and I have to try to cook on wet cow chips?"

Ostler was not in charge of the remuda, but he did, by convention, have the wrangler as his helper. He also slept with him. The cook had insulted the Kid that first night, asking him, "You don't wet the bed, do you?" The Kid had answered, "No, course I don't," red in the face and angry. "Well, you better not," Ostler had told him. "I'll make you sleep out in the prickly pears."

The Kid had not understood his duties at first. That night before they left, excited by his being hired and inspired by Colonel Kittredge's talk, the Kid had not come to bed at all. The first night on the trail, he had not come to bed by midnight, so Ostler went looking for him and found him on his night horse, dead asleep, circling the grazing remuda. He had come awake at Ostler's approach and had immediately protested, "I wasn't asleep, Mr. Ostler. I just closed my eyes a minute." The cook had said, "Well, why the hell ain't you? What in the world are you doing out here?" "I'm just watching the horses." "Watching the horses! Ain't you got no sense, Kid? What do you aim to do? Drive these horses all day and then stay up and watch them all night? Don't you aim to get no sleep at all between here and Nebraska? You leave these horses alone and get to bed." "Well, I just thought they might stray off, Mr. Ostler, the ones that ain't hobbled." "Let them stray off. The night guard is supposed to look at them once in a while, and if they stray off it ain't your fault. You take your night horse down close to the wagon and take his bridle off and tie him to a tree. Then you get to bed." The Kid had turned as he rode off to obey and said, "Thank you, Mr. Ostler." These words had astonished the cook for a moment, and when he recovered himself he scratched his head and said, "Blame, it seems like kids ain't got no sense these days."

The Kid was a wharf rat from Galveston, a gangling boy sixteen years old. He appeared to be mostly long legs and thumbs and elbows. He had spent his early years with an irresponsible mother, who had lived with a succession of men she called his daddy or his uncle or his cousin and who had finally risen to the high station of manager of something she called a "rooming house," where women lived and were continually visited by sailors. When he had found himself old enough to make some money by his own work, he had drifted west, leaving his mother without a thought. He had worked at a dozen jobs. He had helped a Mexican man skin cows, fed and curried horses in a livery stable, trapped with a Negro man for a bunk and all the baked possum and coon meat he could eat. His ambition had been to be a cowboy, but the nearest he had gotten to it was a job shelling corn for a man who owned a few cows.

When various of the men of the outfit had asked him, "What's your name, Kid?" he had told them "Paul Henry Rogers," and they had immediately forgotten it. So his name was Kid. He said "yes sir" and "no sir" to all of them and watched everything they did, trying to learn. When they pulled jokes on him, he grinned.

When he rode by himself, driving the remuda, he could hardly believe where he was and what he was doing. He would say, "I'm a cowboy! I'm really and truly a cowboy! And I'm going up the trail to Ogallala with the Lawson herd!"

The Big Segundo

5

Oh, I crippled my hoss and I don't know how,
A-roping at the horns of a muley cow.
Come-a ti yi yippi, yippi yea, yippi yea,
Come-a ti yi yippi, yippi yea.

They came down out of the high country into the valley of the Llano River, watering easily in the spring-fed creek, then in the cold, clear river. When they made noon camp beside the river, Kittredge had gone ahead to look at a creek crossing. Blackie was his usual jovial self, bullying the others with loud banter, taking advantage of the absence of the trail boss, until Scratchy Wilson rode up to the wagon.

Blackie's smile faded and he glowed at the bewhiskered rider as if he remembered some old insult. Scratchy went to the keg to dribble a little water over his hands.

"Wash in the river!" Ostler yelled. "I ain't no nursemaid to tote water, when we're right alongside the river."

Scratchy turned away from the keg with his look of hurt innocence and found himself confronted by the big segundo.

"I been aiming to ask you something," Blackie said.

Scratchy stared at him and raised his eyebrows as if to say to the others that he was being mistreated from all sides.

"I want to know how come you to walk off this morning when Colonel Kittredge was reading!"

Scratchy mumbled.

"You done what? Talk where I can hear you!"

"I had to go to the bushes."

Blackie was stumped for a moment. "Well, you don't go to the bushes when the Colonel is reading!"

Scratchy mumbled.

"You hear me? I say you don't go to the bushes when the Colonel is reading! You understand that?"

Scratchy mumbled again and started for the river, not so much to wash as to escape the hazing. Blackie slapped his big hand on the man's ragged shoulder and spun him back. Scratchy's legs became entangled with each other and he fell.

"You hear me? I aim for you to understand it! And don't go walking off when I'm telling you something!"

Scratchy's usual manner was that of a man who is accustomed to being fussed at, who is willing to take the criticism and go his lazy way; but as he gained his feet his manner had changed. The watching cowboys stopped eating and waited. Scratchy backed up and possibly thought about the rusty gun at his hip for a moment but didn't touch it. When he spoke his voice was quavering, but he was not mumbling. "I'm quitting this outfit! I ain't no nigger slave!"

"You ain't quitting nothing," Blackie told him. "You heard what the Colonel said: can't nobody quit!"

"I ain't asking the Colonel or you neither. I ain't no nigger slave, and I ain't breaking my back working for this screwed-up outfit. Can't nobody kick me around like that!"

"You'll think you was kicked around," Blackie said. "You try to quit and I'll beat the hell out of you sure enough."

"I'll quit. You see if I don't."

"And besides that the Colonel will probably have you throwed in jail. You heard what he said, and you signed on; can't nobody quit!"

"You just wait and see if I don't!"

Blackie advanced one pace toward him. "Stop saying see if you don't or I'll beat the hell out of you right now."

"I ain't no nigger slave."

Blackie turned away. "If you aim to eat, Scratchy, you better go on. I'll send you back to the herd without any dinner if you don't go on and eat."

Scratchy had gone back to mumbling. Whatever he intended doing, evidently he had decided to keep it to himself.

Blackie had chosen the one man to pick on whom the others were not inclined to defend.

On the morning of their second day along the Llano, Blackie rode ahead with the Colonel toward the herd while the others were still catching their mounts or leading them around to take the humps out of their backs, or perhaps taking it out the hard way. Blackie was following precisely behind the Colonel as if they were a two-man military formation.

"Look at that," Professor said. "Boys, if I were a poet I would write some kind of a verse about that: a big man on a little horse following a little man on a big horse."

"I'm betting money Blackie don't last as segundo," Ostler said. "That horse he's on this morning has got a sore on his back big as my fist. He'll be afoot before we get to Indian Territory. If I was in charge of this outfit I wouldn't put up with that."

"I'll tell you one thing," Dandy said. "He ain't getting none of my string when he wears his out."

"Well, I'll tell you boys a secret," Scratchy said. "He can have my string, 'cept one horse I aim to take for my wages."

"Who you kidding?"

"You'll see. I ain't no nigger slave."

In a few minutes Blackie came riding back to get the cook's ax.

"What's the matter, Blackie?" Dandy asked. "Did one of those boys out there get smart with you?"

Blackie blinked, not understanding. "Cow dropped a calf last night. Damn a bunch of crazy cows that start having calves all over the place."

Baldy asked, "You ain't going to knock that poor little old baby calf in the head, are you, Blackie?"

"Don't give me no bad time, or I'll make you do it," Blackie said. "Hand me that shovel. You all better get out yonder. Colonel Kittredge will get sore if you don't get on out yonder."

Billy Scott had taken care in the three hundred head of young cows he had selected to cut out any animal that looked as if she would calve in the next three months, but someone had not been so careful with the seven hundred other cows. Now the first of them had dropped her calf and added to the trouble of the driving. She trotted around the area where her calf had been covered with just enough soil that she could not smell it, searching, bawling. She didn't want to leave; she kept trying to turn back; she dashed among the other cattle, searching.

As they approached Mason the herd was not road broken as Colonel Kittredge had predicted. In spite of the hard driving, the cattle were gaining strength from the lush new grass, which they seasoned with the white flowers of wild onions and the patches of sour sheep sorrel, blooming with tiny yellow pansy-like flowers. The strength of spring seemed to counteract their familiarity with the trail. The mixed herd was still three thousand separate and perverse wills.

They forded the Llano at a wagon crossing, where the cool water was no more than wagon-box depth at its deepest. Three hours later they passed the little cowtown of Mason with its sturdy stone buildings, and made night camp in the rolling hill country. The land was dotted with dark green cedar and still-leafless mesquite and oak. Ostler, who had stopped in town for kerosene and sorghum molasses, got supper late. Dandy was refused permission to go into Mason and did not argue about it. The guard had been divided into three groups, but still each man got no more than six hours' sleep at night and they were dead tired.

The following morning Kittredge demonstrated further his acceptance of Blackie as second in command. When he had finished his morning Bible reading he said, "Mr. Blackburn, I will be in Mason a few hours writing letters and finding what I can about the condition of the trail ahead. I want you to push these cattle straight through to the San Saba River. Don't graze them and don't let them drink on this side of the river. Push them straight across. If I haven't caught up with you, select a campsite north of the river. Do you understand?"

"Yes, sir. About how many . . . uh . . . about when would we get there—to the river?"

"In the middle of the afternoon. There will be time to graze and water north of the river if you'll push them."

"Yes, sir. Did you aim for us to stop for dinner or . . . uh . . . just go on."

"Certainly, stop for dinner. It's not that far, Blackburn."

So Blackie had it all on his own that day. He left his point position and ranged out ahead, though they were following a clear trail; then he went up and down the string of cattle, shouting orders or encouragement or any pleasantry that came to mind. "Now, there's a happy man," Professor said to himself.

The big segundo worked an hour on the drag, as if to show them how it was done. He yelled incessantly and quirted the stubborn cattle. Once when he tore out to bust down a steer, Scott said to Shorty, "Reckon we ought to go ride in the wagon? Looks like Blackie can handle this end of it pretty good by himself."

Shorty grinned. "He can show off pretty good. But how long would he last at it?"

Scott was thinking that the big man probably would last all day and all night too, if his horse held up. Why in the devil, if Kittredge was such a good trail boss, didn't he talk to Blackie about taking care of horses?

They crossed the San Saba an hour after the noon meal and camped early enough that those who felt a need had the opportunity to bathe in the icy water. Some of them took advantage of it; others splashed a bit of water over their chests and proceeded to try to catch up on sleep. "How come you don't take a bath?" Blackie yelled at Scratchy. "You smell like a damn wolf den. If I was Murph and had to sleep with you, I'd throw you in that river clothes and all!" Scratchy gave him a dark look.

That evening for the first time they felt not driven to snatch all the sleep they could as soon as possible. The second and third guards sat around Ostler's fire and speculated. Baldy was picking his teeth with a mesquite thorn. "I ain't complaining, you understand, Ostler," he said, "but when we going to have some beef to eat?"

Ostler, busy with his pots in the lantern light, said, "If I judge that blame Colonel right, we ain't going to eat any I-D Connected beef. How come you don't shoot us some deer meat?"

"Yeah, Baldy," Cory said. "You got plenty of time to hunt. How come you don't shoot us some deer meat?"

Baldy said, "Hell, we ain't never going to get these cows where we're going anyways. I don't see why we don't eat a few of them."

"What do you mean by that?" Blackie asked.

"Well, did you ever see such a spooky herd?"

"Sure I have. You fellers just don't push them hard enough. The Colonel will get them through all right. Spooky? They ain't run yet, have they?"

"No, and we ain't there yet. But we've come far enough they ought to be road broke."

Shorty said, "You mean you're road broke, Baldy, so the cows ought to be?"

"The Colonel will get them road broke," Blackie said.

The Kid came and squatted in the light of the coals, and Baldy went to work on him. "Kid, how come you cut so much wood around here? Ostler, why you want to make the Kid chop so much wood? You always have a bunch left over."

"I told him to cut some wood," Ostler said. "I never told him to cut all the timber he could find."

"Well, it's all right this time, Kid, but just don't do it again. Hell, we ain't got room to spread our soogins, and all this wood drug up. How does it feel, Kid, to be away out here where the wild Injuns grow?"

The Kid's grin was all over his face. "I ain't seen any yet."

"Well, you got to keep your eyes open. When you see one it's done too late. Zip! There goes your hair."

"Is that what happened to you?" Professor asked.

"No, it was a woman pulled mine out."

"You think you're kidding about Indians," Dandy said. "Right up this river is Fort McKavett, and the other side of that is them damn Apaches, and they're worse than any of them Indians north of here."

"Fort McKavett ain't on this river," someone said.

Professor rolled over and asked Scott, "Where is Fort McKavett, Scott?" They knew that Scott had maps among his gear.

"It's up this river, all right. Maybe fifty, sixty miles."

Blackie said, "Well, are you trying to say Apaches are the worst Injuns they are?"

"I guess it's a matter of opinion," Scott said. "I don't want to meet any of them when they're on the warpath."

Baldy picked up an empty tomato can from the ground; Ostler had put tomatoes and chile pepper in the red beans for a change. "Kid," Baldy said solemnly, "I reckon now is a good a time as any to start on your education. Now, I can see from looking at you, you can't read and you don't know nothing hardly. But don't give up. You can learn to be smart. You can learn to read off of tin cans; in fact, you can learn nearly all the words that's worth knowing off of tin cans. And the best tin can in the world to read off of is a tomater can."

Blackie said, "How come you want to tease the Kid about that? Don't pay no attention to him, Kid."

"I ain't teasing him."

"The hell you ain't! Just because the Kid can't read don't

82

give you any cause to tease him."

"I ain't teasing him. Ask the Professor; he's a book-reading man."

"Well, you stop teasing him. What does it matter if he can read or not?"

The Kid's smile had faded. He said, "But that's all right. I can read, Mr. Blackburn."

"Don't pay no attention to him," Blackie went on. "Just because you can't read ain't anything to be ashamed of."

"But I can! Sure enough. I can read."

Blackie stared at him a minute. "Well, shut up about it! God dammit! I try to help you out and you don't appreciate it. Bragging about it. What the hell difference does it make?"

Blackie's angry talk was interrupted by Baldy's flailing at the smoke from the fire with his hat.

"It ain't no use, Baldy," Shorty said. "It's bound to follow the prettiest critter around. You can't get away from it."

Blackie was silent a few minutes, then seemed to have regained his humor. Someone had found a large horseshoe on the camp ground before dark and had hung it over a wagon spoke. Blackie got it and sat back down, studying the rusty chunk of iron. He said, loudly enough to get the attention of them all, "You think a man could straighten this horseshoe out?"

Someone took it, and it was passed around. Dandy said, "I could straighten it out if I had a forge and anvil and sledge hammer."

Shorty said, "That's a shoe for a Percheron horse. Look at the size of that foot."

Blackie reached for it and began to study it again. The

front portion was worn somewhat more than the rest, to the thickness of about a quarter inch. He felt of the iron, as if in his fingers he had an understanding of its strength. He seemed to be in doubt until someone said, "You can't do it, Blackie."

The big man took the ends of it in his hands, settled his massive shoulders back slowly, and began to pull. In a few seconds, he began to rearrange his fingers on the iron.

Someone laughed.

Blackie started pulling again. The firelight played on his ruddy features beneath his shock of black hair. His teeth were clamped shut. His face became darker red and veins stood out on his neck. Sweat grew in droplets and rolled down his chin. All of his torso trembled as he strained at the curl of iron. It seemed for a long moment that he had done his best and failed; then, after a spasmodic jerk of his shoulders, his hands could be seen to move apart, slowly, then more quickly. The metal began to tear on the inside of the curve, and straighten out. Blackie rearranged his hands, gave a twisting yank at the metal, and tore it into two pieces. He held the pieces high in the air in his two hands. The bright crystal silver of the torn iron sparkled in the firelight, and Blackie's eyes sparkled like those of a child.

The bull session was broken up by the arrival of Kittredge. He brought the news that the trail ahead of them was dry. They would make another short drive on the morrow to Brady Creek, which barely ran enough water for a big herd, then would face hundreds of miles of west Texas, where there had been no more than light spring showers in the past three months. Four herds were already ahead of them on the trail.

The Colonel's suggestion that it was time to get some sleep amounted to an order, and they obeyed.

Colonel With a Dead Commission

6

Oh, I went to the boss and I asked him for my roll,
But he had me figgered out nine dollars in the hole.
Come-a ti yi yippi, yippi yea, yippi yea,
Come-a ti yi yippi, yippi yea.

When the Colonel peered out across miles of terrain, reading carefully its details, his sharp face was like a stone promontory in the badlands, hewed by time and blowing sand, cleaned of all that was weak or soft. It was like the hard residue of reality, after any pretense of beauty or kindness or mercy had blown away. If at some time his lip trembled involuntarily or his head shook with his age, it seemed as if one were looking through heat waves at some stark natural object which could not itself possibly shake.

He sat astride one of his big horses as if it were a part of him. In his thin frame was no hint of strength or lack of strength. He simply rode as if strength had nothing to do with it. His manner of command was a great presumption—that whatever is *is* right, that his understanding and assessment of any situation were identical with the reality of it. If he asked one of the men for information, he wanted fact and not opinion.

Cruel war had done its share to shape his manner. He had

seen men die and their goals not reached because of vacillation in their leaders. Also, perhaps, he had come to consider the lives of men and the efforts of their days not too precious. He was concerned about the condition of the herd and of the trail. The grass was good enough, but watering places for three thousand head of cattle were too far apart. He felt that he could settle them to the trail if he could only drive them hard with some degree of regularity and at the same time find regular water holes. He had seen spring weather in this part of the country such that every arroyo ran water and every low place was a natural lake; now they were all dry. It wasn't too bad, at least not impossible, now while the weather was still cool; but if it didn't rain decently at all this spring, then western Kansas and Nebraska in June would be rough. And the ironic truth of the matter was that if it did rain at the wrong time, the big rivers ahead of them, the Red, the Canadian, the Cimarron, the Arkansas, could be just as rough.

Meanwhile, he had already decided to leave the regular trail north of the Colorado River. The herds ahead of him and behind could go where they pleased, but he intended to follow a route suitable to his herd and the water supply. He knew of bosses in years past who had lost thousands of dollars' worth of cattle for no other reason than that they thought they must precisely follow trails laid out by other men.

The individuals working under him he had already estimated much more than any of them suspected. As a whole, he considered it an average outfit, adequate to the job if they were handled properly. All of his thoughts, as he ranged far out alone ahead of the herd, were concerned with the task he was in charge of, the natural obstacles, his plans for the weeks ahead, sometimes the men he would use in fulfillment of his plans.

Blackburn is strong and he obeys. What else do you want in a segundo? He is loyal out of my presence. He is not intelligent, but such a man will always have some leader to direct his efforts. As for myself, I expect to live forever. His physical strength is to me like the strength of an obedient horse, but it should not be discounted, for some childish fools in any enterprise look to physical strength for leadership, and the real leader will use it for his own purpose. The big fool is ruining his horses. They will all six be cripples in less than a month at the present rate. I shall let him go ahead as long as I am breaking in this herd and this outfit, for an outfit must be road broken as must a herd; I shall use his unhampered drive and energy. Then he's going to get it about his horse string; I shall demonstrate to him how an army officer of the old school dresses down a sergeant. If he can take it like a soldier and adjust himself to my determination, then he will be my second in command for the remainder of the drive.

As for William Scott, let him do his work, I say, and keep his place. If he expects me to cater to him because he knows the owners, he does not know me or the difficulty of the task we are about. I saw officers in the war who had attained their ranks through money and influence; some of them proved that they were not worthy of being privates in the rear ranks. He is going to have to show me, and if he proves to have ability, he still will not be moved off the drag because of deserving better, but because I need him. For if he be a good hand, it is no more than I expect of every hand; he has no commission to do anything but what he is told. There can be only one boss of a cattle drive. As for his being assigned hard duty, is he too good? I need no excuse for assigning any man to a duty.

As for the Professor, his right name is Robert Woodberry, which is the name I use. "Professor" implies some kind of exalted position in an entirely different world, but he is in a real and harsh world today, and I expect him to measure up. Personally, I doubt his learning; I think it is pretense. But, officially, I say it is irrelevant. He's plain Robert Woodberry to me. Let him be alert to keep the cows from scattering. Let him keep his gun oiled. And I better not catch him reading one of his precious books when he should be working.

The Kid, Paul Henry Rogers, will be a man when we have come to Ogallala. He is another of those inadequate, ignorant followers that any leader must learn to put up with. He cannot help his youth, but he signed on, and he shall be excused from nothing. We have no room for pets.

That bald-headed Neil, the clown, is not funny to me, but while I appear to only tolerate him, actually I use his crude talents as I use the strength of Blackburn. I am not so inhuman but that I recognize that our life may be almost unbearable to weaker men at times. It is my duty to put down mutiny with stern measures and to avoid mutiny by such measures as may come to hand, as long as those measures do not hinder the work or seem to betray a weakness in leadership.

As for Juan Martinez, I don't want him speaking any of his Spick to me, but I knew—back at Lawson's place when we had to throw the cow to check the brand and he unlimbered his rope—that he was a top cowhand. And I don't care a whit for what crimes he may have done in the past. He is tough. He is quick. He knows cattle. He doesn't seem to know pain or weariness. I must have such men.

As for Alexander Rice, the one they call Dandy, at least I can say that he is neat. That is not without importance. One man, Wilson, the one they call Scratchy, is so sloppy that he is a disgrace. No man can care so little for the opinion of others about his appearance and at the same time care for his duty to his employer. When I have taken care of more pressing problems, I intend to do something about Mr. Wilson. I'll make an example of him.

They made the short drive to Brady Creek and found such scant water that it was hard to make sure that the cattle had all drunk their fill as they wandered up and down among the timber. Again they made a long, easy camp. Colonel Kittredge didn't like it. The cattle were not tired enough to be manageable. They bunched up too close and wasted too much energy in flighty runs to be able to stand the dry trail north of the Colorado River.

The following morning he could see a herd behind them, south of the creek, so he gave up any attempt to water again and pushed due north for the Colorado. It was twenty-five miles on his map, made forty by their winding course through the hills. It was a hot day for so early in the year, but he pushed them. They wound up through Cow Gap and down into the rough country south of the river. The creeks were dry. The nervous condition of the cattle told on them as he had known it would. Their bunching heated them. By the middle of the afternoon they had stopped breaking from the herd, but they were stubborn and dry and almost ready to stop. It was sundown when the leaders finally smelled the water and went ahead at a trot, followed erratically by the knotted string of cattle behind.

The Colonel judged the day's push and decided that it was the maximum distance for hard driving with the herd the way it was. He might make the country ahead better by shorter drives and dry camps and closer control of the cattle. He rode back toward the drags, warning the men to keep the herd surrounded and prevent them from scattering as they hit the river.

The next morning Kittredge scouted west and found a crossing in a bend where the herd could take the water with the morning sun at their backs. The Colorado was the biggest river they had yet encountered; it carried the water of the various prongs of the Concho. It was fast and clear, but the crossing had a rocky bottom and would present no difficulty.

When he came back to camp, he was met by Blackie, pushing a reluctant Murphy by the shoulder. "Go on, tell him," Blackie ordered.

"Well, all it was, Colonel, I just didn't know where Scratchy might be, and I didn't know if I ought to wake you up or . . ."

"Speak up, man," the Colonel said, sitting astride his horse. "What's happened?"

Blackie said, "It looks like Scratchy Wilson has run out on us, Colonel. Murph here went out and rode the last guard, and him gone, and never even said anything about it."

Little Murphy was serious but vague in trying to explain. "When they woke me up I thought: Well, Scratchy's done gone on guard, and then when I never seen him, I thought maybe you or Mr. Blackburn had sent him some place to do something or something like that."

The Colonel yelled, "Ostler, did Wilson have any gear in the wagon?"

"No, not as I know of."

"Are you missing anything?"

"I ain't missed nothing yet."

The Colonel turned back to Murphy. "Did he keep any belongings in his bedroll? You did sleep with him, didn't you?"

"Yes, sir. All I ever seen was a pair of drawers and three socks he had between the blankets."

"And I suppose those articles of clothing are gone now?"

"Yes, sir. They're sure gone all right. And I think he might of got one sock of mine. I had eight pairs of brown socks, nearly new—one or two of them had a little hole in the toe—I got a ingrowing toenail on my big toe—and I counted . . ."

"So he separated the blankets and took his clothing and you slept right through it?"

"Yes, sir. I guess so. I sure never thought old Scratchy would leave that way. I didn't . . ."

"Why didn't you think he would leave?"

Murphy grinned, just enough to show the gaps where his front teeth were missing, then he met the Colonel's eyes and sobered up. "I just thought . . . I thought old Scratchy was lucky to have a good job."

"That's the first intelligent thing you've said about it," the Colonel told him. "Blackburn, I suppose Wilson's horse was staked with the others?"

"Yes, sir. And he's sure gone now, Colonel. I checked the remuda, and his night horse ain't there."

The Colonel looked around a minute and said half to himself, "That's fine. That's just fine. He's gone on a fifty-dollar horse. When he was first missed, he may have been gone only a few minutes; now he's been gone several hours."

Murphy said, "Well, I didn't think . . . I just thought . . ."

"Never mind what you thought! Ostler, cross your wagon one mile due west of here after the herd is across."

"Float it?"

"No, it may touch your wagon box in the middle of the stream, but go right on through. Turn back downstream to a point about opposite here. We will stay one more night on this water. Blackburn, let's point them west."

"Yes, sir. Uh . . . which direction is that, Colonel?"

"That's the sun coming up over there, Blackburn. It comes up in the east. This way is west over here. Maybe you'd better just follow me."

He had lost his chance to make an example of Scratchy Wilson, a good example. He would have liked to have caught the man and bound him hand and foot and carried him like a trussed pig in the wagon to the next point of civilization, where he could charge him before the law. As it was, he would do the best with the example he could. The matter was not as bad as it could be. If he had been choosing one to quit, he would have chosen Wilson. And it settled some of the problem of Blackburn's mounts; they now had five extra horses in the remuda.

That afternoon he spent poring over his map of west Texas. They were camped on a rise, and occasionally he would peer to the north, once or twice consulting the brass compass which he wore on a black ribbon around his neck and inside his shirt. A short time before supper, he left the herd with only two men and addressed the others beside the wagon. His attitude was formal, and they gave him complete attention.

"Mr. Nicholas Wilson has broken his word, has broken his solemn contract, has stolen a horse belonging to this outfit, and has deserted. Men, he has not only deserted the man who employed him, he has deserted you. Who will do the work that would have been assigned to Wilson? You will. When a man deserts a trail outfit, he has done a dirty, underhanded trick to every other hand in that outfit.

"He has stolen a night horse. Is some rider going to have to try to do his share of the work without one good horse? You understand that problem as well as I do. So you see, we are not only short one hand; we are short one important horse. Well, you can be assured that if the lawmen of this state can find him, Mr. Wilson will answer for what he has done. He's a horse thief, and I will certainly charge him with that crime when we have come to Fort Griffin. Furthermore, I will insist that he be hunted down and prosecuted to the limit of the law.

"Now, one time when I caught a man attempting to desert and steal a horse and had bound him up and was delivering him to justice, he told me he thought he had a right to the horse on account of the wages due him. In case this might occur to any of you in regard to Mr. Wilson, let me set the matter straight. When he signed on, he understood clearly that he had *no* wages due him until we have delivered the herd. *No* wages. Every one of you understands the reason for such an arrangement. The owners have many thousands of dollars tied up in this drive. You risk three months' wages on its success; they risk much more. If any hand has a need for money, he may be advanced it, but he is not due it. Furthermore, the horse Mr. Wilson stole is worth fifty dollars, and he certainly has not earned fifty dollars by any manner of calculation. He's a horse thief. He may think he's free, but the charge will follow him and find him.

"So much for Mr. Wilson." The Colonel was unconsciously standing at parade rest, his hands clasped behind his back. "Tomorrow we start on a dry drive that will take us into the third day before we come to water. I know that this can be done, because I've done it before. But it's got to be done right. We will not push the cattle. I want the leaders held back, and I want them strung out a full two miles. I don't want any two bodies touching in that herd.

"In the morning we will hold them on the river and make sure they have drunk all they will. They must be strung out thin and walking steadily before the sun is high. We will let them drift in the general direction in the heat of the day. The second morning I want them prodded off that bed ground and grazing while the dew is on the grass. Same way the third morning, and we should strike water that day. I know it can be done, because I've done it, and we should have no great trouble this time of the year if every man does his duty.

"The water carried in the wagon will be for drinking and cooking purposes only. Mr. Ostler, you will carry all the water possible and take precautions that it last. Does anyone have any questions?"

They had no questions, or did not ask them.

The next morning when the cattle had watered to the Colonel's satisfaction they strung them out north and a little west. He worked closely with the men, starting with Blackie and Martinez in the lead, setting the direction and the pace. When they had gone two miles, the Colonel insisted that the leaders be held down. Blackie was better at pushing them than at holding them back. He would crowd in, causing them to turn or even stop. And if they stopped he wanted to be after them with the quirt.

"Watch your cows when you move in," the Colonel told him over and over. "Work together with Martinez. You've got to hold them down."

Then the Colonel fell back and let the herd string past him, advising the swing riders on the left, Shorty, who had taken Scratchy Wilson's place, and Art Howard. "Squeeze them out!" he would say to them. "Don't let them knot up! Squeeze them out!" The swing men rode in constant circles, working in pairs on opposite sides of the herd, coming together against a heavy concentration of cows, squeezing them toward the rear, then swinging out to go forward again. The cows on the outside of the concentration would slow up, ducking their heads in away from the riders, and fall back to a thinner line.

To the flank riders, the Colonel yelled the same thing. "Squeeze them out! Don't let them ball up back here." And as they followed his orders, he circled around to the drag and yelled, "Hold up! Let them drift back! Keep the slack out! Don't crowd them!"

They wound along the hilly divide west of Home Creek, which was dry. Occasionally they could see the timbered course of the stream out to the right. The Colonel's shrill voice, insistent yet patient, echoed up and down the string of cattle, and the riders worked harder than they had at any time during the past two weeks. The cattle, whose ease was the object of the work, were not easy to handle; they wanted to go. The young heifers broke from the herd at every point along the string and headed east and west and back south. Most of them carried a dozen or more steers with them as they broke away. They were headed by the riders and crowded back to the string, making another knot that had to be squeezed out.

At the dry noon camp they changed horses, and the Colonel, seeing the condition of the morning's mounts, ordered that another change be made in the middle of the afternoon.

The cattle continued restless in the heat of the day. Then in the cool of evening, when they might have safely covered some distance, they wanted to slow up or stop and graze. The men pushed them till ten o'clock that night to a large bed ground selected by the Colonel on a smooth rise. The second guard got to bed at midnight and were roused up to begin their stint two hours later.

It was still dark when the first guard was awakened for another dry day, and the Colonel read to them briefly by lantern light.

When he was gone out of earshot, the men began to grumble and joke, trying to waken themselves and trying to harden themselves, because they faced another day and still carried the weariness of the previous one. "Boys," Baldy said, "it sure never took us long to stay all night in this place, did it?"

Someone told him, "Just be glad you ain't a horse or a

cow. At least we got drinking water."

And someone else said, "I ain't at all sure but what Scratchy had the right idea."

Blackie killed two newborn calves on that bed ground, splitting their skulls with the butt of the ax, and they buried them in hasty graves to hide them from their mothers. It was barely light when they prodded the cattle up and tried to make them graze; the cattle did not have the eagerness of the morning before. They were sullen as they walked north. They had used up too much moisture the first day.

As the sun came high overhead the drag became the most difficult place to work. The beasts became more and more laggard, more and more unwilling to follow the animals ahead. Then other spots in the long string of cattle became like the drag with cattle slowing or stopping, causing gaps. The loud bawling of the two frustrated mothers was taken up here and there by steers, whose voices were moans rather than calls.

Colonel Kittredge was everywhere as he had been the day before, from a spot ahead of them on a hill, looking at a folded map and his brass compass, to the drag. He yelled shrilly to the men and took no part in the work, but studied carefully how his orders were followed and did not hesitate to repeat them. Dust came straight over the herd from a light south wind; it built up to a high yellow bank worming across the prairie. The men wore their bandannas tight up under their eyes, looking like a bunch of dusty bandits, but the Colonel ignored the dust.

Far to the east they could see the landmark of Santa Anna Mountain. When they took the pressure off before noon, some of the cattle lay down where they were allowed to stop; others wandered aimlessly. A full double guard was required to hold them until four o'clock in the afternoon, at which time the Colonel judged that it was cool enough to continue.

At dark this night the cattle began to stop and lie down long before the Colonel was satisfied with the day's distance. There was nothing to do but turn the leaders back in a circle and try to bed them all. Half of them refused to lie down. They wandered and bawled mournfully. The Colonel gave up trying to bed them at midnight and again set two short guards.

In the darkness of the second guard William Scott had pulled out away from the others and dumped his canteen, a quart of water, in his hat and thrust it over his black night horse's nose. Blackjack got one good gulp and a few more sips as he chomped at his bit inside the wet hat. Shorty rode out toward Scott and asked, "Anything wrong?"

"Nope." Shorty was one of the few men that Scott would not have minded catching him wasting water in such a way. "What do you think? Reckon the Colonel will get us to water today?"

"He probably will, but I wish he'd head more east." Scott remounted and pointed. "See where the North Star is? We've been heading west of north all the way. I believe we could have hit water yesterday if we had held over to the east."

As they fanned them out in the dim morning light to graze, the cattle tongued at the damp grass, licking rather than grazing. They slobbered, leaving white bubbles along the ground, and seemed to lose more moisture than they gained from the dew. When the sun was up and hot, the cattle stopped their moaning bawls for the first time in twenty-four hours. They lagged and stopped but made no attempts to break from the herd. Their swollen tongues began to show out of grotesquely grinning mouths. Many of the cattle had to be quirted to make them leave the dry gravelly bottoms of Hords Creek. They crossed another dry creek, then Colonel Kittredge set out ahead to scout for water.

When the trail boss was little more than out of sight, the herd came out onto a level stretch of land with a shallow sink in the middle, a place without drainage. An area of two acres was bare of grass because of alkalinity in the soil, and sometime earlier in the spring a shallow sheet of water had stood over it. The soil surface was webbed with cracks, its topmost layer divided into six-sided pieces the size of a man's hand and curling up at the edges. Into this area the lead steers trotted; they put their heads down and sniffed and jerked this way and that, searching. Blackie and Martinez whipped at them and yelled, to no avail.

The action of the leaders seemed to send a signal to the cattle behind. They lifted their heads and hurried forward and tried to crowd into the place where water had been a month before. Then in and around the two acres of ground began a mad circus of milling cattle. The rear riders came up. Blackie shouted desperate orders at them. They rode at right angles into the whirling streams of cattle, but the beasts, checked, all tried to go to the center. The men began to cut off bunches to try to hold out of the mill.

The beasts' tongues were hanging out now, blue and swollen and dusty. They seemed to be coming to a bitter crossroads in their behavior and were unmanageable. Their frantic searching turned to listless wandering. Then a curious stubborn purpose seemed to arise in them, a few at a time; they started plodding—south.

At the same time Kittredge came back, galloping his horse. He had been gone not much more than an hour. He screamed at the men, "Stop them! Turn them! It's only three miles to water!"

A moderate wind blew out of the south; had it been from the north the cows would have smelled the water. They had come in their distress and pain to an instinctive kind of action that made them blind to small dangers in the immediate vicinity. They were no more afraid of man or horse than is a rabid animal. They went as relentlessly as lemmings following their destiny toward the sea. They may have gone south through memory of the water they had left, or they may have gone into the wind through a dim instinct that made them, in distress, want to smell the land they were entering. The plodding determination filtered back through them like a disease spreading, and they surged out of the place where the shallow lake had been, now a pit of dust with one dead trampled cow.

The riders fought them on tired, dry horses, according to the Colonel's orders. Scott came even with the big dun steer in the lead, dallied his rope around the saddle horn, and cast his loop over the steer's horns. He rode to the side the length of his rope and stopped the grullo, making a rope barrier twenty-five feet long. The cattle pushed against the rope without even lowering their heads, and Scott saw he was lucky that he hadn't tied his end fast to the saddle. As the grullo was sliding and about to go down, Scott released the rope and let them go on. He threaded among them and reached down and took his loop from the big steer's horns. The steer did not seem to notice but plodded ahead.

The riders lashed them in the faces with quirts and the knotted ends of ropes; the beasts did not feel it. They would walk straight into a horse. They moved back the direction from which they came, doggedly, in a solid front. Checked or turned briefly in one spot, they surged out in others. The cowboys could see that it was hopeless.

Blackie tailed down a steer, and his horse's legs crumbled. The big man came out of the saddle and, cursing, flailed at the pony with his quirt. When he had beaten the worn-out pony to its feet, the Colonel came up beside him.

"Mr. Blackburn, round up the men. Tell them to leave the herd alone. I want to speak to them right here."

When they had gathered, all but the Kid and Ostler, they saw that the old trail boss looked stern and they expected a severe tongue-lashing, but his voice, though harsh and shrill, was almost expressionless and had in it a kind of tight patience.

"The herd cannot be stopped short of the Colorado River. I have seen this before and know whereof I speak. We can hold them together and we must. And we can prevent them from overrunning another herd back at the river. I want every man to catch his strongest horse; that's important. We can't stop the herd, but we can control them. We'll lose nothing but a few days' time.

"I will send the wagon and the remuda ahead to water, and they will overtake us. Rice, I want you to help the Kid take the horses to water." He pointed. "It's due north, not over three miles. Don't rush them at their drinking and don't let them run after they have drunk. You should catch us in the middle of the afternoon.

"All right, catch your strongest horse, whether it's a night horse or some other, and let's stay with the cattle."

William Scott came near to disobeying the order to catch his strongest horse. It was with a heavy heart that he dropped his loop over Blackjack's head. He patted the horse on the shoulder, thinking: Three miles from water and I've got to take you south clear to the Colorado River.

The riders caught the cattle and followed them, followed ahead of them and to the sides and the rear. There was no herding to do. There was no noon meal. The cattle moved in their relentless drift, driven by their mysterious single purpose, pitiful and dazed, into the wind. They passed the camp of the night before and drifted on in the heat of the afternoon.

Dandy Rice rejoined them late in the afternoon, and they could see the chuck wagon and remuda a half mile to the side. The Colonel sent them one at a time to eat whatever Ostler had prepared and to change to a freshly watered horse. It was almost dark when Scott got to the wagon. Ostler handed him a cup of coffee, a plate of beans, and two sourdough biscuits.

"I got to have a little water for Blackjack," Scott told him.

"You know better than that. I ain't running no horse trough."

"It won't take much, Ostler. Maybe two or three gallons. You filled everything up, didn't you?"

"Sure I did. But this water is for humans. You know better than that, Billy."

"Aw, come on, Ostler, my horse hasn't had a drink for three days."

"I tell you this water I got is for humans."

"I got to have some, Ostler. Just two gallons. You've got two kegs. I bet you've got fifty gallons on this wagon, and those crazy cows are going to walk all night. They'll hit the Colorado tomorrow morning. Why should you carry all this water back to the Colorado River?"

"Blame! Can't you understand this water I got is for humans? You're supposed to turn that horse loose with the remuda and catch one we watered. Your horse can make it back without water."

"Aw, come on, Ostler. You watered your mules. Let me have one gallon. He hasn't drunk in three days."

"Damn a knotheaded cowboy that can't understand you when you talk right in his face! Ain't I told you this water is for humans? The Colonel would skin me alive!"

"Just one gallon, Ostler. I'll do you a favor some time. The Colonel's not going to know anything about it."

"They's a dozen horses that hasn't had water. What about them? I'm about to run out of my patience on you. Can't you understand nothing?"

"He's been three days, Ostler. I don't want him to walk all night again tonight without water. One gallon. Come on. What do you say?"

The cook looked straight up as if he were in anguish, heaved an exaggerated sigh, and said, "I got a three-gallon bucket hanging under the back end of the wagon with a cloth tied over it. Might be a little water in it if it ain't all sloshed out."

While Blackjack sipped in the bucket, raising his head and letting the water dribble back, the cook moaned, "God damn! I think I must be going crazy in my old age. Listen to that nasty horse snorting and slobbering in my dipping bucket. You think a cook is dirty about grub sometimes; he ain't half as nasty as a knotheaded cowboy. Hurry up and get that ignorant horse out of that bucket and eat that grub and get out of here."

They went south with the herd through the night. When they passed the bed ground of forty-eight hours before, the two cows who had borne calves there circled, sniffing silently. The two had to be roped and dragged forward, two ropes on the horns of each cow, and forced to join the rest of the herd. Outside of this, there was no herding to do. The herd moved on relentlessly through the early morning hours and into the daylight, neither slowing nor increasing their speed, not even as they came in the middle of the morning into the valley of the river.

Finally, they stopped, spread up and down it. They stood up to their knees in the cool, clear rushing water. They nosed at it.

One Cowboy's Dilemma

7

Oh, it's bacon and it's beans and it's gravy every day;
I'd a soon a be a eating prairie hay.
Come-a ti yi yippi, yippi yea, yippi yea,
Come-a ti yi yippi, yippi yea.

I t was harder than Scott had thought it would be—not the work, but the position he was in. He couldn't keep his mind out of the Colonel's problems. He worked on his own maps whenever he had a chance, drawing with a pencil sharpened keenly against a pocket stone, correcting the curves of streams, noting distances and crossings and water conditions.

He would have given a month's wages when they had first left the Colorado, going west of north, to have put his head together with the Colonel's, to have put their maps together, to have talked it over with him. The maps were not accurate; they represented scanty army surveys and a great deal of guesswork, a hundred faulty memories about distances and the nature of terrain and watercourses. The state of Texas was engaged with the federal government in a land dispute, which had resulted from an earlier survey's placing the hundredth meridian a hundred miles in error. But more important than meridians to cattlemen was the mislocation of water and the fact that two maps seldom agreed as to whether a small stream were steady or intermittent, whether it flowed the year around or only in rainy weather.

Then, if he had been able to compare information with the Colonel, one of them could have scouted ahead to check on their conclusions. He had seen a map one time whereupon the course of Pecan Bayou and Jim Ned Creek, which runs into it, were almost certainly plotted wrong, and he believed that the Colonel must have such a map now. But, anyway, a lot of important information could have been gained by a day's scouting. The Colonel was making it harder than it needed to be. What the old man needed was a segundo he could trust.

The day after they came back to the river, they lay over in the area, making a tally and letting the cows regain their strength. Scott asked Dandy, "Was there plenty of water in that creek where you watered the horses—up there where we turned back?"

"Yeah, enough for a herd of cows. Why?"

"It was Jim Ned Creek," Scott said. "Which direction would you say it ran?"

"Come to think about it, it angled back south."

"It ran southeast?"

"Yeah, I guess it did. What do you think the old man will do now, Scott?"

"He'll go east, I think. Away east. I thought he would the first time."

"What makes you think that? How you know there's water east of here?"

Scott laughed. "That creek where you watered the horses runs into this river. They call it Pecan Bayou down there. We can go east and hit it and follow it right up."

He turned out to be right. Kittredge grazed them east two days along the river, watering twice a day. These were easy days. The men took baths and slept a full eight hours at night. They had time to lie on their backs and look at the stars and listen to the small frogs and the crickets and the locusts, which were beginning their long warm-weather music.

Scott had a strong memory during those days, awakened by the dry drive they had made and also by the Kid. He had almost forgotten. It was fourteen years ago that he had made the drive, half of his life ago, thousands of miles of cattle driving ago. It wasn't the drive that he had forgotten, for he had been part of a drive which blazed a trail that would go down in history, something he was proud of; but he had almost forgotten the Kid part. They had called him Kid. He must have grown up on that drive, for no one had called him Kid afterward. But he could see in the Kid from Galveston, Paul Henry Rogers, the keen eagerness, the innocence, and he remembered it and understood it.

And he had almost forgotten how thirst-crazed animals can look and act. Remembering those cruel days long ago, he knew that they were lucky today to have this Lawson herd intact and under control. Old Oliver Loving had been in charge around the herd, and Goodnight had scouted out ahead, pointing a trail to New Mexico, which would finally go up into Colorado and beyond. And he, Scott, the Kid, had had no idea that he was a part of something that would be remembered forever by men who raise cattle, for his whole boyish heart and soul had been saturated with the simple desire to please Mr. Loving, to show that he could be a good cowhand, to do his part.

At first Goodnight had sworn that he would hire only army veterans, and Scott had sworn in turn that he was eighteen and had been a Confederate soldier for a year. The two cowmen had laughed, and then they had argued. It was during that period when his having missed the war hung like a dark cloud over Scott's life. And finally Loving, the older and more experienced of the two partners, had done that which he rarely did; he had overruled Goodnight. Scott was hired.

They had pushed southwest from the Middle Concho toward the Pecos, for a dry drive that was pure hell. The cows had suffered horribly, and the horses. He had had a galled spot in his crotch that spread with the long hot hours in the saddle clear down to his knees, burning with the salt of his sweat. On the third dry day, when it had become doubtful that they could get the whole herd through, Mr. Goodnight had cut out the strongest two-thirds of the cattle and taken them on to Horsehead Crossing on the Pecos, with four men, leaving the rest of them with the drags. But Mr. Loving had said, "We can get them through, boys. It's not far to go now."

Then when they were so close that they all thought they could, the pitifully weak cows smelled the water too soon and ran for it with all their remaining strength, straight south to where the Pecos ran between high banks. They could not be stopped. Scott had seen his own horse almost crowded over. They could not be stopped, but went over the bank to drown or be caught in the quicksand.

He had dismounted to look at his horse's lame foot and had cried like a baby, thinking he was alone. But Mr. Loving had come up behind him and said, "Don't let it worry you, Kid. A man can't afford to fret about a few crazy cows."

And, pretending that he hadn't been crying, he had said, "But we brought them so far, Mr. Loving. We worked so hard trying to get them through."

The old man had said, "Well, you save some and you lose some," but his face, as he stared at the dying cattle in the river, showed that he cared more than he said.

That must have been the instant that the Kid, still a boy in years, became a man, when he understood that the old man cared as much as he, in spite of what he said. A year later, when Scott learned that Oliver Loving was dead of a Comanche bullet, he had no tears, but he remembered the look on the old man's face that day when he stared out into the Pecos River and said, "Well, you save some and you lose some." The irony of that statement had remained with Scott. You say something like that, but when you have done your best, you are not satisfied with losing any at all. When you start to do something and find that it is harder than you thought, you try harder, and the goal is made precious by the work and sacrifice and pain that go toward it; and you are never satisfied with losing any at all.

When they had crossed Clear Creek, the Colonel headed them northeast, and they made the drive to Pecan Bayou in one day. They crossed and turned up it northwest, looping out away from the brakes and timber to graze and bed and returning once a day to water. Again they crossed the main body of Pecan Bayou and went on northwest along one branch, Jim Ned Creek. Seven days from the day the thirst-maddened cattle had turned back, they reached that point three miles ahead, where the remuda and chuck wagon had watered; they had lost exactly a week through the cattle's stubbornness.

The Colonel had been watching the penning of the remuda in the rope corral and the catching of mounts, and evidently had decided to establish some order in the procedure. When the men came, each with his lariat, to start the usual confusion, the Colonel yelled, "Put those ropes back on your saddles! I want two men to do all the roping. This man and this man!" He pointed at Scott and Martinez. "Call out your mounts to them!"

The penned horses bunched up, holding their heads together. Often one would sense that he was wanted and would duck behind another and lower his head. Scott threw a soft loop, sweeping it forward from the ground behind him, and he had learned to let it roll over the neck or back of one horse and around the neck of one beyond. He felt satisfaction that the Colonel had chosen him for the job, but the words "this man" rankled. "This man and this man!" As if the trail boss did not know his name or the name of Martinez. Or maybe the old man was trying to pretend that he hadn't been watching and didn't know that they were the best two men with a lariat rope in the outfit.

It was that same day, in the late afternoon, that Cory made his fantastic proposition to Scott. They had ridden a half mile down to the creek to wash out some socks and underwear.

Cory asked, "You know that country real good out west of here, don't you, Billy?"

"I've been through it a couple of times," Scott said.

"What I mean is, you could take a herd of cattle to New Mexico, with your maps and what you know about it, couldn't you?"

"Yeah, I guess so. Sure I could, if I had a herd to take."

"Hell, didn't you help start that Goodnight-Loving Trail?"

Scott laughed. "I rode on the drag. I was pretty young."

"Well, you know this herd is going to run one of these days, Billy. This is a spooky bunch if I ever saw one. They're bound to run."

"I wouldn't be surprised. I guess the Colonel has done a pretty good job of choosing bed grounds and everything so far. They've been ready, ever since we started."

"A man could make them run just like that." Cory snapped his fingers. "That's all it would take. We could get us a herd to take to New Mexico."

"What in the hell are you talking about, Cory?"

"I'm talking about us getting us a herd, me and you and Shorty. When they run we could cut us out about five hundred head and go west. That's how simple it would be."

Scott laughed again. "That's a kind of dangerous dream."

"By God, it ain't no dream! I'm serious. Shorty would throw in with us. I know he would if you said it was all right. And we could do it, Billy. How could they catch us? The outfit would have their hands plenty full just holding the rest of the herd with us gone. Hell, they probably wouldn't know we was gone for two days."

Scott studied him, grinning. "Good thing you got two pardners like Shorty and me to keep you on the straight and narrow. You'd be in a jailhouse somewhere, or swinging from a cottonwood tree."

"Swinging from a cottonwood tree? How could they catch us? You can get out of this state without papers on cattle. You might not going north, but you can going west. And you can sell them out there too. You can find buyers out there that won't ask you no questions. Hell, that two-bit Colonel couldn't do a thing. He might report us when he gets to Fort Griffin, but we'd be long gone. It would be easy."

"You reckon we could beat a telegraph message from Fort Griffin to Fort McKavett or Fort Concho or Fort Stockton out the other side of the Pecos? It's a damn good thing you got pardners like Shorty and me, Cory."

Cory was quiet for a moment; then he narrowed his dark eyes and said, "Well, I still think we could do it. Maybe I think better of us three than you do. I know we could handle five hundred cows. And we can shoot; we could get the rifles Ostler carries in the wagon. And I believe you could find us a way to get around these forts you're talking about. Maybe it wouldn't be easy, but maybe we could do it anyway."

"Well, you think it would be honest to steal five hundred cows?"

"God dammit! I'm not joking, Billy. Honest, hell! Most of the big owners in this country got their start roping mavericks that wasn't theirs. What's right about owners like Greer and Brown setting on their broad ass at home, while fellers like me and you drive their cows and work our fingers to the bone under a high-faluting Colonel that thinks me and you are lower than a snake's belly? Look at old Scratchy Wilson. I know he was a sorry son-of-a-bitch that wasn't worth his grub, but just because he quit he's a horse thief. What's right about that?"

Scott was still grinning. "Cory, you're just like a lot of boys that get kicked around a little, so what do they do? They do the first stupid thing that comes into their head to try to get even. And that gets everybody down on them. Hell, why don't you be smart and play the game according to the rules or just check out? But it's one thing to quit, and its another thing to steal five hundred head of cattle."

"Yeah, if you steal cattle you're a cattle thief; if you quit you're a horse thief. What's the difference? I've heard of a man getting hung for stealing a horse."

"Well, a man's not a horse thief because the Colonel says he is. He's trying to scare the boys that don't know any better. The owner of the horse has got to swear out a complaint, and the owners don't think quite like the

Colonel does."

"All right, then what do you say we quit? Me and you and Shorty. I'd like to see that smart-aleck Colonel and his dumb segundo run the outfit and us gone. Maybe it would show them something if we quit. You don't owe the owners anything after the way they done you."

"No, I don't figure I owe them a thing. I might even make up my mind to quit, but what's the hurry? Why don't we just stay around and watch the show?"

"The show? You mean working like a slave for this messed-up outfit and driving this spooky herd is a show?"

"It won't be the same outfit by the time we get to Nebraska. The Colonel straightened out that horse-catching mess today. Things will change. Of course, they may not be any better, but they'll change."

"Why in the hell don't he make you segundo if he means to straighten out the mess, and put Blackie on the drag?"

Scott laughed some more. "I don't care about being segundo. I haven't got any worries. Let Kittredge and Blackie do the worrying."

"Naw, you don't care about being segundo. Hell no, you don't care. Let Blackie be segundo. Let Blackie wear out the horses. He's done wore out his string and now he's riding Scratchy's; whose horses will he start on next? I reckon you'll loan him Blackjack. But you don't care about being segundo. Not you."

"Not me. Who knows? Maybe I can learn something from the Colonel."

"Oh, yeah, I expect you will. You'll learn a lot from that smart Colonel. And Blackie too. We'll all learn how to work cattle from the Colonel and Blackie."

When they had come almost back to camp, Cory said, "If you make up your feeble mind to quit, let me know, and I'll go with you."

They went northwest to the head of Jim Ned Creek; then jumped across the divide through the confines of the mountain pass called Buffalo Gap. This was the pass through which Goodnight had guided the Goodnight-Loving outfit to blaze the trail west, and it was also the route of the Butterfield Trail and the Southern Overland Mail.

Past Buffalo Gap they came to the southernmost headwaters of the Brazos River, along which they watered, going northeast. They passed and saw, across the timbered creek bottoms, the gaunt stone chimneys of abandoned Fort Phantom Hill, standing like forgotten sentinels.

They crossed Spring Creek, Long Creek, Chimney Creek, Fish Creek. Mosquitos started coming out from the river to find them in their camps. The Kid snaked up bundles of small cedar boughs to lay over the coals of the camp fire. Ostler fussed as much about the smoke as he had about the mosquitos.

Bluebonnets were beginning to bloom, also purple violets and little clusters of lavender flowers called Sweet Williams and down in damp areas along the water, white buttercups.

They passed Fort Griffin. Its buildings of whitewashed stone stood high on the hill as if in disdain of the sorry scattering of shacks it had spawned in the valley below. Kittredge led them to a camp north of the Clear Fork. Again Blackie was in full charge for a day while the Colonel went in to buy supplies and make his report on the horse thief.

Following the day when Blackie was in charge, Scott began to question himself strongly about his position in the outfit.

It was not so much that he wanted a better position as it was that he was conscious of the misunderstanding. He and the Colonel had gotten off on the wrong foot. It was hardly his fault, considering the disappointment about the broken promise; but it was hardly the Colonel's either, considering that he knew nothing about the broken promise. Maybe if he caught the Colonel alone and apologized for the way he had acted that day when he went back after Blackjack, showed the Colonel the letter from Lawson, just laid his cards on the table, told the Colonel that he wasn't asking for anything but just wanted the misunderstanding cleared up . . .

He unfolded the letter, now becoming worn and deeply creased, from his pocket and tried to imagine how it would sound to the Colonel. It read:

Dear Scott,

Just a line to let you know that the herd is all arranged for and we should begin road branding April 1. I hope that you can get here on that date or no later than the 5th for sure. You will want time to check supplies and gear to be carried in the wagon, to choose your mounts, and become acquainted with your men. Also, as you say, it is better to have the expense of an extra week on the trail than to run the risk of having to trail too fast to meet the July 1 delivery.

As for the heifers and young cows, Johnson understands that any calves belong to him and are no expense to us. Watch the six-year age limit. I wouldn't throw a single cow to check her teeth and I wouldn't argue—if you're not sure, just cut them back. You will have to talk right up to Johnson. I think it is high time for drovers to be as businesslike when they buy, as they are required to be when they sell.

I don't have to tell you to avoid cows that will calve in three months. You can buy up to thirty head over three hundred, if they look good to you. Make sure you agree clearly with Johnson on the tally—he is honest but a sharp trader.

Please give my regards to . . .

Scott folded the letter and put it back in his pocket. It would sound like he was asking for something if he showed it to the Colonel. He didn't need to show the letter in order to apologize. But what in the devil did he have to apologize for? This line of thought led him to a kind of bitter anger, and he consoled himself with the same idea he had expressed to Cory: Things will change.

They were coming up out of the cedar country. No longer were the distant hills and ridges dotted with the dark evergreen. The land through which they had been passing and which lay ahead of them was rolling hills, broken by ridges from which they could see far into the distance, and they were impressed by its vastness. They would come upon one grassy ridge, only to see another a mile ahead; upon that one, to see another; but then they would come upon one and be surprised at the distance they could see across the undulating terrain to the hazy purple horizon more than a day's drive ahead.

When the wind breathed her long breath in the buffalo grass, the land seemed to come alive like a swelling sea. The relentless sun filled the air and bathed the land as he fills sea air and bathes wide water. The men peered through slitted eyes into the distance. Some places the horizon was near; some places it was far and uncertain—as in a heavy ocean. They understood that beyond the horizon was more of the same, and beyond that more and more. The distance spoke to them. Its meaning lay in its mystery, in the possibility of experience contained in it.

The trees along the watercourses, cottonwoods, elms, hackberries, oaks, redhaws, sycamores, pecans, were bursting out with tender leaves. Out on the prairies, scattered mesquites were starting to bloom. They found enough water holes along Elm Creek to water one night, then pushed ahead to the main course of the Brazos River.

The Brazos had a broad bed, wide enough to carry the water out of the staked plains from a score of small streams like Crawfish Draw and Frio Draw and Yellowhouse Creek, as well as from its larger tributaries, White River, Salt Fork, Double Mountain Fork. But the broad bed now was mostly dry white sand, gleaming in the sun. At the crossing, the water lay in still pools and two shallow streams in the center. Tracks indicated that a herd had passed no more than a week before without trouble.

The Colonel rode back and forth three times; then decided to cross the wagon at the cattle crossing, rather than send it to the ferry at Round Timbers. Ostler didn't like it and moaned about quicksand, but he went right on through.

They crossed the river on May 4. To Scott it seemed that they were running a little behind time, not seriously, but considering that you push a herd the first week and that you fatten them in the last months of the drive, they were behind. If he had been in charge of the herd, he would have wanted to be crossing the Red on this day.

They Run

8

Oh, it's cloudy in the west and it looks like rain,
And my damned old slicker's in the wagon again.
Come-a ti yi yippi, yippi yea, yippi yea,
Come-a ti yi yippi, yippi yea.

Kittredge held them north of the Brazos two full days after the crossing, grazing them and returning to the river to water. The grass was good, indicating that fair rain had fallen here earlier in the year, but the creeks were as they had been farther south, dry or only holding small pockets of water. On the afternoon of the second day he watered them and pulled them out on a new grazing area, expecting to push across to the Wichita River the following day.

Most of the men had been expecting rain and dreading it, on account of memories of long wet rides in other years, but Scott sympathized with the problems of the old trail boss, who gazed in silent speculation at the cloudless sky. To put weight on the steers and get them through on time you had to graze them north in a slow regular manner, but to do it you had to have water holes between the rivers.

On the eastern edge of the area they grazed that afternoon was a vast shallow depression as if made by a huge scoop taking the surface layer out of the terrain of gentle hills. Its walls were eroded banks as high as ten feet on this side and its floor was bare red earth with a scattering of small chaparral and bunch grass, some spots of igneous rocks, but mostly bare alkaline soil. In the middle an eroded dry stream bed wandered, visible only because of the shadows of its shallow banks.

It was a hot and muggy day. Clouds hung low in the west. They grew as afternoon wore on. Kittredge surveyed the wide depression in the earth and ordered his men to push the cattle a half mile back from it for bedding. The old man kept looking at the clouds. They were growing. In them dim lightning winked. He sent half of the men to the wagon for early chow.

As Scott rode with the bunch back toward the wagon he was sweating, though it didn't seem hot any longer. His horse stirred dust out of last year's grass, but the air was full of moisture. Not a breath of wind blew. The sweat in his clothes, which wouldn't evaporate, was cold. The air gave him a feeling of apprehension. He was thinking: It's bound to rain in this part of the country in April and May, but it hasn't rained two cupfuls yet; when it comes, it will come hard.

Ostler fussed at them. "Looks like you all expect me to feed you any time of the night or day."

"Why don't you tell the Colonel your troubles?" Dandy asked.

They were not in the mood to get a good argument going. Baldy observed, as if trying to put some life in the group, "One of these days we going to have weather wholesale."

Scott said, "I think the old man smells some weather now."

They had only filled their plates and found places to sit or squat when Kittredge rode up among them. "I want every night horse saddled," he said. "Cory, Rice, get out there and bring them in right now. Let's don't waste much time eating." He rode back toward the herd in a lope.

The two men named put their grub on the drop table at the end of the wagon. Cory said to Ostler, "How about keeping the bugs and gnats out of my chow?"

"I will," Baldy said.

"No, you won't neither. You fellers let that nut ruin my chow, and I'm going to whip somebody when I get back."

The clouds had grown and spread; they could be seen to the north and south as well as the west. From some uncertain direction came the low rumble of thunder. Scott was roping out the night horses when Kittredge rode up to the wagon again. His voice was louder now and shriller. "What's the holdup here? I want you men on the herd! Ostler, when every man has eaten, move this wagon back down to lower ground near those trees. Do you see where I mean? Lash your tarp down good and have that Kid drag up some wood under the wagon. Then you catch one of my horses and stay with the remuda."

When he had ridden back to the herd on Blackjack, Scott thought he could understand the Colonel's nervousness. The air felt even heavier now and as still as death. It made him pant to get enough air in his lungs. The cows had stopped grazing and it was too early to bed down. They poked their noses high and sniffed the air. The thunder muttered more clearly, and occasionally a steer would snort as if in answer to it.

The sun was hidden in the west. Overhead the sky was slate gray in its highest reaches, and at a lower level thin scud raced as if fleeing heavier clouds to the west. To the north and south tall clouds had passed; these were touched by the sun, towering high like piles of clabber cheese, glowing. Rays from the hidden sun fanned in long arcs in the heavens. Over the whole landscape was diffused an unnatural light that seemed to emanate from the rolling land and the air itself, this light made every object stand out vividly, each cow and each rider, and made an ominous contrast with an angry dark cloud which lay due west.

Thunder came louder, like a log chain dragged over a drum. Scott saw a chain of lightning play in the clouds to the north, its end jabbing among the lower reaches, searching. He counted the seconds, five seconds to the mile, to see how far away it was, but when the sound came it was a long rumble that built up to a stuttering noise, then rolled away grumbling among the clouds, and he could not mark when it began or ended.

They circled the herd slowly, half in one direction, half in the other, singing each his own choice of song. Scott was singing "Barbara Allen."

> In Scarlet town where I was born
> There was a fair—maid dwelling,
> Made every youth cry well away,
> And her name—was Barbara Allen.

He passed Shorty, who was singing "Dixie" in his own

unique rhythm.

Mistress married William Weaver; William were a gay
deceiver.
Look away, look away, look away to Dixie land.
When he put his arms around her, he smiled as big as
a forty-pounder.
Look away, look away, look away to Dixie land.
Oh, I wish I was in Dixie . . .

He passed Professor, who seemed to be singing for his
own amusement more than to the herd.

Now he's gone to court a widder,
And I hope that he don't getter.
Shovel and a hoe and a handle of a plow,
Suit much better than a wife just now.

The clear sky in the east had shrunk to one blue patch.
The dark angry cloud due west was rising toward them; it
was full of lightning. The light faded, as at dusk, and some
half of the cattle lay down; others wandered restlessly,
tensely expectant. One full-grown brindle steer bawled as
a calf to its mother.

Scott was thinking: They've been ready to run ever since
we left; I don't know what's held them back. But this just
might be the night. It was a fairly good place to bed, two
miles from the river, and the draws between the gentle hills
were shallow. The only bad terrain was that depression to
the east with the red clay banks. If they ran, God knew
what direction they would go. If I were bossing this outfit,

he thought, I would be personally waiting out there toward those red brakes. He looked to see the spot where he would have stationed himself and he saw Kittredge out there alone, dim in the fading light, but unmistakable because of his thin stiff form on his big horse. Scott had to admit that the little old man was the one big reason why the skittish herd had not yet run. But this could be the night. That big cloud due west was going to hit head on.

Blackie came around in a trot, passing and intercepting the other riders. His voice was a penned-up yell, toned down by the need for calm. "Sing church songs, God dammit!" he grated. "Sing church songs!"

They sang church songs. The thunderstorms which had surrounded them and now threatened to engulf them from the west produced awe and some degree of reverence in the riders. They could see up into the vast reaches of the clouds, see the varied lightings, see the upward depths full of murky streaks and puffy fingers, writhing in contrary currents. They could hear the rumbles of thunder that seemed to penetrate even into the ground. They understood the belief of many peoples in the past that the sun is a god and the storm is an angry god, a belief not caused by simplicity of mind, but by a nearness to these forces, an involvement, sometimes a feeling of standing naked and alone in nature.

Three-fourths of the herd had bedded, but the others had no intention of lying down; they were watching the approaching storm. They bellowed to one another across the backs of their complaisant fellows and jerked their heads this way and that, watching, not to be surprised.

Scott untied his slicker and eased into it without stopping. The air was no longer perfectly still, but he could not tell which direction the wind was from. It seemed to blow down from overhead in little uncertain gusts. The slicker felt good, the gusts were icy cold. He patted the black horse on the neck and said, "Blackjack, old boy, I'm glad you're carrying me tonight."

He passed Shorty, who was singing "Nearer, My God, to Thee," in the same slow rhythm he had sung "Dixie."

Though like the wanderer, the sun gone down,
Darkness be over me, my rest a stone;
Yet in my dreams I'd be—nearer, my God, to thee,
Nearer, my God, to thee, nearer to thee.

He passed Professor, who was singing "Amazing Grace," with some cynicism in his voice, but not without belief that the song had power to soothe the beasts they guarded.

Amazing grace! how sweet the sound that saved a
    wretch like me.
I once was lost but now am found, was blind but now
    I see.

Sheet lightning played in the clouds continuously, back-lighting their bulging gray forms, and thunder had become a constant rumble of sullen threats, near or distant. Somewhere a chain of lightning came sputtering down, as if tearing itself loose from restraints above, and spent itself in a crack like a whiplash. That hit something, Scott thought. The cloud which bore down on them from the west had its upper reaches obscured in the racing scud. Low around its front a rolling belt of clouds reached eagerly forward. The belt was boiling with white and gray puffs, and out of it fell streaks like threads lost by the carelessness of some mad spinner of cotton.

Below the roll cloud was a spreading expanse of solid color, dark dirty gray tinged with green, ominous in its dead hue, as if it were the silent deadly center of all the threats of the clouds. When the expanse lighted up inside it revealed light purple highlights. To Scott, the green tint meant hail. He tightened the neck string of his hat snug under his chin and began to sing "Rock of Ages" to the cattle. The nervous steers and cows were moving about, sometimes stumbling over the ones that were lying down. A big drop of rain spattered against his hat.

He could hear the faraway rushing of wind. There in the west a line of green foliage, willows and cottonwoods, suddenly came alive, bending and flattening, jerking. The wind came toward the herd in sallies, drawing long invisible fingers through the grass, making ripples. It hit quickly, with surprising violence, as if it meant to tear the clothes from his back. Blackjack's mane tossed back and forth across his neck; the horse bowed his head and kept his steady walk. The wind changed directions as if spirits fought in the air; it whipped the scattered raindrops into stinging level flight.

Darkness was closing in, though it could hardly have been later than sunset. Intense light of lightning emphasized the darkness. The chains came straight to the earth about them and thunder boomed immediately. Then a tremendous clap of thunder broke over their heads in a burst of light and shook the earth. It seemed to say, "Right now! Right here! This is it!" Scott said to his horse, "God, it means business!" He could smell the scorched air.

A voice screamed two hundred yards away, "They're running!"

Scott drew up and peered into the dim confusion. A new rumble had joined the sounds. Then lightning flashed and he saw that it was true. One moment three-fourths of them had been lying on the ground. In the next instant the fear signal had passed through them and they were all up running in the same direction—east.

Blackjack was ready to go after them, and Scott let him have his head but veered him farther away from the herd. It was his belief that most of the trouble resulting from a stampede came from too many cowboys trying to turn them too soon, thus splitting and scattering them. He wanted to stay as far away from them as he could without losing them. Now, in the first violent expression of their fear, nothing could stop them successfully.

He could see them clearly when the lightning played. Their bodies were a dark tumbling avalanche, topped by wet shining horns. The horns were like stubby spears carried by some ancient panic-stricken horde of warriors. Sometimes he saw a rider, too close in, and once he heard Blackie's loud cursing.

The sound of the cattle blended with the sound of the storm. They ran without voice, but their twelve thousand split hoofs and their six thousand horns popped and clacked and combined into a rushing thunder. Rain fell in streaks, catching the dim light, drifting and jerking in the wind. When it came straight down it bounced on the turf and spattered up like steam along the ground. They were running under the storm and with it.

When the run began Scott was near the rear and he veered toward the upper side. He was thinking about the scooped-out depression and the red clay banks. If he was judging right, they would strike the lower portion of it where the banks were shallow or eroded away, but Kittredge might be up there planning to turn them enough to miss the brakes altogether. He urged Blackjack ahead and was gaining on the cattle.

Hail began to hit him in the back and on the shoulders. His horse jumped and broke stride when the first balls struck his rump, then he ducked his chin and went ahead. In the lightning flashes, Scott could see that the hail pellets were the size of quarters; they mixed with the sheets of rain, bounded crazily on the earth, flew before the wind. When one hit solid, it hurt.

Blackjack crouched all at once and slid to a halt. In the next flash, Scott saw the drop in front of them. They had come farther than he had thought. He dismounted and led the horse to a better place to descend the five-foot bank. The herd was pouring over two hundred yards away, and he thought the banks were lower. When he remounted again his boots were balled with clay.

The wind slackened some and the hail stopped, but rain poured out of the sky. Blackjack ran heavily in the mud. Scott didn't press him. As long as he could hear the running cattle or see them in the flashes, he was satisfied. Behind him he could see another rider, just far enough that he couldn't identify the man, but he hadn't seen anyone else for some time.

The herd ran for what seemed like half the night, but must have been no more than an hour. The storm had passed them and pulled away grumbling and winking. Light rain still fell. Scott was even with the leaders. He couldn't see so well as before because the lightning was faint, but he was sure that no other rider was trying to turn them from the other side. He pushed in against the leaders. They veered. The rider behind him came up to help. It was Shorty. In another hour they had turned the leaders in a circle that met the trailing cattle. The beasts were trotting, or jogging, tired, all following one another.

A near full moon had come up, making a big white spot in the thin drifting clouds. Scott rode over to Shorty. "Let's let the damn crazy critters mill, Shorty. We haven't got enough help to stop them anyway, this big a bunch."

"How many you reckon we got?"

"Maybe half of them. I thought we had them all, but if we did, we'd see some more of the outfit around. I wonder where everybody is."

"There was another feller with this bunch half an hour ago," Shorty said. "Some damn fool without a hat or slicker. I seen Blackie try to turn them a couple of times away back there; he split off a bunch both times."

"How'd you get down that clay bank?"

Shorty chuckled. "I come over it in a dead run. Didn't know it was there till we hit bottom."

"I didn't see any cows down, did you?"

"Naw. But I wasn't seeing much of anything right about that time."

They spent a cold long night waiting with the milling cattle. Scott dismounted and walked to warm himself and rest his horse. Rain had blown inside his slicker in spots, and his britches legs were soaked. The wind was gentle. Moonlight filtered softly down through quiet clouds. He felt as if he were a thousand miles away from any human being. He heard Shorty singing over across the herd, and he began to sing, as much to himself as to the cattle.

The cattle slowed to a walk by themselves. Then one stopped and began bawling, and shortly after all had stopped. A kind of mournful complaining came into them to replace the fear. They wouldn't bed on the wet ground. Here and there one wandered, hunting for a separated companion.

Toward morning fog formed in the low places. Wisps of it drifted with the gentle wind. As the first morning light was discernible, seven young cows came over the rise to join the bunch Scott and Shorty held, driven by a lone rider, the "damn fool" Shorty had mentioned. It was the Kid. His wet clothes were sticking to him. He was hunched over his horse shivering. Scott and Shorty met him.

"Where in the hell's your slicker?" Shorty yelled.

The Kid grinned. "Well, Mr. Ostler was mad, and he wanted me to hurry, and I didn't have time to get it."

"I bet you have time to get it next time. Where in the hell's your hat?"

"It blew off some place. I've got to find it. I sure hope Mr. Ostler ain't too mad about me getting lost from him and the horses."

"I wouldn't worry too much about Mr. Ostler," Scott said. "Look at those britches tucked into your boots. I bet your boots are full of water."

The Kid threw his gawky legs up over the front fork of

his saddle, one by one, removed his boots, and dumped a cup of water from each.

"Kid," Shorty said, "you want some good advice, don't take them boots off no more till they get dry, or you won't never get them on again."

The Kid grinned at it all. He was obviously pleased at being with them, but he said anxiously, "I hope you all tell Mr. Ostler I helped bring some cows back. He don't think too much of me anyway."

Scott gave the Kid his slicker, and the Kid accepted it without apology. "My gosh, Mr. Scott, I don't believe I ever got so cold in my life! I didn't think it could get that cold in the spring this way."

When it was lighter, they saw that the Kid had a beautiful black eye, where he had been struck by a hailstone. "I thought somebody was chunking rocks at me," he said as he fingered his eye tentatively. His horse had mud, beginning to dry and wrinkle, all over one side. They had been down back at the red brakes.

Scott and Shorty made a rough count as soon as they could see well enough. They agreed that they could see between seventeen and eighteen hundred head. The cows had begun to graze. Scott figured there were too many for the three of them to drive, and then he wasn't sure which direction to go. If the other cattle were this far east, Kittredge might want to go on north from here rather than retrace their path back toward the trail. He left Shorty and Kid with the bunch and began to backtrack the path of the stampede. He would be able to see where the herd had split and maybe contact some of the other men.

He had gone about two miles when he saw Ostler driving

half the remuda, and he cut over to intercept the old cook. Ostler's first words were, "You haven't seen anything of that sorry Kid, have you?"

Scott laughed. "Why? You and him get lost from each other?"

"Lost!" Ostler snorted. "Ain't no telling where that crazy Kid went. He ain't got no sense. Sorriest horse wrangler ever I seen." Something in the old man's voice gave the lie to everything he said. "I hope he had sense enough to go back to the wagon and stay out of the way."

Scott could tell the old man had been thinking about it for some time. He laughed again. "Looks like you lost about half the horses."

"I never lost none of the horses." He pointed down in the draw a quarter of a mile ahead of them. There was the rest of the remuda. Ostler said deliberately, "I got one horse too many. I got one with a saddle on."

Scott squinted and saw it and quit laughing. "Well, you can rest your mind about the Kid. He's back out yonder helping Shorty hold more than half the herd. He put in a hard night's work last night."

Scott caught his grullo and turned Blackjack loose. For the first time since they had left south Texas, the grullo didn't pitch. He rode on down ahead of Ostler. The big muddy sorrel with the saddle on was lame in one front leg. The saddle was too muddy to identify, but behind the cantle swung leather saddlebags. Only two or three of the outfit carried saddlebags. Scott could only think of one man—Kittredge.

He caught the horse without using his rope. One bridle rein was broken off short. When Ostler came up, they unbuckled the flap of one of the saddlebags. The first thing they saw was the Colonel's leather-covered Bible. They strapped it back shut. They looked at each other, frowning, and did not speculate aloud.

Ostler went on driving the remuda and leading the sorrel; Scott returned to the muddy path of the stampede. Where the main body of the cattle had run the grass was almost gone, trampled into the mud. It had rained plenty. Out on level ground the old buffalo wallows were full, making little round pools that sparkled in the morning light. Some five miles farther on, at a place where the herd had split, Scott ran into Baldy.

Baldy had left Cory and Dandy with about five hundred head. He whistled when he heard about Kittredge's horse. "Man alive! That old Colonel is going to be mad if he had to walk back to the wagon."

"I hope he can walk," Scott said.

"Yeah! Say, wouldn't it be hell to pay if that old Colonel had a broke leg or something?"

They rode several miles farther and entered the lower stretches of the big depression which the cattle had poured across early in their run. Here the red earth looked as if it had been plowed. Cow tracks were six inches deep and full of water. Their horses picked their way, hoofs making a sucking noise in the mud. Halfway across this area Blackie converged with them. The big segundo's slicker was shredded. Evidently it had been beaten across many a steer horn during the night.

He yelled, "Where in the hell was you all at last night?" They didn't answer, and when he had come up to them he went on, "I damn near turned them a dozen times, but I couldn't get no help. And when I finally get a bunch of them stopped, here comes half the outfit to help me. Looks to me like we got some cowboys that are scared to get close to a cow."

"Somebody split them up pretty bad," Scott said.

Blackie didn't get the hint. "I tell you one thing: Colonel Kittredge is going to be plenty mad about it."

When they told him about the Colonel's horse, Blackie scowled and stared at them. "It probably ain't the Colonel's horse. It was somebody else's horse. The Colonel is probably out yonder some place with most of the cows."

"It's the Colonel's horse, all right. Ostler and I looked in the saddlebags. He's only about a mile back there; go see for yourself."

Blackie only frowned at them suspiciously. The three of them went on across the muddy waste toward the banks on the other side. First they saw a dead steer, his head twisted with one horn stuck in the mud, his legs already stiffening in the air. Then they saw a crippled heifer that tried to rise at their approach, but could not. Blood snorted from her nose. They were almost upon it before they saw the human form in the mud.

Baldy whistled low.

Blackie said, "It's the Kid! It's that damn crazy Kid!" He sat on his horse and stared.

Scott dismounted and went to it. He was not in doubt about who it was; he could see the white hair and gray pointed beard under the mud. Nor did he really need to check for signs of life; the main stream of the herd had come over the bank onto the body. He looked at the other two men. They were dismounting, hesitantly, reluctantly.

Scott gathered up the body, working it loose from the mud. When he had it in his arms and had risen, he was swept with amazed awe. It was not that the body was broken and covered with mud and blood, but it was light! It was almost nothing! No more than a hundred pounds! All of the overbearing will and spirit, the drive and the knowledge that even he had begun to respect—all of it had been wrapped up in, dependent upon, this pitiful container. The old man had been physically not even as much as the Kid.

Scott made his way up the broken bank. Baldy hunted for a good place to lead the horses up. A hundred feet above the clay bank grew a scraggly live oak, which had parted the cattle and preserved a strip of grass. Here Scott laid the broken form. He rearranged one of the legs, which stuck out grotesquely to the side. Then he wiped his hands on the grass to remove the blood that was so dark as to be almost black.

Baldy and Blackie came up to stand and stare. Scott looked back to the west where the storm had hit the herd. He could see the draw where the chuck wagon must be; he could see the dark path of the herd leading up to him and out east, where the riders and cattle were scattered. All of it, even the bald-headed man and the big black-haired man there, looked new and strange to him now.

Kittredge Is Done Right by

9

It matters not, I've oft been told,
Where the body lies, when the heart grows cold,
But grant, oh grant this wish to me,
And bury me not on the lone prairie.

That was a hectic morning. Baldy shot the crippled heifer between the eyes, and Blackie was all over him, screaming, "Who told you to do that? Didn't the Colonel tell us a long time ago not to fire no guns off, without he said to?" As he came to accept the death of Colonel Kittredge, the big segundo became touchy, seemingly uncertain about what to do next, and certainly jealous of his own position.

Scott went after the chuck wagon and found that one of the mules had broken his stake rope. He found the mule two miles down the river and finally got them harnessed. The wood the Kid had put under the wagon the night before was useless. It lay soaked in six inches of water. Scott brought the wagon up three hundred yards above the spot where the body of Kittredge lay, to a place where it would be seen by the men as they came in.

Blackie, and then later one of the others, kept watch by the little live oak. Three buzzards were circling half a mile high. They were probably interested in the two dead cattle. With more gentleness than he had shown in a long time, Blackie removed the few belongings from the

Colonel's pockets.

Martinez and four others brought in the bunch of about seven hundred that Blackie had stopped. Ostler brought in the remuda. By knocking dead wood off of standing trees and peeling off the rotten wet bark, he got enough wood to build a smoking fire. By the time he had some grub ready, Cory and Dandy brought a smaller bunch of cattle and threw them in with the first bunch. Water was no problem for the herd now; it stood in small pools in every low place.

The men did not talk about Kittredge much, but they spoke to each other in subdued voices, and sometimes, frowning, they stared down toward the little scrub oak where his body lay. Baldy expressed their feelings when he said, "It sure seems like something is missing around here, don't it?"

Scott said to Blackie, "I guess as soon as we get some grub inside us, some of us ought to go out there and relieve Shorty and Kid. It must be fifteen miles."

It made Blackie angry. "You trying to tell me what to do?"

"Not especially."

"Well, you better not! I got enough things on my mind without somebody trying to get smart. I'm in charge of this outfit, and I don't want nobody to get smart. We got a man to bury, and we're going to do right by him. You ever stop to think of that?"

"Well, maybe if you'll cool down you'll stop to think of this," Scott said. "You haven't got much more than a third of the herd here. The rest of them are away out yonder, held by just two men, and they're hungry. I think they better be relieved before night."

The men seemed to look to Blackie for a decision. Professor said, "I suppose we could wait till tomorrow to bury the Colonel, Blackie." And Baldy said, "Yeah, I reckon he would keep till tomorrow, Blackie."

Blackie frowned at them suspiciously and said, "Just don't none of you all get smart, that's all I say. I got enough on my mind." He sent Scott with four men out to relieve Shorty and Kid. This large bunch of cows, which had been stopped by Scott and Shorty in the bottoms of Kickapoo Creek, seemed to be the easternmost bunch and probably represented the last of the scattered cattle. Scott carried two bedrolls on one of Kittredge's gentle horses. The tired Shorty and Kid came straight back to camp, and the others drove the big bunch until dark, then bedded them for the night.

Ostler and Kid carried a shovel full of coals and some wood down to the scrub oak and built a fire at dark. The plot of grass on which the body lay was small. They had to spread their bedroll right beside it or else in the mud. They chose the mud, twenty feet from it. Coyotes yapped and yodeled all over the country that night. Perhaps the rain had increased their activity, or perhaps the damp air carried their shrill voices farther. They seemed to be on every hill. Some came down into the red clay depression that the stampede had crossed. Ostler and Kid didn't sleep well, even though they had skipped a night, for listening and making sure the fire was up. In the morning they saw that the two dead cows had been ripped and gutted two or three hundred feet from them.

That morning Art Howard and Booger Red were assigned to digging a grave. Blackie marked it off beside the scraggly oak and left them with the long-handled shovel. It was customary for a man hired purely as a cow-hand to resent, and even protest, working with a shovel. He was inclined to think such work should be done by a Negro or a Mexican or by a white man too old or too young or too dumb to work as a cowhand. But if Art and Booger Red resented the work, they were too much subdued by the dead form lying there to say anything. Blackie came back in an hour and said, "You ain't making it wide enough. What you think we're going to do? Bury him edgeways?"

Art laughed at this, and Blackie bawled at him, "It ain't funny! Dig it plum out to here! I aim for us to do right by Colonel Kittredge, and I don't want nobody to laugh about anything."

"I thought that's where you marked it off," Booger Red said.

"Well, it ain't. And anyway, I aim for you to dig it plum out to here, and I aim for you to do it like I say. And throw the dirt in one pile; don't throw it all over everywheres."

They immediately set about enlarging the hole to suit Blackie. After he had gone they worked steadily, trading the shovel back and forth at brief intervals. At three feet they hit solid sandstone. The damp rock could be marked by the shovel, but showed no crack or other hope for cutting through it. They went to get Blackie. The big man looked at them, suspiciously, as if they were somehow to blame. He marked off another spot for them higher up on the hill.

Before noon Scott and the others brought the big portion of the herd which had gone farthest east and threw them in with the others, which were grazing loose herded. After an early noon meal, ten of the thirteen men in the outfit assembled to do some kind of final honor to the man who had led them. Art and Booger Red had tried digging in two other locations, had found the layer of sandstone even more shallow, and had returned, at Blackie's orders, to the original hole with the supposed intention of digging through the stone. "It don't look to me like you all dug much," Blackie said.

"Hell's fire!" Booger Red said. "You can't dig in that rock with that shovel, Blackie."

"You can't if you don't try! You ain't hardly scratched it!" The big man laid down the saddlebags he had brought, seized the shovel, and stepped into the hole. He stomped viciously on the shovel, scraped with it, then stomped again. Two minutes of work did not yield more than a half shovelful of the damp stone. He began to jump on the shovel with both feet, sweating profusely.

Ostler said, "Blackie, you're going to ruin my shovel. You can't dig rock with a shovel like that."

He panted, "I am doing it, ain't I? Can't you see this goddam grave ain't deep enough?"

"Well, I got to have that shovel, and you're fixing to ruin it. You're fixing to bend the end of it right back. I got to have it to dig holes for my fire and everything. What you think I'm going to use for a shovel when you ruin it?"

Blackie jumped on it again, and the point bent back as Ostler had predicted. Blackie flung it out of the hole. "You can straighten the goddam thing! That's what you can do. Kid, go up to the wagon and get me the ax. You all stand around and complain, and I'm the only one here that's man enough to dig through this rock, and you just stand there and complain and say what are you going to do without a shovel."

The Kid asked, "Did you mean the ax we cut wood with, Mr. Blackburn?"

"What in the hell ax do you think I mean? What other ax is they? You damn crazy Kid! If you don't get moving when I tell you to, I'm going to straighten you out."

When the Kid had gone, Ostler said, "I don't see no use to talk to him that way, Blackie."

"I'll talk to him any way I want to."

"I don't know what you want with the ax, anyway."

"You don't know what I want with the ax? For Christ's sake! Are you trying to get smart with me too? I'm going to cut through this goddam rock with it. This ain't no decent grave!"

Baldy said, "Blackie, that rock's two foot thick down yonder a ways where it breaks out."

Blackie paid no heed to him but stood there in the waist-deep hole with his hands on his hips, his shoulders still heaving from the work, while the others stood waiting. When Kid returned with the ax, Ostler said, "Just a minute, Kid," and took the ax from him. "Blackie, you done ruint my shovel. I might straighten it out enough to use till we can get another one, but if you chop that rock with this ax I can't get it sharp no way at all."

Blackie began to come out of the hole. "You going to give me that ax, old man? Or am I going to have to take it away from you, and punch you in the nose besides?"

Scott said quietly, "Just a minute, Blackie."

"You want a punch in the nose too, huh?"

"Well, you say you want to do right by the Colonel. If you think it's decent to have a knock-down, drag-out fight here over his body, get started. But it seems to me like we might have a little talk and straighten out some things before you ruin that ax."

"What do you mean? If I tell him to give me the ax, he's got to give it to me. If Colonel Kittredge told him to do something, he done it and never argued this way. And he's got to do what I tell him."

"It's not that simple, Blackie," Scott said. "You're not the Colonel."

"You trying to say I ain't in charge of this outfit?"

"If you'll cool down a minute, I'll tell you what I'm trying to say. First, I'd like to ask Ostler something." Scott turned to the cook. "Are you drawing more pay than a regular hand?"

Ostler spluttered a moment. He was still clutching the ax as if to protect it. "That ain't none of your business."

"Well, I've worked for outfits where the cook was second in charge. I just wondered if the owners were paying you to take any more responsibility than a regular hand. Blackie's got the Colonel's papers and stuff now; he's going to know what your monthly wages are. But the way you're arguing, you don't seem to think Blackie's in charge of the herd now."

"He's going to get a punch in the nose over it, too," Blackie said.

"It ain't nobody's business but mine," Ostler insisted.

"All right, if that's the way you want it," Scott said. He could feel that the others standing around were interested in what he had to say but were not necessarily behind him, none except Shorty. Still he went on with it. "I think some of us would like to know just what your plans are, Blackie.

141

Yesterday you got sore when I mentioned that Shorty and Kid were out there alone with the biggest part of the cows. I don't know whether you meant to leave them out there another day, or what. Now, you don't seem to mind ruining equipment we've got to have to continue this drive. I'd like to know just what you plan to do."

Blackie had calmed down somewhat at the suggestion that it was not decent to fight over the body of the Colonel, but he was still surly and suspicious. "Maybe it ain't none of your business what my plans are."

"I think it is, if these other boys see it the same way I do. We all signed on to work for Kittredge, not you. And the owners didn't make you segundo. Now we've all got some wages earned, so we've got a stake in this drive. And that's not all; you can't do a thing without the outfit. You may punch some people in the nose, but you can't take the herd anywhere without us. We've got a right to know what you plan to do."

There was a mumbled chorus of, "Yeah, we got a right to know."

Blackie looked at the nine men around him, blinked a couple of times, and said, "I plan to do right by Colonel Kittredge; then I aim to take that goddam bunch of cows to Nebraska, just like he was aiming to do."

"Well, you'll want to notify the owners that Kittredge is dead as soon as possible," Scott said.

"Why?"

Professor laughed. "I think Scott's right. We may accept you as a big shot for a while, Blackie, but we want to know whether the owners are behind you. Maybe you better hightail it to the nearest town and get in touch with them."

Some agreement was indicated among the other men by their words, but Scott objected. "I'm pretty sure we ought to keep the herd moving. We're running a week, and maybe two, behind schedule right now. If we don't get the herd to Ogallala by July the first, the owners are in trouble. We could write at Doan's Crossing and pick up an answer up in Indian Territory somewhere, at least by the time we hit Camp Supply. I'm willing to go along with Blackie, myself, if he'll agree to write at Doan's Crossing."

Blackie seemed to jump at the proposal. "Yeah, we can write at Doan's Crossing."

And so, out of the petty argument over the shovel and ax came what seemed to be a loose agreement: that Blackie would be the boss but would not be accepted quite as Kittredge had been; that his judgment might sometimes be questioned and that he might be given advice; that someone would write a letter at Doan's on Red River, expecting instructions farther up the trail. Scott had purposely left it vague as to who would write.

When the men had informally agreed that Scott was right, Blackie, as if to deny that he had ceded any authority, said to Ostler, "I guess everybody's had their say; now you can let me have that goddam ax."

Ostler had not said anything since the suggestion that he, as cook, might have some special authority from the owners. He handed over the ax. Blackie fell to work, sweating profusely in the hot and humid air. They stood around watching him swing the tool, as if he were a show of some kind. Since it was obviously a hopeless task and since Blackie had taken it upon himself in an arrogant manner, no one offered to help. It was like that night when he tore the horseshoe in two. But this time he was less successful. After a quarter of an hour the edge of the single-bitted ax was blunted and dulled so that it was a quarter of an inch thick, and the big man tossed it aside. He scooped up the chips of rock with his hands; all his work had deepened the hole less than an inch. He studied it a minute and said, "That's deep enough."

Ostler had picked up the ax. "I wish you'd look at that. How am I going to cut any wood with a thing like that?"

"I ain't seen you cut any wood noway," Blackie said. "Kid does it, and he don't cut it; he breaks it."

When they turned to their next task, all of the men changed. They had almost forgotten the purpose of the big hole here on the prairie. They stopped any arguing and spoke quietly. The body of Kittredge appeared as one that is already returning to dust. It was thoroughly dirty. In spots the mud had cracked and warped and peeled.

They spread out a double blanket on the ground beside it and gathered around and set to work to lay it on the blanket, without anyone giving directions. They supported the body in the middle, as if it would bend, but found that it was stiff as a plank. Never having wrapped such a thing, they were clumsy. After laying it on the blanket, they brought the long end over, then found themselves stymied. They lifted it and pushed the blanket under; then did the clumsy, obvious thing: rolled it, with the one stiff elbow sticking out to impede the progress, along the ground to wrap it.

They picked it up then with firmer grips, having the blanket to grasp, and, stumbling in the loose earth, some six of them lowered it into the hole.

Blackie took the leather-covered Bible out of the saddle-bags, handed it to the Professor, and said quietly, "Read some stuff out of here."

Professor looked at it a minute with lips pursed and began to flip through it. Finally he read:

"Man that is born of a woman is of few days, and full of trouble.

"He cometh forth like a flower, and is cut down: he fleeth also as a shadow, and continueth not.

"And dost thou open thine eyes upon such an one, and bringest me into judgment with thee?

"Who can bring a clean thing out of an unclean? Not one.

"Seeing his days are determined, the number of his months are with thee, thou hast appointed his bounds that he cannot pass.

"Turn from him, that he may rest, till he shall accomplish as an hireling, his day."

The Professor looked around a moment, then closed the book. After some silence, Blackie said, "Somebody that can pray good ought to say a prayer." No one volunteered, and at last someone suggested that they should sing a song. After some hesitation, for they felt ill at ease and at the same time bound to continue some further service, they agreed upon "Rock of Ages." Someone began it in a monotone, and the others picked it up louder. They sang it in ten different voices, those who knew the words carrying them through all the way and the others joining in when they could.

The song had satisfied their need for a funeral. Blackie took up the long-handled shovel and tried to fill it with the loose clods. Its bent point made this almost impossible. He took the ax and, placing the shovel blade against the trunk of the oak, pounded it and straightened it to nearly its original shape. No one laughed or said, "I told you so."

He filled the shovel and dumped it, thoughtlessly, into the grave. The clods bounded on the blanket. Blackie drew back, suddenly surprised and awed. He put in two more shovels full, carefully, then handed the shovel to Murphy, who stood nearest. Murphy grew white as he continued the work; he looked sick. After some minutes one of the others took the shovel, and the hole was filled and mounded over.

They carried rocks to cover the mound from an outcropping two hundred yards away, all of them but Murphy, who sat down white and trembling. At the common labor they became more at ease and began to say things about the Colonel. They prefaced their statements with, "He was a hard man to work for but . . ." and "I'll say one thing about the Colonel, he . . ." The particular things they said about him were thus: "He knew cattle, all right"; and "He was a man you had to look up to"; and "He knew how to get a herd to market"; and "He must have been a brave man to be a colonel"; "Sure he was; he died trying to turn the goddam cows away from that bank."

The rocks still left something lacking. They set about cutting from the scraggly oak a big limb that amounted to about half the tree. This job was nearly impossible with the blunted ax. Blackie took it and, not by cutting but by crushing with the blunted edge at the expense of great labor, produced a post. The post was frayed at the ends as if it had been gnawed by some giant rat. They inserted it in the loosened earth at one end of the grave and propped it with stones.

Blackie found a clean sheet of writing paper and a pencil in the saddlebags and said to the Professor, "I guess we ought to put where he come from and when he was born—stuff like that."

"All right. Where did he come from and when was he born?"

It developed that no one knew. They had no doubt that he had actually been a colonel, and that about him there must be many important facts that should be recorded, but no one knew. In fact, no one even knew the day of the month he had died, except Scott. Professor wrote: "Colonel Horace Kittredge" and "Died in a stampede" and the date.

They wedged it into a split in the oak. It might last six months in the rain and the wind.

Scott did not know why he had stepped in to stop the argument between Blackie and Ostler, why he had worked to get the loose understanding that they would follow Blackie's orders for the time being, why he had insisted that they move north while they contacted the owners. He had no doubt that any return instructions from Greer would name him trail boss, but the only thing he could think of was the colossal stupidity of Greer and Brown. Even though they had been somehow suspicious of Kittredge, at least of his age, and had wanted him, Scott, to go along because they could "count on him," they had not made the slightest provisions for the difficulties they feared. They had left him at first in a position where he could ride drag or else slowly prove himself to a hardheaded Colonel, and now they had left him where he could let the herd go to hell or else take it away from a big dumb segundo, who could tear a horseshoe in two with his bare hands. His predicament now was worse than it had been under the Colonel. Except that it wasn't his predicament at all. It was theirs. If the herd did go to hell, it was still theirs. If they happened to send him word to take charge—if they sent it before Blackie had messed things up so bad they could never be straightened out, then, all right, he would take the cattle to Ogallala.

Looking at the crude grave with the crude post at its head, Scott suddenly felt a pang of emotion not based on his thinking, having nothing to do with the strange relationship that had existed between himself and the dead man. It was almost a feeling of brotherhood with the old man who had been trying to do a big job, had been doing it in a creditable way, and had come to the end of his life in the middle of the job. Briefly, he felt nearer the old Colonel than to any other of the men in the outfit, seemed to know him down underneath the crust of formality, even felt toward him as he had felt about Oliver Loving.

This brief understanding brought a memory of the old Colonel's words: "This is my herd. Do you understand? My herd." But this memory kindled a flash of emotion, stronger and even less rational, a revolt that might have been expressed with, "Not only is it not Blackie's herd now, it wasn't even his, the Colonel's. It was mine. From the first. By promise and by right. It's mine because I can do it. It wasn't the Colonel's then, and it's not Blackie's now."

But this feeling never became words in Scott's mind. It

flared and then hid itself under his pride, seething under his consciousness. He thought that he could wait patiently for authority from Greer and Brown. He thought he could wait and not care, maybe offer casual advice, but let Blackie have the command, and humor him.

That afternoon Blackie announced that they had better get rested; they were pushing out early in the morning. Scott asked casually, "What do you mean to do, Blackie? Run a tally when we string them out in the morning?"

Blackie stammered around. He had not thought about a tally at all. He turned out the crew to make the count. Blackie caught one of the Colonel's horses. He had three strings now, including eight of the night horses, since all of the Colonel's had been the big gentle part-thoroughbreds. Some of them kidded him about it, but Blackie frowned and barked orders and refused to see any humor in having so many mounts.

Martinez and Blackie counted, sitting their horses on either side of the stream of cattle, running the knots of tally strings between their fingers, one knot for a hundred head. Scott worked squeezing them down into the stream, trying to make them walk single file, and he ran a rough tally of his own. He counted three thousand and sixteen; he had seen three or four stray brands. They could not have lost more than one or two head besides the two that were killed.

Martinez reported three thousand and fifteen. Blackie said, "Are you sure about that, Martinez?"

The Mexican grinned, his white teeth flashing. "Pretty sure, *Pendego. Hijo de puta.*"

Blackie ran over his knots again. "That's what I got," he said.

. . .

The next morning in the dim light, Blackie was up and standing by the wagon when Ostler awakened the rest of them. In Blackie's hand was the leather-covered Bible. He opened it and looked through it a minute, closed it, walked over by the fire, opened it again. He seemed once or twice as if he might be about to read something, but then he would close the book and look around. Finally he walked over to Professor and thrust the Bible out to him. "Why don't you read us a little out of here?"

Professor was pulling on his boots. "Hell's fire, Blackie! Do your own Bible reading. I don't want to read that stuff."

"Why not? You trying to say they's something the matter with it?"

Professor laughed. "I've got a complete Shakespeare. I might read you a sonnet or a soliloquy."

Blackie sputtered a moment and said, "By God, you don't have to read it. I just asked you. You don't have to get smart." He put the Bible away and took out one of the Colonel's maps, which he opened and began studying.

Baldy asked, "Did you point the wagon tongue north last night, Blackie?"

Blackie looked around at the cloudy horizon, then glared at Baldy.

"I ain't trying to get smart with you. I just asked you a simple question. I just asked if you pointed the wagon tongue north so's you'd know which way to go."

"By God, you never asked Colonel Kittredge things like that, did you?"

"No, I never. But he had a compass. Besides, he knew the way to go from landmarks and things."

At the word "compass" Blackie stopped glaring and began searching frantically in the saddlebags.

Dandy asked, "Didn't you get the compass, Blackie?"

Blackie didn't answer and didn't speak at all until after they had caught out the horses. Then he assigned Booger Red to ride on his point position and told them to string the herd out and go north.

"But which way is north?" Booger Red protested.

"By God, the trail is right over yonder ways! Have I got to tell you everything? If you don't know the way to go, Martinez does. Ask him. Wait, Murph, I want you to hep me."

"Hep you do what?"

"I'll show you. Get the shovel and come on."

Murphy got the shovel and said, "What you going to do? Why don't you let somebody else hep you, Blackie? What you going to do?"

"Shut up your bitching and get your horse and come on!"

The outfit strung out the cattle. Looking back, they could see Blackie's and Murphy's horses tied to the scraggly oak. The two had removed the stones from the earth mound, and little Murphy was shoveling away the earth.

The point men found the sign of another herd and turned right to follow it, knowing they could not be far in error. The brighter area of the sky told them the general direction, in spite of the clouds. When they stopped at noon camp, Blackie and Murphy still had not caught up.

Scott caught Ostler to one side and talked to him, trying to be casual and friendly and not rouse the ire of the old cook. "We ought to hit Doan's Crossing in four or five days if we don't run into trouble," he said.

"Oh, we'll run into some kind of trouble with Blackie running the show," the cook predicted.

"We want to make sure he writes at Doan's. We're getting shorthanded to work the herd, and you may be the only one that has a chance to check on him and make sure he writes."

"Why wouldn't he write?"

"Well, for one thing he may not be able to write, Ostler. He may not know how."

"How come you think that?"

"Just a guess."

"Well, I don't know as it's my place to see he writes. I got enough worries trying to cook for this blamed outfit."

"You may be the only one that has a chance to check on him, especially if there's some other herds camped close to the river. We wouldn't want to crowd them, but you'll have to go in after supplies. He's got to notify the owners, Ostler."

"One thing I know, I'm going to have me a new ax and a new shovel, if they's any to be bought."

"Will you see that he writes or maybe help him?"

"I reckon so, but I don't know as it's my place."

Blackie came in alone before they finished eating. He said nothing until someone asked, "Where's Murphy?"

"He claims he's sick."

"Well, did you go off and leave him when he was sick, Blackie?"

"I stopped a half a dozen times with him when he said he was sick. He kept on saying he was sick so much I couldn't hardly get him to do no digging. He kept stopping. I never seen such a man with a weak stomach. If I hadn't said I'd punch him in the nose, he wouldn't of done no digging at all. The last time he said he had to stop and throw up, I told him he could go to hell before I'd stop and wait on him any more, and him not throwing up anything anyway, just wasting time. I got too much on my mind to set there wasting time."

Blackie had gone out to the herd when Murphy finally rode up. The little man was as white as a piece of paper and trembling, or jerking. He dropped the bridle reins on the ground and clambered up into the wagon to lie on the bedrolls.

"Did you all find the compass?" Ostler asked.

Murphy looked at him with eyes as big and dark as those of some old starving cow. "It was smashed," he said.

Horse Thief

10

There's a stray in the bunch and the boss said, kill it,
So I shot him in the rump and he landed in the skillet.
Come-a ti yi yippi, yippi yea, yippi yea,
Come-a ti yi yippi, yippi yea.

Murphy had ridden in the wagon all that afternoon, sometimes groaning with the jolts. It had drizzled, and Ostler had put back up the wagon sheet, which he left off as much as possible to allow things to dry out. Periodically, Murphy had thrust his head up over the wagon box and pulled aside the canvas, trying to vomit but unable to.

As they ate supper, first one, then another of the men called, "Come on out and eat something, Murph. You'll feel better to eat something."

Finally he came out. He didn't say anything but kept slowly shaking his head, as if to indicate that he felt worse than any words could describe. There were stewed apricots that night, and he downed a quantity of these and one sourdough biscuit. Then he sat quietly a while as if to see what effect the food would have on his stomach.

Blackie said, "Well, I'm damned glad to see you're all right, after wasting the whole afternoon. We're short-handed in the first place, and then you ride in the wagon."

Murphy shook his head a moment, then said, "I ain't all right. I just don't feel good at all, Blackie. Once I get out of sorts, I just don't seem like I can get going again." He sat there a few moments, silently rubbing his hand up his narrow forehead and through his thin brown hair. He held his mouth open and panted lightly, like a sad dog. Finally he said, "I got some folks that lives down the Red River a ways. Might be I ought to go down there, Blackie. I just ain't feeling worth a hoot."

Blackie jumped on the idea viciously. "What the devil do you mean—go to some folks down the Red River?"

Murphy shook his head slowly.

"I say, what the devil do you mean? Listen, Murph. Get this in your goddam head: you ain't quitting this outfit. We're done shorthanded—two men. Scratchy quit, and I sure can't do my work and the Colonel's too, so that makes two men we're short. And I ain't going to put up with no talk about quitting."

"Well, I don't know," Murphy said. "I just didn't think

I'd be much use to anybody, feeling like I am. I sure don't feel good. And I got these folks that lives . . ."

"Well, you can just forget it. You ain't going to quit, and you're going to make a hand. I can't drive these goddam cows without some hands. The Colonel told you before we started: can't nobody quit."

Murphy slowly shook his head and said nothing.

"Just remember that: can't nobody quit. I don't want to hear you say no more about it."

The herd was no different for having trampled a man to death; the men could see this. The dun cow with the pile of wrinkles between her eyes still stopped erratically to bawl. The spooky, high-headed steer with blinders still came out of the herd in his fast trot, jerking his head this way and that. The dark Spanish heifers with the keen eyes still flitted about like spoiled girls, carrying with them their entourage of steers when they broke from the herd. Whatever it was in the cattle that had enabled them to kill a man had been in them all the time; it had only revealed itself.

One change had been going on in them since they left south Texas; they were losing the weakness of winter. They had grazed virgin spring grass for more than a month. Now the wild rye and other grasses were beginning to head, with fat green grains full of rich milk. The cattle were gaining strength to do what they wished. Any extent to which they had become trail broken had been negated by the power they had gained to follow the wild urgings that remained in them.

It was wet in the camp south of the Wichita River, from the drizzle that had fallen intermittently during the day.

Fireflies winked down in the timber, and June bugs were drawn into camp to buzz around the smoking fire and the lantern.

They ran again that night. It did not require a storm. All it took was one cloud, far to the south, with faint flickers of lightning and one clear rumble of thunder. At the sound of the thunder they were up and gone, west this time into a fresh wind.

The men were on a three-guard schedule. Scott, Cory, and Baldy were supposed to be holding the herd. Everyone else was asleep and no other night horses were saddled, in spite of the general fear that this might become a "running" herd.

Scott brought Blackjack plunging full tilt up around the rear of the running cattle. There was a moon, but its light came faintly through the broken clouds. He saw the form of another horseman and yelled, "Let's turn them north! Push them against the river!" The horseman wheeled to follow him and he recognized the familiar slender figure of Cory.

Scott had taken note the evening before of the sweeping horseshoe bend, fairly open of timber, with broad sand bars next the river. He pushed his strong black horse into a dangerous dead run in the darkness in order to come even with the lead steers. He took off his slicker and began to flail with it while he yelled, trying to check the leaders so that the herd would become more compact and trying to veer them down toward the river.

It was a wild ride and a ticklish one, for he had to let Blackjack sense the footing and choose his way where he must, and at the same time Scott had to guide him to accomplish the purpose of a man rather than the purpose of a horse. Like a good cutting horse, Blackjack would stay with a steer and hound him, but Scott was thinking about three thousand beasts. Again and again he and Cory pressed against the leaders, split them down toward the river, then pounded ahead to press against the steers which had gone straight and become new leaders. From nowhere out of the darkness, Baldy came to help them.

They made their last stand at the western lip of the horseshoe bend. Here with hoarse yells and flapping, crackling slickers they turned the last of the cattle that were determined to go straight ahead and watched the rear half of the herd follow past them in an arc down onto the river sand and out around the sweeping circle of the mile-wide horseshoe.

When they were confident that all the cattle would follow the circle, Scott led the other two riders back to guard the other side of the opening of the horseshoe, but this precaution was unnecessary. Forced into the big circle, the cattle continued turning of their own accord. Trying to stay out of the hard running in the sand, they decreased the size of their circle until the head of the herd met the tail, and they were trapped into a giant mill, going hard and furiously, but going nowhere.

The three riders sat their heaving horses, listening to the pounding, clattering rumble of the thousands of beasts between them and the river. The men were sweating. The air was cool, though damp.

"I'll be damned," Baldy said. "If anybody ever tells me about this, I'll call him a liar. You fellers realize we've stopped these crazy, spooky cows, and they ain't but three of us, and we ain't more than two miles from camp?"

Scott said, "We're just lucky we had a natural corral to

pen them in."

"I don't call it luck," Cory said. "That fool Blackie would have had them split up all over the country."

The herd had been milling an hour, and from the sound had begun to slow up, when the three riders heard Blackie and the rest of the outfit coming, running their horses toward the sound of the cattle. Scott yelled, "Hey . . . Blackie! Over here!"

When the big man drew up, the others behind him, he said angrily, "Why in the hell ain't you all going after them? Did you have to wait for me?"

They laughed. Baldy said, "Go after them? We got them. How come you all to get out of the sack? Don't you trust me and Scott and Cory?"

Blackie eased down toward the herd enough to convince himself that they were going nowhere, then took back to camp all the outfit except the three-man last guard, who had handled the stampede as if they were a crew of twenty.

When dawn came sneaking through the eastern clouds the cows had already quietened, then they could be seen scattered around, bedded or grazing. One cow proved to have a broken leg and later had to be shot. When they tallied them, Martinez counted three thousand and fourteen, which Scott believed to be correct. They really had been lucky, but if the herd was going to run at every rumble of thunder they were in serious trouble.

That day, in addition to the tally, they butchered the cow they had to shoot, slogging around in the mud caused by the intermittent light rain. They kept only the tongue and liver, hindquarters and hide. Out of the rawhide Ostler would fashion a "possum belly," a sling under his wagon box in which to carry cow chips in the timberless country ahead.

Crossing the river with the cattle proved to be no trouble. There was no swimming water, which fact indicated that the rain must not extend very far to the west. But the wagon was more trouble. They began to move it across before time for the noon meal and it became bogged in the low ground immediately; the mules could not get good footing. The riders tied on with lariat ropes from four saddle horns, and after two hours of hard work had snaked it across and onto high ground north of the Wichita.

Then Ostler began a long fight to establish a fire. He had it going once, and the rain came down again long enough to put it out. The cook fussed and fumed; the rest of the hands sympathized with him, offering all manner of help and advice, thinking of the fresh beef they would have at their late dinner. Finally they rigged up a shelter of cotton-wood poles, gnawed off with the blunt ax, and the tarp which had belonged to the Colonel's bedroll. Spirits were usually low in a wet camp, but the fresh liver and tongue, with potatoes and cornbread, which Ostler finally delivered in a foul humor, seemed fit for a king.

"Damned if I don't believe some of this liver would put old Murph back on his feed," Baldy said.

"Murphy?" Blackie said. "Is Murph out at the herd? Come to think of it, I ain't seen him all day. Where in the hell is he?"

"Why, he's still sick," Baldy said. "He's still in the wagon."

"In the wagon?" Blackie strode to the front of the covered wagon, put his foot on the doubletree, and swung up to peer inside. "Murph, is that you laying in there in this goddam wagon again? What in the hell do you think you're doing? Get out of there. Right now!" He stepped back to the ground.

Murphy's head stuck out and Blackie insisted, "Come on. You heard what I said. Get out of there, right now! How long have you been laying up in there hiding?"

"Why don't you leave him alone, Blackie?" Professor said. "Can't you see he's sick?"

"Sick? I'll make him think he's sick. How long have you been laying up in that wagon? Don't tell me you was in there when we had all that trouble pulling that wagon across the river."

Murphy shook his head sorrowfully.

"That's just about what I call the goddam limit! Us working our tail off trying to get the wagon through the mud and you laying up in there just making it heavier. Like you was some big auger! Murph, I ain't going to put up with it. Come out of there like I tell you."

"Hell's fire, Blackie," Baldy said. "He's sick. You can see that."

"He ain't sick! He just never wanted to dig when I told him to dig, so he said he was sick. Well, I ain't going to put up with it. Murph, are you going to come out of that wagon, or am I going to pull you out by your goddam hair?"

Murphy slowly climbed out.

"Damned if I don't believe some of this liver might put you back on your feed, Murph," Baldy said.

"It makes me sick just to smell it," Murphy said. "What I need is eggs and butter and things like that. I got these kinfolks lives down the Red River and . . ."

"Don't start that 'kinfolks' with me again," Blackie said. "I told you I don't want to hear no more about it. Butter and eggs! I ain't going to put up with nothing like this. I'm shorthanded, and I got a spooky herd, and I got wet weather, and lots of other things to worry about. I want you to eat and go out there and stand your guard tonight and not be acting this way no more."

Murphy picked at some of the food and rode his tour of guard that night but did not sing to the cattle. And when his guard was over he did not unroll his bed, which he had to himself, but crawled back into the wagon to sleep. The other men talked about his illness or pretended illness. One belief was that he needed a good dose of sulphur and molasses. Scott believed that, unless Blackie stopped riding him, they were going to be short another hand.

One further event marked that second camp on the Wichita, a small but startling and beautiful event. Most of the men had eaten breakfast and saddled up and gone out to the herd. The last guard, Scott, Cory, and Baldy, was in camp with Ostler.

Suddenly the three men stopped eating and cocked their ears to the wind. From somewhere, maybe from out toward the herd, and from an indefinite distance, came the clear, sweet tones of a French harp, or mouth organ, playing, "When You and I Were Young, Maggie."

They looked at each other in astonishment. Baldy said, "What in . . . ," and was stopped from making any more noise by the "Shoo . . ." of the others.

It was the last thing they had expected to hear; not that it was so unbelievable that a trail driver might have a French harp and be able to play it; but it seemed that music didn't belong out here. They were in the far reaches of a rough wilderness. Of course, music might belong anywhere, but it was something like the impossible eggs and butter little Murphy had wished for. They had heard no music for a long time except their own voices, which generally were not very musical and in some cases were positively raucous. Yet there it was: the pure plaintive notes of the familiar song. Each of them knew the words so well that the little harp seemed to be singing them in a girlish voice.

> . . . Is built where the birds used to play, Maggie,
> And join in the songs that were sung,
> For we sang as gay as they, Maggie,
> When you and I were young.

> But now we are aged and gray, Maggie,
> The toils of life nearly done.
> Let us sing of the days that are gone, Maggie,
> When you and I were young.

Lumps grew in their throats. When the sounds died away, they moved their heads this way and that, trying to catch the tune again. Scott said, "Who in the world could that be?"

Baldy said, "I don't know, but that sure does sound pretty out here, don't it?"

Ostler climbed up on the wagon and looked around, trying to see the source of the music. Cory said, "I heard that French harp one night when we were down on the San Saba, but I just barely heard it, and I finally decided it was a bird or something."

Later they found that some of the others had heard the music too, but no one would admit to being the musician. At noon camp there was much conjecture and accusation, but each of them said, "Hell's fire! If I could play one of the things and had one, I'd be playing it." Some of them finally accepted the unsatisfactory explanation that a settler out hunting or maybe a man on the dodge had wandered near their camp.

The following day, beyond Beaver Creek and the first thing in the morning, they ran again. They seemed to have been started by nothing more than the early morning sun on some clouds. The last guard was eating breakfast, and the other riders were starting to string out the herd, when suddenly they became frightened and unruly. They ran north into the rough country around Paradise Creek. They scattered badly over an area of several square miles but the outfit managed to keep up with all of them in the daylight. Nothing was lost but another day's time, which was required to bring them back together and establish order.

But after they had crossed the Pease River and had made night camp no more than ten miles from the Red, the herd stampeded again. A thunderstorm built up in the middle of the night, and the cattle burst out of their bed ground and ran west wildly. The moon was hidden for the first hour of their run, and they split again and again. Some cows and riders went up Wanderer's Creek; some went through the timber and across the creek.

Scott found himself at dawn with a fair-sized bunch, which he and Professor had managed to quieten down.

When the bunch had set to grazing, making little noise, they were able to hear, out north across the creek, the distant sound of more cattle running and harsh but faint yells. Scott left Professor with the bunch they had stopped and set out to investigate in the dim light of the cloudy dawn.

On the first rise beyond the creek he could see below him about five hundred head of cattle running in a fast mill. Little Murphy was riding around the edge, not doing much. But cutting through the center of the frantic cattle was Blackie, yelling curses, cutting at the beasts with his quirt, slamming his heels into his horse's sides to force him through the cattle at right angles to their run. From his voice and violent movements it was clear that the big segundo had lost his temper.

Blackie's horse became caught in a fast current of the cattle and was unable to move, except as he moved with them when he was bumped by their bodies and horns—this in spite of Blackie's flailing with his quirt at horse and cattle. Scott thought the man's position dangerous. If his horse lost his footing . . .

He pushed Blackjack into the circling stream of cattle and began to clear a path toward the big segundo. But when he came as near to him as the distance across a room, he saw that Blackie seemed to have no interest in getting out. The big man had concentrated his anger on a single red-roan steer, which was penned against his horse, and was quirting him across the head with all his might, as if he had forgotten where he was or what he might be trying to do. He yelled hoarsely, his voice punctuated by his violent movements, "God damn your . . . filthy stinking hide! . . . I'll learn you . . . how to stampede! . . . I'll learn you

. . . who's the boss . . . if I have to beat . . . you to . . . death!" The nose of the dazed steer ran blood and from one eye a red spray left dark spots on his yellow-red face.

"Blackie!" Scott yelled. "Blackie!" Then he turned and made his way out of the mill.

In another minute the particular victim of Blackie's anger had escaped from him, and the big segundo gave up and pulled out. He was panting and his face was beet red. His horse limped.

"Let's let them run down by themselves, Blackie," Scott said.

"By God, I was going to stop them from milling, but that damn Murph wouldn't give me no help."

"I don't think they'll hurt anything, a bunch that size and all grown stuff."

The steer which had been whipped in the face drifted out to the edge of the running cattle. Blackie said, "There's one goddam steer I learned a lesson."

"He won't go on the contract now," Scott said. "They won't take any crippled stuff."

"Hell, I never hurt him. He damned sure ain't crippled."

"He's got one eye gone. They'll call him crippled."

"Listen, God dammit! You trying to tell me what to do and what not to do?"

"I'm trying to tell you they won't take any crippled animals on the contract," Scott said. "And we've lost too many head already. We're getting down too close to three thousand head, and not halfway there. And after we cross that Red we may need some to trade to the Indians."

"I ain't giving no goddam beggar Injuns a single head," Blackie asserted.

"We may not have a choice about that. When we get up there in the territory that belongs to them, shorthanded and with a spooky herd that scatters all over—if we don't give them a few beeves, they may just take as many as they want. They've got all the advantage."

"We ain't going to have no spooky herd. I'm sick and tired of it. We're going to doctor up some legs on about twenty head; by God, maybe fifty head. I'm through messing with these stampedes."

Murphy rode up beside them, looking listless and forlorn. Scott answered Blackie's last assertion in a quiet, almost casual voice. "I don't think you're going to doctor any legs, Blackie. If you started cutting tendons, it would be just like throwing away the contract. They *will not* accept any crippled animals."

"Who the hell are you to tell me I ain't going to do it, if I decide to do it? I tell you something else I'm going to do. You act like you're worried about the tally being short. They's range cattle around here. By God, when we round up this mess this time we're taking ever cow we find, I don't care what the brand is. Everybody else does it, and I don't aim to come up short."

Scott laughed. "I hate to have to tell you, Blackie— seems like I object to everything you say—but they're going to cut our herd at Doan's, right down to the road brand."

"Listen, God dammit! Don't you think I been across the Red River before? I even been across right at Doan's Crossing! They ain't nobody cuts any herd at Doan's!"

"If you would read a newspaper once in a while, Blackie, you might find out things are changing. They've got an association up in this country, and they're going to cut us right down to the road brand. And it'll be legal."

"What the hell do you know about it? I guess you've about forgot who's running this outfit, Scott. You better change the way you act. I don't like the way you're acting right now. I thought at first you was one of the best hands I had, and now you keep on acting smart. If you don't change your ways, I think me and you are going to have trouble."

"The feeling is mutual," Scott said.

"What the hell do you mean by that? Is that some more of your smart talk?"

Scott laughed.

Blackie pointed the butt of his quirt at Murphy and said, "By God, the next time I tell you to come on and let's stop a bunch of cows from milling and you just hang around like a sick dog, I'm going to take this here quirt to you!"

Two days were required to gather up the scattered cattle, and according to Blackie's orders some thirty head of miscellaneous brands were added to it. But into their noon camp in Eagle Flats south of Red River rode a good-natured man and, behind him, a silent Ranger. The good-natured man declined to eat with them, presented credential papers, one of which was signed by a judge, and told Blackie that the herd would have to be cut down to the I-D Connected brand.

"Well, I sure don't understand it," Blackie said. "We started out with this many cows, and we're leaving twenty or thirty head with our brand in Texas. Any herd will pick up strays, and ain't nobody complained before."

"The law has been flouted for years," the man said, never losing his smile. "I sympathize with you. I'm not here to cut your herd; that's your own responsibility. I'm an inspector and I will have to look at your herd, when it's convenient to you. And it will have to be clean before you can take it farther north.

"We try to meet the herds this far out," he went on, "so no one will be held up at the river. Incidentally, the ford is passable now, but the water is slowly rising. I will look at your herd when you are ready to string them out." The man seemed positive about everything he said, as if to give the lie to his smile. He had evidently made the speech quite a few times before. Blackie was not impressed by the man or his papers, but he understood the silent Ranger without any need for words.

They handled the herd, which had been grazing loosely, as for a tally. The inspector proved to be as sharp-eyed as he was good-natured. He made sure that every creature not under the road brand was cut out to the west and not allowed to rejoin the stream going north. The outfit pushed them hard for the river. They were taking into the disputed area of Greer County, claimed as part of Indian Territory by the Federal Land Commission, three thousand and nine head by Martinez' tally, out of three thousand and twenty-five they had started with south of San Antonio.

They passed the adobe house and new plank store of old man Doan, whose business was supplying trail herds, and pushed the cattle into the river. The Red was the first of the big rivers they had to cross which were a part of the Mississippi drainage. It was a river that pulsed through the seasons, having little regular source in springs or melting snow; yet its broad bed, flanked in places by bluff banks, carried at times a torrent of water out of the red arroyos and canyons of the high plains. The riders could see driftwood stranded far above their heads, and the green foliage on trees far back from the present water level was strangely painted murky red halfway up the height of the trees.

The flat bed of the river was marked in spots by willow clumps, caught with all manner of fine drift. The water lay in pools or flowed slowly in several separate channels, but it was beginning to lap up over the flat bars, rising. They drove the horses in the lead, and the herd followed with one minor difficulty. One cow lost her footing in the last current and tried to come to shore in the shallows under a bank, but Scott and Professor, on the drag, snaked her out before she could become bogged and hustled her after the others.

They pushed the herd on to a night camp on the almost level plain several miles beyond the river, for any herd behind them would push across fast to avoid the rise and might run into them. Blackie took the Kid and went back to the wagon even before the last of the cattle had crossed; so that these two and Ostler were the only ones who had a chance to touch the little bit of civilization at the crossing.

They built a towering fire to guide Ostler to the camp ground. He came in an hour after dark, his wagon heavy with enough supplies to last to Dodge City. Later when the camp was quiet, Scott pulled on his trousers and boots and approached the old cook, who was arranging coals around a pot so that it would simmer through the night. The old man looked up and fussed at him. "You fellers sure don't know nothing about building a camp fire. You got enough blamed coals here for a dozen camp fires. I can't get clost to it."

Scott kept his voice low. "Did Blackie write to Greer?"

"What do you care? What you want to worry about that for?"

"You know why I want to worry about that. I want a straight answer, Ostler. Did Blackie write to Greer?"

"Why, hell yes. He said he would, didn't he? I tell you something else: I got me a new shovel and a new ax, and I never even asked him if I could. I just took them and he paid for them."

Scott was not satisfied with the answer, but he went back to bed. He lay for some time looking up at the stars that showed through the half-cloudy sky. One cowboy was snoring peaceably. A locust kept up a continuous keen hum; another broke in at intervals with a deeper buzzing noise. Faintly, one of the first guard could be heard singing. In spite of these sounds, Scott felt quite alone, as he had felt when he was realizing the meaning of Kittredge's death, and he was troubled. Out of the confusion of his drowsy thoughts came that pang of bitterness which had become associated with the words "It's my herd! Do you understand?" He was not able to sleep until some time after the first guard change, when Shorty crawled into the pallet beside him.

The next morning he caught Kid alone when they were releasing the unwanted horses from the rope corral and asked him, "Did Blackie write a letter, Kid? Back there at the store?"

"I don't know, Mr. Scott. I was helping load the stuff."

"You wouldn't lie to me, would you, Kid?"

"No, sir, that's the truth. I don't know."

Scott laughed. "I think I guessed who was playing the

French harp around here a few days ago, Kid. If I caught you lying to me, I just might tell about the French harp."

The Kid blushed deep red. "I ain't lying, sure enough. Mr. Blackburn might have wrote. He talked to the man there a while, and there was a woman too. I had to unload the bedrolls, because Mr. Ostler wanted to load stuff different, and I had to carry stuff. About all I done inside was get my new hat. Mr. Ostler made Mr. Blackburn pay for it. But I don't know if he wrote a letter, sure enough I don't, Mr. Scott."

So he would have to wait and see. He might have asked Blackie, but he was sure that he would get the same answer he had gotten from Ostler, and some bit of pride prevented him from pressing the question further.

It was at the noon camp ten miles into Greer County that Blackie missed Murphy. The big man stood up with his tin plate in his hand and asked, "Where is that damned Murph? Is he out at the herd? I ain't seen him all morning."

No one answered him, and the big segundo suddenly set his plate down and ran for the wagon. The tarp was off. Blackie sprang upon the brake bar and began poking among the gear. "Murph! God damn you! I told you I ain't going to put up with this! I aim to show you what I mean! Murph? Murph?"

The big man dropped to the ground and confronted the men. Something was dawning on him. "Who seen Murph last?"

"He was on guard last night," Dandy said.

"Hell's fire! ain't anybody seen him since then?"

No one admitted having either seen him or missed him. Kid was driving up the noon change of mounts, and

Blackie yelled at him, "Is Murphy's night horse gone?"

"No, sir."

"Have you seen Murphy this morning?"

"No, sir."

A tin wash pan covered with porcelain enamel, half full of dirty water, sat on the corner of the drop table at the rear of the wagon. Blackie seized the pan and dashed it against the ground in rage. "Goddam, there ain't nobody around here knows a thing! There ain't nobody pays a goddam bit of attention to what's going on, but me! I can't get no help, anything I try to do!"

He untied his horse from the rope of the temporary corral and said to Ostler, "Get out Murph's bedroll and see if his stuff's gone." He mounted, jerked the horse around, and set out for the herd in a dead run.

Ostler searched out the bedroll, grumbling, "Blackie can pick up that pan, or one of you fellers can pick it up, or it can lay right there. I ain't picking it up. I ain't no nursemaid for him ner nobody else. I ain't never been no nursemaid, and I sure ain't starting in to be no nursemaid now." Murphy's things were gone from his bedroll.

When Blackie returned from talking to Art and Booger Red, who were watching the herd as it grazed, he seemed to have satisfied himself that the little cowboy, Murphy, was gone. He dismounted and faced them. "Everybody check your gun and mount up. We're going after that son-of-a-bitch!"

They stopped eating and sat and stared at him.

"I mean it! We're going after that damned horse thief!"

Professor laughed his sarcastic laugh. Baldy asked, "Why do you want to bring him back, Blackie? He wasn't doing no work anyway, the past week. He won't be no use to us even if we find him and bring him back."

"By God! we ain't going to bring him back. We're going to hang him! For a horse thief!"

They all stared at him, and Baldy expressed their common feeling with the words, "Little old Murph? You mean you aim for us to hang little old Murph?"

"Hell yes, I do! You all know what Colonel Kittredge said. Can't nobody quit. We're going to teach him a lesson he won't never forget. He's going to get what a horse thief's got coming to him!"

"Hell's fire, Blackie!" Baldy said. "He never took his night horse. Probably he only took that old flea-bit paint he had in his string."

"A horse is a horse! And he's going to pay for it!"

Professor said, "Don't you think we'd better take the rifles, Blackie? That Murphy will likely put up a pretty stiff fight."

"Hell yes, get out the rifles, Ostler."

"I ain't going with you," Ostler said. "I hired on to cook, not to ride no horse."

"I never said you was going. I said get out the rifles. But, by God, you'll go if I say for you to! What are you all setting there for? I said to get ready to mount up."

They looked at one another. Ostler, Martinez, Dandy, and Baldy began to make some small pretense of obeying. Scott, Professor, Shorty, and Cory did not move. Kid was hiding around behind the wagon.

Scott said, "You were saying a while ago that you're not getting enough help from the rest of us, Blackie. I guess that means you'd be willing for some of us to help you by talking this over a little."

Blackie frowned at him suspiciously, standing with his hands on his hips.

"Since Murphy's got maybe a twelve-hour start on us," Scott went on, "how long do you think it might take us to catch him?"

"By God! we'll catch him if it takes two weeks!"

"Well, do you think Art and Booger Red can hold the herd all right by themselves for two weeks? I guess one of them could hold three thousand cows while the other one slept. Of course, we may have Indians around here and we've got a spooky herd. Are you going to guarantee our wages, Blackie, if we lose the herd or if we don't make the delivery date? I was thinking we might be ten days or two weeks behind schedule right now. I remember you didn't know what day it was when Kittredge died, but I'm sure you're keeping up with everything now, since you're in charge. I know you must have it figured out what day you plan to cross the Canadian River and what day you plan to pass Camp Supply and what day you plan to hit Dodge and so on, in order to meet the delivery date. Why don't you explain to us what your plans are and what effect it will have on your schedule if we go chasing down Red River after Murphy?"

Blackie didn't know how to take it. He was angry and trying to think of something to say as Scott went on.

"I don't understand you, Blackie. You must be a new kind of trail boss. You can hang Murphy—hell, you can crucify him—and it won't move the herd one mile north."

Blackie had found one thing to say. "By God! I'm the same kind of trail boss that Colonel Kittredge was. That's what kind of a trail boss I am. He was a great man!"

"Yes, he was a great man. I've got a good idea, Blackie. Why don't you go after Murph by yourself? You can handle him easy by yourself. You can hang him or anything you want to do, without any help. The rest of us can be pushing the cows up the trail till you catch up with us."

"Yeah, I guess, by God, you want to be in charge while I'm gone, don't you?"

Scott said quietly, "I believe I could handle it, but I'd be happy to go along with Shorty here or Martinez, whoever you say."

Blackie was thinking about it.

Baldy said, "Hell, you don't want to hang little old Murph, Blackie! Think about them hound-dog eyes he's got, and them big ears, and them three teeth he's got kicked out. It would be like hanging your own grandma. He ain't heavy enough to get the kinks out of a rope anyway." Some of them laughed at this; they were not taking the hanging idea seriously now.

Blackie looked at all of them. Finally he said, "I ain't made up my mind what to do yet. I may just let him go. He ain't made me no kind of a hand for a week anyway. I know one thing; they's one or two fellers in this outfit is always getting smart with me, and one of these days they're liable to get a punch in the nose. I'm pushing this herd as fast as I can, and I got a hundred things on my mind, and I ain't going to put up with nobody getting smart with me."

So the hanging plan was dropped. Scott was not displeased that Blackie had made such an obvious fool of himself; there had been something ludicrous about the idea of hanging the little cowboy. When he, Scott, got the authority to take over the herd, and he couldn't stand the thought that he might not—when he did he wanted the men behind him; he wanted it obvious to everyone that Blackie couldn't handle the job, for he did not intend to use Blackie as segundo.

He didn't want any trouble, no taking of sides, not even any argument when the time came. When he got authority from Greer, if nobody was displeased other than Blackie, he thought he could handle the big man. And that's what he wanted. Rightly handled, Blackie, with all his strength and energy, would be a good cowhand—and they were getting short on hands of any kind. But he must get authority. How could anyone expect him to handle a person like Blackie without authority.

The Fight

11

Oh, the peckerwood's a pecking and the children are a crying;
The old folks a fighting and the hogs are a dying.
Come-a ti yi yippi, yippi yea, yippi yea,
Come-a ti yi yippi, yippi yea.

As they went north the talk in camp was of Indians. The previous decade had seen some of the most fierce fighting of the American frontier. Trouble with Indians was an old thing; they had heard stories by fathers and grandfathers. But since the War between the States a new desperation had come into it. The best mounted, best armed, most independent Indians that had ever existed in the country had been facing increasing encroachment by the white invaders, with no place left to go, and had turned like cornered animals. They had forgotten old tribal differences; Kiowa braves had followed Comanche chiefs to burn and kill in the southern plains; Cheyenne braves had ridden behind Sioux chiefs against their common white enemy in the north.

It had been a time of treachery, sudden new warpaths, broken treaties. The question on the plains now was whether the last of the great chiefs understood, or accepted, that they were defeated and must obey, must stay on their reservations and accept such humiliation as came. Cochise had made a lasting peace, but Geronimo ran free in the mountains; Crazy Horse had been taken and killed, but his superior, Sitting Bull, was still free, somewhere.

The concensus in the I-D Connected outfit was that the only good Indian is a dead Indian. They had no argument over this opinion; they had believed it all their lives. They did disagree about the degree of danger they were in and about the proper approach in dealing with the redskins. The more thoughtful among them believed that their job was to get the herd across the Territory with as little friction as possible. If there was fighting to do, it should be left to that group of men which they thought of with mingled admiration and disdain, the U.S. Army, commonly referred to as "them god-damned Yankee soldiers."

They had all been in the Nation before except Kid, and they took turns trying to scare him or reassure him. He grinned through it all. Scott told him, "If you see an Indian in Texas, Kid, look out! He's on the warpath. But if you see one here, don't worry; he's where he belongs."

Coming into the hills, before they crossed the North Fork, Kid came riding hard from the direction of the remuda, slid his horse to a halt in the evening camp, and screamed, "I seen one!"

Baldy asked, "You seen one what, Kid? A horny frog?"

"I seen a Injun! I sure did! Right on that hill over yonder. I wasn't far from him, either. He just set there on his horse and looked at me, then he rode . . ."

"Simmer down, Kid," Baldy said. "You're liable to stampede old Ostler here, and then we won't get no supper."

"You probably seen a bush," Dandy said.

"I thought it was a bush," Kid panted. "First, I thought it was a man setting there, but it never moved, so I thought it was a bush. And after a while he turned his horse around and kicked him—I seen him kick him—and it was the biggest Injun you ever seen, and he rode off over the hill."

They teased Kid, pretending they didn't believe him. He protested for an hour, then only grinned, even when Baldy told him to watch out, because he had exactly the kind of hair Indians like to collect.

But in the days that followed they all saw them. They took the herd through the extreme western fringe of the Wichita Mountains. Here the red granite hills rose around them, slopes covered with lichen-encrusted boulders, dotted with scrub oak and cedar. The herd was strung out, passing west of a ridge, the crest of which was a half mile away. Two Indians sat their horses on the crest, watching them pass, as still as statues. One had his horse turned sideways, facing the other one. The two did not move until the drag came even; then they turned and rode away to disappear behind the ridge.

Blackie didn't like it. An hour later, at noon camp, he threatened, "I'm going to start carrying a rifle, if them bastards don't stop spying on us. They'll get too close, and I'll drop one."

"At least they ain't trying to hide," Shorty said.

Baldy suggested, "Maybe they're trying to learn how to trail dogies."

Scott was afraid they were waiting for a stampede and a scattered herd or perhaps waiting for a chance to get at the horses. He expressed these ideas so that Blackie would understand but with enough tact so that the big segundo could not accuse him of "getting smart."

After that, as they came up through the area of Elk Creek, they saw the Indians daily, sometimes one alone, sometimes two, always in clear view on a rise a half mile or more away. The outfit began taking the precaution of herding the remuda more closely at night, hobbling and sidelining those horses which were inclined to stray any distance.

The herd had run once since Doan's, between the North and Salt Forks of the Red. They seemed to be looking for another excuse, though now the weather had cleared up. They found the excuse south of the Washita River, the smell of a skunk in broad daylight. The herd ran west, came against the river, and turned south. Blackie had gone out scouting and so was not there to apply his violent methods of controlling the cattle. The rest of the outfit, recognizing the need to keep the herd together, stayed with them until they began to tire, then stopped them and had restored order before nightfall.

The following day they crossed the Washita and pointed them toward the broad Canadian. The Indian "spies" were still with them.

Where the Canadian River, sometimes called the South Canadian, ran out of the Texas Panhandle into the Indian hunting grounds, it swept in three giant bends, going north ten or fifteen miles in each case before it curved back south. The trail to Dodge City led through the easternmost of the bends, deviating from a more direct route in order to follow better watering for herds and to avoid the dry sand hills north of the river that made traveling hard labor. The trail crossed at Wagon Road Crossing on the road from Fort Sill to Camp Supply.

They were in noon camp near the headwaters of Deep Creek when a trail hand from a herd ahead rode into camp. His herd was held up by high water, and his foreman had sent him with a message to put on the telegraph at Fort Reno. Instead of riding cross-country he was back tracking on the cattle trail to where it cut the Fort Reno-Fort Elliot road. Of the river ahead, he reported, "Man alive, you ought to see that old South Canadian. She's a mile wide, and whole big trees going down her. Damnedest thing ever I seen!"

He reported that five herds of cattle and one composed of nearly a thousand head of horses were ahead, waiting for the river to go down so they could cross. After a hasty lunch, the man bragged on Ostler's cooking and headed on south, wanting plenty of time to find the military road before dark.

Squatting with his tin plate poised in one hand and his fork in the other, Scott mused, "That's a real bad situation: ten or fifteen thousand cows and nearly a thousand horses stacked up waiting to cross up in that bend."

Some of them shook their heads in agreement. Blackie made no sign of agreeing or disagreeing.

"If they run," Scott said, "they haven't got much place to go except all over each other. We're not going any closer, are we, Blackie?"

"What the hell do you mean—not going any closer? We're fifteen miles from the river."

"Well, that's about the distance I'd want to be. I'd pull off the trail three or four miles right here and wait till they thin out, or hunt up another crossing."

"By God! Maybe you would, but what you can't seem to get through your thick head, you ain't in charge of this outfit. You think I'm going to pull off the trail and let everybody else get ahead of me? Goddam, if I ain't got enough worries now with Injuns following me."

Scott replied calmly, "Did you ever see that many cows and horses stampede together?"

Blackie didn't answer.

"I saw it once, Blackie, on the Chisholm Trail; when all the strangers got mixed up it made them more skittish. They scattered over five hundred square miles, and it took three weeks to get them straightened out."

Blackie's face had become deep red, as it always did when he grew angry. He rose and said loudly, "All right, let's don't waste so goddam much time eating! Let's get out there and get them cows headed north."

They camped that evening on the high ground in the

middle of the giant bend. They could see around them on three sides, from five to eight miles distant, the wide river or the scant timber along its course. In the west the river, in the vicinity of Wagon Road Crossing, was a surging torrent, darker than the land, carrying on its surface bright sparkling patches from the setting sun. Their view was a majestic panorama, a giant three-sided corral with vast pastures of grass dotted with the waiting herds. Smoke rose in a thin wisp from a half-dozen camp fires.

For Scott, the beauty of the scene was marred by his imagination. He could see the possibility of the biggest stampede of all time and thousands of cattle trampled to death. There must be between them and the river some trail bosses who were bigger fools even than Blackie, or maybe they had enjoyed such easy drives that they were lulled into a false sense of security.

Scott knew he had to press Blackie further. They were getting too short on time to take a risk like this. The big segundo was getting more touchy about advice, day by day, but he, Scott, was getting tired of being tactful.

Ostler had pulled the pots out of the fire and they were ready to eat. It was still daylight. Scott asked, "What are your plans now, Blackie?"

"What the hell do you mean—what are my plans?"

"I mean since you've seen the layout here, surely you don't mean to stay here. What do you plan to do tomorrow?"

"By God! I plan to go straight on and get as close to the river as I can, so's we can cross when it goes down. But all the reason you want to know my plan is so you can show off and give me some more smart-aleck advice. And I'm warning you for the last time; I'm sick of it!"

Scott felt anger growing slowly but clearly in himself. The anger was as much at himself as at Blackie. Why had he allowed it to come to this? Why hadn't he tried harder to straighten out the question of leadership before they were in clear danger of losing the whole herd? Why hadn't he worked on their reason and intelligence? On Ostler, whom the men looked up to? On Professor, who surely could see Blackie's inadequacy?

His anger was rushing through him. It was as if he could feel the blood throbbing in every vein and artery in his body as he said, "The job of bossing this herd is too big for you, Blackie. I thought we talked it over down on the Brazos and decided to get together on the problems we ran into—until we hear from the owners. Did you even write to Greer at Doan's?"

"That ain't none your goddam business! You're fixing to get it, cowboy! You're just about a hair away from a good punch in the nose!"

All of the men were standing there watching and waiting, except the three on the herd: Shorty, Art, and Booger Red.

Scott said, "I'm going to tell you why I seem to give you more trouble than any other man, Blackie. I've ridden segundo for seven years, to Abilene and Wichita and Dodge, and last year clear to Montana. I was hired by Lawson, himself, to boss this drive; then I got screwed out of it after he died. I'm taking over, Blackie. These men here know you can't handle the job. I've got proof right here that Lawson thought I could boss a herd and get it through."

He took the letter from his pocket, removed it from the envelope as deliberately as he could, smoothed out the creases, and thrust it out toward Blackie.

The big man took it and, with one movement, crumpled it into a ball and tossed it into the coals of the cook fire. The ball of paper grew brown at the bottom and flamed up immediately.

Then Scott did a stupid thing. It had been stupid to hand the letter to Blackie—some perverse devil had prompted him. But, seeing the letter in flames, Scott did a thing more stupid still. He swung with all the strength of his body, reinforced with his coursing anger, and struck Blackie straight in the face. Straight in the nose.

The blow had no more landed than he could see, through the haze of his emotion, that he had made a mistake; but with this realization was the satisfaction that he had landed solidly. The big man's nose spurted blood as he reeled back.

He might as safely have struck a grizzly bear in the nose. The big man bulled back upon him, cursing incoherently, not setting himself or feinting, but flailing with arms that were like the trunks of trees. Scott dodged two blows, then took a looping one on the left shoulder that lifted him off his feet. He landed as if he had been thrown from a bronc and, seeing at a hasty glance the big man's boots striding down upon him, he rolled on the rough ground to escape. As he scrambled to his feet, Blackie's fist ripped through the loose front of his shirt, burning his skin like a cannon ball passing.

He steadied himself on the balls of his feet, ducking back and forth, and managed to get in a jab that smeared the blood at the bottom of the big man's nose. From the corner of his eye he could see Cory coming up beside him, and he yelled, "Get out! Get back! It's my fight!" He didn't see whether Cory obeyed, for in that same instant he caught a solid blow to the side of his head that sent him reeling again to the ground, dazed.

He had rolled to his side when the big man crushed down upon him. He took hard fists in the back and chest, but squirmed violently to keep his opponent from pinning him.

Blackie slammed a long blow at his head, missed, and lost his balance. Scott took advantage of the big man's clumsiness to twist free of the weight and come to his feet. He had to stay on his feet if he could and try to use his superior speed and agility. He danced in and out and sidestepped another wild rush, getting in a blow to the big man's side; it felt as if he had hit a brick building.

He got a glance of the spectators standing around them in the dusk. All of them were standing hunched, intent, their big hats pushed to the backs of their heads, yelling, waving their arms. He could not hear what they were saying, but imagined they were watching as if it were a dogfight. He cursed himself again for a fool.

Blackie closed, swinging, but more warily. Scott felt his leg bump one of the cooking pots and, as he retreated, saw Blackie step on the edge of it and spill out the beans. Ostler's voice could be heard above the other yelling, "Get out of camp to fight, you fools! Get out of camp!"

The old cook was right about them being fools, Scott thought. He thought it while he was in the immediate act of dodging and feinting, while he was feeling blood run down from his ear to his back, while he was listening to the roaring in his head and his own grunting and the big fighter's curses and the cushioned sounds of fists landing. It was as if he were split, part of himself in a wild melee, part of himself detached and observing a stupid, senseless brawl. He had a serene confidence, even as he felt the harsh blows that could crush through his guard as if his arms were limp rope, that he was the better man in every way except one: physical strength; and he was indeed a fool to have challenged the big man in this manner. But the stupid mistake was made. It left nothing now but to try with every desperate effort he could muster to bring about some miracle and whip the big man.

A pile of dead limbs, which had been snaked up in the loop of a lariat, lay between the fire and the wagon. Scott ducked a sweeping arm and hit the big man in the side with more of a shove than a blow. Blackie moved into the wood pile, stumbled, and went down.

Scott screamed at him, "Get up and fight, you bastard!" It was his only chance—to get Blackie blind mad.

Blackie's hand closed over a stick and he slung it. Scott dropped low, barely in time to avoid it, and the big man came up and at him, arms wide, like a man trying to pin a calf in the corner of a corral. The big man's hair stood up in a black rumpled mass; he looked like some strange maddened animal, with black in the center of his face where blood was clotting. He mouthed meaningless sounds.

Scott tried to spar with him, but Blackie had become smarter about it, rather than blind in his rage, and moved relentlessly forward with arms outspread. Scott thought of his gun; he didn't know whether it was still at his side. He decided against reaching for it, but wished he had made it guns instead of fists. It still would have been a senseless fight, but the odds would have been even.

He couldn't back up forever. He threw up his left, ducked, and slammed his right into the big belly in front of him. Then he felt the powerful arms close around him. He was lifted and thrown straight down, sickeningly. He was trying to move along the ground when something, a boot or a fist, caught him in the side of the head. He felt the blow on both sides as the grass stubble ground into the other side of his face like a steel file.

He thrust his legs up, kicking, not knowing for the moment where his opponent was. Then he felt knees in his chest and a great weight, hands like steel hoops at his throat, hands jerking up and down, pounding his head against the ground. The dusky sky, which outlined the frenzied dark form over him, faded to complete blackness.

There were a few seconds when he could hazily feel cold water in his face, and talking, and he knew Shorty was there. The next time he became conscious he came out of it slowly, aware of the creaking and jolting of the wagon, hearing it more than feeling it, for he lay on something soft. He thought dimly that he was lying in a very uncomfortable position, but with his first tentative movement he was rudely jerked awake by the pain. It was brilliant daylight and before his eyes was the coarse tarp of bedrolls. He discovered that rather than having been uncomfortable, he had been resting easy; now he could find no easy position but seemed to discover a new area of pain with any movement.

He explored himself slowly. Underneath one swollen

cheek, he had a loose tooth. His right ear was torn and crusted with blood, as was the back of his head. His left side was so tender to touch or movement that he knew he must have some broken ribs. His body was a mass of bruises but he thought he had no other broken bones. He rose to one elbow and spoke to the drooping back of the cook. "Where are we, Ostler?"

"Oh, you come out of it, did you?" The old man pulled the team to a halt and turned around, grinning. "If you ain't a purty sight! But you ought to see old Blackie's nose. You done a good job on his nose, even if he did whup you."

"Where are we? Where are we going now?" The swollen cheek made his words come out slow and thick.

Ostler laughed. "We're pulling back to Deer Creek. This morning Blackie said he'd decided it was dangerous up yonder close to the river and all them herds bunched up."

Scott managed a smile. "Wonder where he got that idea?"

"Ain't much telling. Old Blackie is sure worried about them Injuns. We seen another one this morning."

"What did all the boys in the outfit think about the fight?"

"Well, they thought it was a danged good fight." The old man rolled his quid in his jaw. Small droplets of amber juice clung to his mustache. "You got friends in this outfit all right, Billy. When Blackie went to beating your head on the ground, Cory put his gun right in Blackie's ear and pulled the trigger, but the damned thing snapped. About the time he got the hammer back again, we pulled him off and while we was trying to get it away from him, it went off and it never snapped that time—shot a hole right through the top of my little washtub. Kid got on Blackie too; Blackie flung him off like some old bear cuffing a pup, you know. It finally taken all of us to get Blackie off of you, after you was knocked out."

"What I meant was—what do they think, all the boys, about Blackie running the outfit?"

"Well, I don't know, Billy. They know you was right, about crowding the river that way. But they know Blackie whupped you, too." The old man spat and whipped up his mules.

Scott began to move around in the jolting wagon, working his bruised muscles. His mistake had been in the way he had handled the letter from Lawson. He had been stupidly angry when he handed it to Blackie. What had he expected the big segundo to do? Fall on his knees and admit that he couldn't read? He, Scott, should have used the letter to get all the men behind him and should have made sure that the letter to Greer was written at Doan's Store. His actions the evening before had been as foolish as had Blackie's when he whipped the big red-roan steer in the face and blinded him.

When Ostler began to make camp Scott began slowly to climb out of the wagon. "That's the thing to do," the cook said. "Get out and move around. It's just like a horse with a setfast on his back; he'll pitch when you first get on him, but when the sore warms up it don't bother him none."

"I'm just like Blackie," Scott told him. "I don't want any of your smart-aleck advice. Where's my gun?"

"Right in the front of the wagon box where I was setting, but I ain't . . ."

"You ain't what?" He fished out the gun and dropped it

into his holster.

"Well, you don't aim to . . . ?"

"No, you can rest easy. I tell you one thing: I've fought that big son-of-a-bitch my last time with my fists. It's a wonder he didn't kill me. But I'm not going to start any gunplay, not unless he crowds me. I could kill him and it wouldn't move that herd one mile toward Ogallala."

Ostler stared at him, puzzled, finally shook his head and laughed. "Anyway, it was a damned good fight."

Blackie came in with a half dozen of the riders an hour before dark. Scott was leaning against a rear wagon wheel. Some of them made a few joking remarks about the fight, watching keenly the two men who had fought. Blackie's nose was flattened and swollen to monstrous size; he walked around without his usual loud bluster, avoiding the eyes of Scott. Scott said nothing to him. Thus a kind of self-conscious truce was introduced between the two.

Blackie had sent two men out to help bed the herd and the rest were drinking coffee, waiting for chow or staking out their night horses, when they heard the sound—or felt it.

It was a kind of constant tremor, so faint to the ear that it might have been the wind in the grass of the rolling prairie. But in spite of its faintness, it was bigger than a wind; ten miles to the north and west some great movement was taking place. The staked horses and those still in the rope corral were standing with heads high and ears pricked forward.

"What the hell is that?" someone said.

"Sounds like a cyclone or a earthquake."

"How could it be a cyclone? They ain't a cloud in the sky."

Scott began the labor of working his saddle out of the wagon. "I don't know about the rest of you, but I'm going out and sing to the cattle."

Shorty rushed to help him with the load. "You sure you can ride, Billy?"

"Yeah, I'm all right. But I sure could use some help to get this thing on Blackjack."

Scott was saddled and mounted before Blackie woke and began yelling, "Catch your horses! Everybody get out yonder and sing! Catch your horses! Kid, get out to the remuda!"

The herd was already bedded on a broad grassy rise, quiet and resting. The men lost touch with the peculiar distant sound as they circled and sang. They talked about it as they passed, some certain that it was cattle running, some coming to believe that it was really nothing at all. But when one of the riders moved out away from the bedded herd and dismounted to relieve himself, in the quiet and with his feet on the ground, he could hear it still. It went on for hours, finally fading away in the far south and west in the middle of the night.

The spooky I-D Connected cattle slept like lambs. They arose one by one around midnight, arched their backs to stretch, and lay back down on the other side. As they had run in the past, senselessly, at the scent of a skunk or seemingly at nothing at all; so now, unexplainably, they slept within human hearing of one of the greatest stampedes of all time.

They pieced together the story during the next two days, part of it, from scattered riders who were searching for lost cattle. One of the strange riders, who took noon chow with them the next day, was an owner. He seemed half dazed and could only say, "Yesterday I was a rich man. It was them damned horses that made it so bad."

South of the swollen Canadian that night two men had died: one a young man from Waco, one a Negro cook, whose chuck wagon had been overrun and slashed to splinters. An uncounted number of cattle had died; one place they had piled into an arroyo till they filled it and the maddened animals following had crossed on their dead bodies; another place a giant mill had crushed nearly a hundred head. The wildly neighing horses had set them off again and again. The six outfits involved faced a roundup that would take a full month's time and cover an area from the Wichita Mountains to the Texas Panhandle.

Quicksand

12

My hoss throwed me off at a creek called Mud;
My hoss throwed me off around the 2-U herd.
Come-a ti yi yippi, yippi yea, yippi yea,
Come-a ti yi yippi, yippi yea.

Four of them sat their horses at the crossing and studied it: Blackie, Martinez, Baldy, and Scott. The river was fully a half mile wide, its waters full of silt and sand. Almost no timber grew along its low banks, only a few willows no bigger than switches, some of which also grew far out in the murky water and showed its shallow depth. Caught on a bar near the middle was a big pine tree, which had grown to maturity hundreds of miles away from these treeless plains.

The water generally was shallow and sluggish, but ripples in its dark surface betrayed the location of channels where swift water ran. The river had the peculiarity of other broad plains rivers in that it swelled downward as much as up; when the flow of water increased, channels cut deep into its soft bed rather than rising at the bank. These channels shifted constantly, to silt up and disappear as the flow slowed.

Blackie asked Baldy, "Reckon it can be crossed?"

"It don't look good to me," Baldy said. "Places out there would bog a saddle blanket. Ain't that right, Scott?"

"Well, the quicksand's not much different whether it's up or down. I think we could cross it in the morning when the cows can see the other bank real plain. We can throw the horses in first. It's been crossed worse than that."

"How many days are we behind?" Martinez asked. He was looking at Scott rather than Blackie.

"A good two weeks," Scott said. "We ought to be in Dodge right now."

"Man, you said a mouthful," Baldy put in. "That's the place we ought to be right now—Dodge City—bellied up to one of them long bars or one of them sporting gals."

Blackie was feeling of his nose and studying the water. "I ain't made up my mind," he said. "I may decide to cross her first thing in the morning."

Scott dismounted and began removing all his clothing except his shorts. His hurts from the fight no longer bothered him, except for his tender ribs. "I think I'll take a little swim right now," he said as he loosened the girths slightly on the big black horse. He had caught Blackjack with a swim in mind when they started down to inspect the river. Baldy and Martinez grinned at him. Blackie stared and said nothing.

He urged the horse into the knee-deep water and gave him his head. Out two hundred feet Blackjack began feeling his way gingerly with his forefeet. Suddenly the bottom seemed to go out from under them and the horse dropped in a void of sand and water. The bank of one of the hidden channels had given away beneath them. The heads of both horse and rider were splashed with water before they started rising again. Blackjack was standing up, kicking with his back feet for the bottom.

Scott did not use the reins but patted the horse on the neck and spoke to him. "Let's go, boy. Let's go." The big horse straightened up and started swimming, angling into the current. Scott pulled his head up slightly as he saw shoal water, and the horse scrambled at the hidden soft bank, at last finding footing. They came up dripping water onto a bar not stirrup deep.

The big horse slid into the next channel on his haunches, as if he were stopping on a rope. And so they went up and down a dozen times across the river. Coming out of the last deep place near the north bank, the horse lunged up several times and Scott slipped off, holding to reins and mane until the horse found enough solid footing to pull himself out. Then Scott regained his position in the saddle, wincing with the strain on his tender side.

He rode up and down the north bank a few minutes, studying the soil, then made the return crossing. The three men were sitting exactly where they had been when he started across. They had been watching his every move. He said casually as he dressed, speaking to no one in particular, "We won't have any trouble if we can keep them moving. Right where I came out is the best place."

The next morning Blackie announced that he had decided to cross the Canadian—some of the damn fools who had been in the big stampede might bring part of a herd back and crowd them; besides, he thought maybe they might escape the Indian spies who appeared daily to look over the herd.

They headed the cattle for the crossing, strung out, with the horses in front. The water showed no rise since the day before, and Scott believed that the channels should not be so deep or swift. He went in the lead with the remuda along with Kid and Martinez, with the halfway permission of Blackie based on the idea that he, Scott, knew the river better than anyone else. The horses plunged right into the deeper currents, churning and splashing the muddy water into foam. As soon as Scott saw that the horses would have no difficulty and would come out at the right place, he fell back beside the line of moving cattle, downstream of them. He kept the big horse moving back and forth, pushing at the knots of cows that were swept down by the current, making them angle back into it. Martinez fell back to help; Baldy and Professor had come out from the south bank. They were all riding near naked.

As the first of the cows were reaching the north shore, some of those a hundred yards behind the leaders began to bunch in the last deep place. They lunged at the soft bank, trying to come out of the swimming water onto the bar, but could not get room enough for free movement. They drifted downstream, fighting frantically in the crowded water. At this point the line was broken, and the cattle behind pushed into the drifting mill.

Scott waved his hat at the men on the south bank and yelled as loudly as he could. They finally understood, or figured it out for themselves, for they cut off the line of cows into the water. Some of them rode out to turn the line away from the mill.

Scott and the three with him swam their horses into the swimming knot of cattle, urging them with yells and quirts, purposely allowing those downstream to drift in order to relieve the crowding. The cows were a jostling thicket of horns and heads on the water surface, bodies hidden; their nostrils flared and their eyes bulged from the exertion. Scott felt the horns and bodies bump his legs, a slashing hoof stab at his boot toe, and he knew Blackjack was feeling the same thing, but the horse never flinched. And in the midst of fighting the cattle he was relieved for a time of the mental burden of their confused leadership, and he exulted in the physical exertion. His pride was almost savage, a feeling that came from his sure belief that he was riding the best all-around cowhorse in the world. Ostler's assertion that a man's injuries would warm up and give no pain, as a horse's sore back was supposed to do, must have been correct, for he felt nothing but the cool muddy water splashing against him and the lunging of the horse under him.

As the stronger of the cattle pulled up into shallow water they left room for the others to come out more easily. The riders began to line them back toward where the others had left the water.

Baldy's horse tried to come out of the current at a different place, and the man finally left the saddle to give his horse a better chance. Baldy clawed his way onto the shallow bar and turned to pull on the horse, but at the same time the horse lunged and jerked the reins free. Baldy sloshed through the shallow water, screaming, "Catch my saddle! Somebody catch my saddle!" The horse went downstream, fighting the invisible bank. The cattle in the shallow water nearby spooked at the sight of the nearly naked, dismounted cowboy, but they could not run much in the water and sand.

Scott, nearest to the loose horse, freed his dripping wet rope, made a loop, and on the second cast settled it around the horse's neck. The horse seemed to lose his frantic haste when he felt the rope and pulled himself out onto the sand bar, where he was remounted by the grateful Baldy.

Some thirty of the cows, not having immediate attention, headed straight through the shallows for the dry shore. They felt bad footing and paused, sniffing ahead of them. A few of them ran ahead and got out all right; some of them turned back to follow those who were being herded upstream. Five head paused too long in their tracks. When their sharp hoofs had sunk six inches into the sand, their struggles served only to bog them deeper. In two minutes, the five rested with their bellies against the sand.

When the riders had pushed the rest of the cattle out, they then had some five hundred head across, and Scott suggested that Baldy and Professor stay on the north shore since Kid was the only other man across.

"What about them bogged cows?" Baldy asked.

"They won't be any problem, as near as they are to dry

land," Scott said. "We'll have to get some hobbles or something to tie up their legs before we can snake them out."

"They won't go anywhere," Martinez said without a smile.

Baldy got a good laugh. As he rode off, he said to Professor, "That damn Scott is a real good man in a river."

"He'll do," Professor said.

"Do, hell! Martinez will do. Or maybe even me or you would do. But Billy Scott is the kind of a man I want to have with me when I get in a river like that baby there. You know what I wish? I wish old Scott had whupped that damned Blackie and taken over this outfit. That's what I wish."

Professor laughed, and Baldy didn't understand the laughter, especially when Professor said, "If this be treason, make the most of it."

As they crossed back through the river, Scott and Martinez agreed that the crossing should be made with bunches of two or three hundred head at a time. Scott let the Mexican pass the advice on to the big segundo, who agreed to try it. Shorty, Art, and Booger Red got hobbles and rope from the wagon and crossed to begin the labor of snaking out the bogged cows.

The remaining hands cut three hundred head from the herd and tried to ease them into the water. The cattle stopped, sniffing suspiciously at the water's edge. Then a couple of the Spanish heifers in the lead whirled away from it and plunged back among those waiting. They milled across the dividing line between the wet sand and the dry sand. Blackie cursed and swung his quirt, but to no avail; it was clear that some stratagem was necessary.

The fact that they had lost three men out of the outfit was making a difference now. There were twelve left, but Ostler was still busy breaking camp. With three men across the river holding the cattle and horses and three working with bogged cows, there were left only two to hold the big herd and three to attempt the crossing of small bunches.

The three, Blackie, Scott, and Martinez, pulled the balky bunch back a quarter of a mile from the water, turned them around, and pushed them fast. They were trotting when they hit the river sand. They took the water, though reluctantly. Some of them were still trying to turn back when they hit the bad channel three-quarters of the way across. The three riders, perhaps the three best in the outfit, could not prevent them from scattering as they came out on the last bar. Again, some of them paused, and two of them stayed, caught tight in the grip of the sand, muddy water lapping their sides, though the water was no more than six inches deep. The snaking crew were only now hooked to their first stranded cow; it was apparent that they would not be able to keep up with the bogging animals.

Blackie told Professor and Baldy to hold the crossed cows near the water, so that they could be seen from the south bank; then he took the river crew back after another bunch. Ostler joined in the work dressed only in long underwear, which he like many older men wore the year around. He took the jibes of the other hands at his "under-riggings" with a snort and said, "You damn fools will wish you had on some decent clothes before the day's over. You'll get sunstroke."

They cut out another bunch and ran them for the water. These were mostly heifers, less afraid of the water but more inclined to scatter. Scott and Blackie rode frantically in the deceptive river; each seemed determined to outdo the other in sheer work. Scott was the better mounted, but Blackie had no less energy; and in such work, in hard herding where a loud yell was valuable, the big segundo could do the work of two. He seemed to be trying, as a trail boss should, to show them how to do it right. Sometimes Martinez cut his dark eyes around at Ostler and flashed his white teeth in a grin. He was not grinning at the figure cut by the old cook with his gray bushy hair and gray bushy whiskers, splashing through the water in his long-handles, but at the seeming competition between the two younger men. Ostler would grin back and snort, "Couple of crazy fools!" They left four of the heifers bogged in the sand, scattered downstream with the others.

The next bunch they cut out refused to take the water at all. They found it necessary to go across and bring back thirty or so horses to lead them in. Baldy, Professor, and Kid were having trouble holding the crossed cattle in sight on the north shore and still preventing them from getting into the dangerous sand. With the horses leading, they crowded another bunch into the water and across, again leaving three stuck near the north side. But the next bunch refused to follow the small band of horses; they would not be persuaded at all.

After some minutes of yelling and urging, Blackie cut out around the balking cattle and, riding in the shallow water, slung his loop over the horns of a big line-back steer, yelling, "Damn you! If I can't drive you, I'll drag you!" He spurred his horse against the rope. The steer set back against the pull, slid forward in the wet sand, ran splashing in the water in a zigzag pattern, then balked again, leaning back and jerking his head. Here, out a hundred feet into the shallow water, the steer won the contest of stubbornness, for his feet steadily pushed down into the soft bottom. Ostler rode in to try to urge him forward from behind, but with no success. Martinez was trying to contain the bunch on the bank, and Scott had ridden out after the horse band, which was straying in the river. Blackie realized barely in time that his horse was sinking; he slipped off and led him back to dry land. The steer was bogged to his belly.

The big segundo was angry. He sulked in silence while Scott, Martinez, and Ostler casually talked over the situation before him. They had crossed about half the herd, leaving more than a dozen in the sand. The crossing, bad enough at first, had probably been made worse by the stirring of the hoofs. The cattle were balking more now because the sun was in such a position that the other bank, in actuality the northwest bank, was less easily visible.

"We've got work for all afternoon, just crossing the wagon and dragging out bogged cows," Scott said.

"I don't want them mules to the wagon," Ostler said. "They purt near bogged me in the Brazos and the Wichita too. That damned red mule will balk anytime it comes into his head."

Martinez agreed with them. "We cross the wagon and pull out bogged cows today; we cross the rest of the herd mañana." Blackie could do nothing but agree.

They ate the noon meal. The meal took considerable time since guards holding cattle on both sides of the river had to be relieved. Blackie sent only Professor to hold the cattle north of the river after lunch; he was told to hold them away from the water, let them graze loosely, and call on the snaking crew if he needed help. Blackie sent the same snaking crew after the one steer he had bogged and then to continue their morning's work. He sent Cory to watch the south herd, and the rest of them began the task of crossing the wagon.

Scott changed his saddle over to his grullo; the blue horse was slowly becoming a good cowhorse. Then he started helping to unload the wagon. Blackjack had not been free fifteen minutes when Scott saw Dandy catch him. "Hey, not him, Dandy," Scott yelled. "Get your damn rope off of my night horse."

"It won't hurt him to pack a little gear across the river."

"No, you don't! Turn him loose. He worked last night and all morning. He's not going to pack any gear."

"Hell, I worked last night and all morning, and I got to work this evening too. Your horse ain't no better than I am."

"You had beans and sow belly for dinner, too, but he didn't," Scott pointed out. "That's my horse; get your damn rope off of him. You're not supposed to be catching horses anyway; Martinez and I catch the horses. Get that rope off his neck, unless"—Scott paused to laugh, but did not ease up on his insistence—"unless you want me to punch you in the nose like I did Blackie."

Dandy laughed and turned the big horse loose, but jibed, "I don't think you can afford to punch many people in the nose like you done Blackie. There's your damned old horse. He's pretty good looking, even if he is lazy. I'd give you twenty-five dollars for him."

"I'd take two hundred and fifty."

"Hell, they ain't a horse this side of the Mississippi worth two fifty."

"We nearly agree," Scott said. "There's not but one."

They packed a dozen of the horses they had been using to lead the cattle with gear from the chuck wagon. Most of the packs consisted of two bedrolls with pots and food wedged in between. One scrawny paint horse, which had been in Scratchy Wilson's string, pitched wildly at the end of the lead rope before he decided he could not dislodge his burden. After filling all the canteens at hand, Ostler ran the clear creek water out of his water kegs, shaking his head sadly, and said, "I bet that old Canadian water will settle out six inches of mud. You all can just take your last look at this clean water."

They led across the packed horses, also driving the rest of the free horses and the four mules in order not to have to leave a guard with them, and had no difficulty. Some of the bedrolls got splashed, but they had been wet before. The precious flour and meal and coffee were kept dry.

Then they scattered up and down the river to drag in such drift logs as could be found out of the water and dry. They lashed them under the bed of the wagon, clear of the ground and free of the wheels. Some argument ensued as to the need for the logs. Some said that with the wide iron tires, iron straps, and iron reinforcements the wagon would not float; some had the idea that it would float, but very low; some thought it didn't matter whether it floated or not. But Ostler, who had assumed some authority in this particular operation, insisted that every precaution be taken.

They tied on with their lariats, four in front and three on the upstream side, and took it into the broad muddy stream.

Being able to choose their own route, which they were not always able to do with the cattle, and now knowing the vagaries of the water and sand, they brought the wagon across without mishap.

But while they were still untying their lariats and loosening the logs, near where they had piled the gear which had been packed over, they heard yells from back down on the river. Leaving Ostler with the wagon, they mounted and raced to find out what was wrong. When they came to a position where they could see the course of the river downstream, they saw Professor riding wildly along the river a mile away, trying to keep the cows out of the water. And it was proving too much for the lone cowhand. The snaking crew were mounting to go to his aid but they were going to be too late. A dozen of the stubborn beasts were already scattered in the shallow water, and a stream of them was coming into the dangerous sand behind Professor as he rode to turn a bunch ahead of him.

They rode wildly after the scattering cattle. Blackie was cursing all the while. It took an hour to round them up and move them in a compact herd again back from the river. They counted thirty-one head left in the sand, strung out for a mile, bogged to their bellies.

Professor was as angry as was Blackie. Professor had had a rough time of it trying to guard something between a thousand and two thousand cattle. Heel flies or something had gotten after them. At least, they had seemed determined to go out and stand in the quicksand. His horse was a white mass of lather. Blackie put two men guarding the crossed cattle, and the rest of them joined the hard, tedious job of pulling cows from the river. Ostler harnessed his mules, hooked them to the empty wagon, and brought it to help with the pulling.

Not even a single leg of a cow could be pulled from the quicksand by pure force. Such force might have caused a leg to be disjointed and pulled off, because of the peculiar holding power of the sand. Each leg had to be dug out with the only digging tools they had, their hands, doubled up, and tied securely with horse hobbles or short sections of well rope. If a leg were dug out and left alone two minutes, it would again be firmly set into the river bed. Even the animals' tails had to be dug out, coiled, and tied. Then, by a rope around the horns, the cow would be pulled through the shallow water and mud to dry land.

It was hard dirty work. Their shirts were wet from sweat and their pants from the river water. If a man were out of the water long enough for his clothes to dry, he had white salt lines on his shirt and whitish brown lines on his pants from the minerals in the water. Over everything was the sand; they felt as if they had it from their hair to their feet. They kept up their spirits by harmless horseplay and kidding. Baldy frequently yelled, "Watch out! If you get bogged, we going to leave you. We ain't digging out nothing but cows."

Kid was around it all, clumsily working twice as hard as anyone else and accomplishing half as much. He had mud all over him, even on his new hat. He had taken up the habit of some of the other men cursing the cattle and would sometimes say, "You damn sorry, lop-eared, knock-kneed, goat-necked critter. If we ever get you to market, I hope I never see another stupid longhorn steer long as I live." But even as he said this to some big wild steer, caught helpless in the sand, he might be patting on the bulging side of the animal as if it were a dog.

All of the men who had begun the crossing by taking off shirts and pants had wisely put them back on in the middle of the morning. Kid had taken his off again to help with the bogged cows. One and another of the men warned him about sunburn, but he did not go after his clothes until Ostler finally screamed at him, "Go get your damned clothes right now! Before I take a double rope to you and learn you some sense!"

The snaking operation was enlivened at intervals by the aggressiveness of the steers when they were released from the quicksand. Invariably, when one of the animals felt his feet free on dry soil, he would stagger to his feet and charge the nearest thing that moved. The cowboys would scramble for their horses. Some of the steers would charge a horse. Some of them were driven to join the herd; some were enticed. When a man narrowly escaped the horns of one of them, he was the butt of a great deal of laughter.

But the steer's resentful actions proved serious. One of those which had bogged at the first crossing early in the morning was the big dun steer that Blackie had blinded in one eye. The steer had been held immobile several hours before they got to him. He lay there a moment on the dry sand after his feet had been unbound, as if contemplating the undignified treatment he had been subjected to. Baldy rode up in front of him, flapping his hat and yelling.

The steer rose on wobbly legs and charged. Baldy was ready; he wheeled his horse and started toward the herd, but the steer would not be led away. He turned to a nearer target. He charged the horsemen one after the other, jerking his head, losing an enemy on his blind side but wheeling to find another. He gained strength as the circulation came back to his legs. Finally, he settled on the wagon as the cause of all his troubles and would not be led away from it.

Ostler whipped his mules and galloped them straight away from the river with the big dun steer in pursuit. Scott followed, gathering up his lariat, intending to try to catch the angry steer by the forefeet. Ostler was turning the bouncing wagon in a wide circle. The steer had lost sight of his target for a moment, and the cook might have lost him except for the slope of the ground. He was about to overturn the top-heavy wagon and had to swerve the team back toward the animal. The steer charged, angling in from the front, his head low and his tail high. He caught the off wheeler, the stubborn red mule, his right horn going four inches deep into the ribs, and ripped him straight back to the flank.

The mule made no sound but plunged wildly in the harness. Ostler leaned all his weight back on the lines. The wounded mule plunged again and again as the other mules responded to the lines. He trampled his own entrails with his back feet, jerking them out of the gaping wound.

The steer had made a second slash at the wagon, at the back wheel, and had undergone a severe twisting of his neck in the spokes. He pulled off one horn as he got free; then he ambled out toward the herd, bloody, shaken, and seemingly satisfied.

They shot the mule. Ostler was wrought up about it. Some of them had noticed that the dark brown gelding, which had been Murphy's night horse, had white hairs on his shoulder, possibly the marks of a collar; and it was proposed that this horse be used to the wagon. Ostler swore that he would pull the damned thing himself before he would try to work a horse with three mules, but eventually his protests weakened. There was nothing else to do.

They secured the horse and found that if he had ever worked in harness, he had not liked it. It was necessary to put a burlap sack over his head before he would submit to the harness and to being hooked in with the mules. The team was now so nervous as to be almost useless in working with the bogged cows, so Ostler took them to haul water and establish night camp. They worked until dark, leaving only seven animals still bogged; these were in such places that they seemed not to be sinking any deeper.

By suppertime, Kid had found out what they meant about the sunburn. He kept saying, "Seems like I can't get the sand out of my clothes. I can't stand having them touch me all over." Ostler had him take off his clothes and greased him down with axle grease.

That night they went back to two guards, so that each man got only three or four hours' sleep; even so, with the herd split up on two sides of the river, the guards were too thin. They rode tired that night. Their muscles had become hardened to the saddle but not to river work, and each man discovered aches in muscles he didn't know he had. Scott heard Shorty making a low moaning in his sleep; the stubby cowboy held both hands over his stomach. But past midnight, when they fell out for guard, Shorty was as cheerful as ever.

Scott rode that night, not even knowing what he sang, thinking about the light guard and the split herd, the possibility of their running, the fact that the cattle to the north were more tired because they had crossed the river, the chance of a strange herd coming up from the south, the necessity for watching the remuda carefully here in the Nation. This last guard was split with three, counting himself, north of the river and two south of the river, a proportion that he thought was correct because of the threat to the horses, which were being held on the north side near camp. Sometimes he could see the river, a dark expanse under a quarter moon, but nothing south of it. Finally, he told Shorty where he was going and went down and rode his big black horse through the wide sand bars and channels and out toward the south herd. When he came near enough to hear a lonely voice singing, "Swing low, sweet chariot, coming for to carry me home," he knew that everything was all right, and he turned and crossed back over to the north.

The work of the second-day crossing was nearly a duplication of the first. They did not lose an animal at all except for the red mule that was gored.

One cow, which had stayed in the sand overnight, bore a calf. It was born dead or had drowned in the shallow water. She had found no chance to smell of her calf, and so seemed not to have had her mother instinct aroused. When she was snaked out and released, she got shakily to her feet. She dragged a string of navel gut and afterbirth behind her through the sand as she staggered off toward the other cattle.

They finished the crossing early enough to push two miles northeast along the river before night. The men looked back down toward the river and made various remarks, calling it "her," except for Martinez, who called it "him." "She can be a bitch when she wants to," they would say, or, "I hope we don't run into another one like that old gal."

Baldy said, "That feller that made up the saying 'come hell or high water'; I guess he must of been thinking about the little old South Canadian."

They felt a sense of accomplishment at having crossed it in two days. They thought of it as one thing they had done—they had crossed it. But as individuals they had crossed it many times in two days, and the one hand who had crossed it more times than any other, Billy Scott, had crossed the wide, muddy river twenty-seven times.

The Spotted Horses

13

Well, I met a little gal and I offered her a quarter,
And she says, Young man, I'm a gentleman's daughter.
Come-a ti yi yippi, yippi yea, yippi yea,
Come-a ti yi yippi, yippi yea.

Their hopes of having left the Indians behind were destroyed the same morning they turned north away from the Canadian. A lone Indian sentinel watched them from a rise a mile away. At noon camp Cory came in from the drifting cattle at a gallop, motioning out ahead of them. There across the trail, spread out as if blocking their way, were some thirty mounted braves.

The camp immediately buzzed into activity. "Who can talk to them red-faced bastards?" Blackie asked. He was excited.

"I can talk to them some," Scott said. Even the word "some" was an exaggeration; he had watched a few palavers and knew a half-dozen signs, but he had no intention of leaving the problem to Blackie. "Martinez might help, too," he went on. "Maybe they can speak a little Spanish."

Blackie issued orders that the herd be bunched closer and the remuda be brought in between the herd and the chuck wagon. As they broke out the rifles, Scott reminded them, "Remember what Colonel Kittredge said about not shooting without orders."

"Yeah," Blackie said. "Don't nobody get trigger happy."

As Blackie, Scott, and Martinez mounted they saw that three of the Indians had already broken out of the line and were coming forward, kicking their heels into their horses' sides. Scott immediately urged the dun he was riding toward them in a run; he wanted to meet them away from the wagon; the less they knew about the outfit, the better. Blackie and Martinez were right behind him.

At some three hundred yards from the wagon they met. The Indians slid their horses to a halt, raising dust, as if they were giving a demonstration in horsemanship. The one in front, obviously the leader, was mounted on a fine paint stallion and carried himself proudly; he wore a spreading bonnet made of the tail feathers of birds. On his right was an old Indian with white hair and wrinkled visage, but keen fierce eyes. On his left was a young one, no more than seventeen years old. They wore their long black hair divided in two and tied at shoulder length. Caught about their shoulders with a kind of natural grace they each wore a sheet, evidently once white but now a mellow brown.

The three had an awesome appearance, full of the dignity and the coarseness that had come from living their entire lives in the sun and wind of the plains and around smoky fires in skin tepees. They inspired respect, perhaps like that given a rattlesnake. These three were not armed, but out in the line of braves across the trail could be seen the glint and unmistakable form of rifles held across the legs of the savage riders.

The one who seemed the chief held up one hand as he brought his horse to a halt. He and the young man, who were riding bareback, slid to the ground. The old Indian, riding a crude saddle covered with rawhide, remained on his horse.

As the three cowboys dismounted, Blackie said to Scott, "Tell them no *wohaw*. We ain't giving no beeves to no beggar Injuns."

The young one said in perfect English, "You tell the big man there are no beggar Indians here."

"You speak good English," Scott said.

"I have been to the school of the Cherokees."

"The Cherokees are very fine people," Scott said.

The young man said, holding himself proudly and without any hint of a smile, "The Cherokees are a bunch of old squaws."

Scott smiled. He thought the statement about the Cherokees was designed to put the trail drivers on the defensive, as had been the dash toward the chuck wagon by the three Indians. The mounted braves strung out across the trail were enough in number to cause plenty of trouble. It was going to take some diplomacy as well as some bluff.

The chief made guttural sounds and the young man said, "My father invites you to sit down on our land."

The cowboys squatted on the toes of their boots, and the two Indians sat flat, cross-legged. Scott thought it was time to try to take the initiative. He said to the young Indian, "We are pleased to talk to you. We want to ask a question. Why have your scouts followed us? It doesn't seem friendly. We saw them first away down in Greer County, in Texas."

The young man and the chief talked a minute. It was not a matter of a direct translation, more like a discussion of strategy.

The young one said, "The agent says there is no such thing as Greer County. It is a mistake of the *Tejanos.* Some day the Great White Father will give that land to the Indians. The white agent says so and my father believes that it is so."

Scott said, with more definite feeling in his voice, "But you are Cheyenne!" As he said this he pointed at them and drew his right index finger several times quickly across his left, making the "cut-finger" sign of their name. It was a little bluff; now they would not be sure but that he could understand their talk. "And you followed us not only in Greer County, but in the reservation of the Kiowa and Comanche and Apache. Didn't you get lands at Medicine Lodge? Didn't you go on the warpath and then make peace again and agree to stay on your own lands?"

At the words "Medicine Lodge" the white-haired Indian on the horse emitted a shrill grunt as if in disgust. He must have understood the words. He was looking down at the powwow with a kind of silent savagery, as if he would gladly take part in a massacre but was being restrained. The other two paid little attention to him for the moment.

Blackie said, "Tell them no *wohaw,* Scott. We sure ain't got no beef to be giving away." Even though the young Indian spoke perfect English, Blackie was looking to Scott as if he needed an interpreter. "And tell them that damned old man don't scare us."

The chief had understood some of Scott's last speech. He began to converse with his son. His dark, heavy face was calm.

The young man said, "My father wants you to understand that we are like brothers now with the Kiowa and Comanche and Apache, as we have long been with the Arapahoe. We have not harmed you on their lands or on our own lands. We watch you so that we can come to you, as right now, to get the payment you owe us from bringing cattle into our land."

"I wonder," Scott said, "what the Colonel at Fort Reno thinks about you leaving your reservation? Does he know that you leave the land you agreed to stay on?"

After some more consultation, the young Indian said, "My father is pleased that you speak about the man who wears the eagle at Fort Reno. For that man is well known to my father; they spoke together not more than one moon ago. Are you, too, a friend of the Yankee Colonel?"

Scott could see that the young man was as sharp as a locust thorn. He had answered his, Scott's, bluffing references to various Indian tribes with the word "*Tejano*" and now "Yankee." The young man evidently was perfectly aware of a possible coolness between a Texan and a Yankee colonel, even though both were white men.

"The Colonel is not a personal friend of mine," Scott admitted. "But he will keep the peace. He will punish anyone in this land who does not keep the peace."

"Yes, our friend who wears the eagle at Fort Reno will keep the peace, and my father agrees to this. We only want those who bring cattle here to pay us what is right, and then there will be peace." The young man made a majestic gesture, indicating the chief. "My father is a great chief. His name is Seven Killer. He is the nephew of Black Kettle, and he sat behind Black Kettle at Medicine Lodge. He has asked you to sit down on our land so that he can tell you the right payment for bringing cattle through this place."

It was like a ceremony that must have been repeated over and over in the past. The chief spoke several words directly to the trail drivers; among them was the word *wohaw,* and he held up ten fingers. He had named his price. It was ten beeves.

Blackie said, "By God, I can understand that! Tell him, 'hell no,' Scott. We ain't got no ten cows to spare. Tell him I said, 'hell no.' Tell him that's the last word: 'hell no.' "

Scott said to the young man, "We'll discuss this payment idea, but you'd better tell the chief right now that ten cows is more than we can pay. We will pay something reasonable."

The old man on the horse had begun to make sounds. He started out with a low, moaning chant; then spread his hands out to the sky and seemed to talk directly at the midday sun. He seemed to stare straight into the sun. The short guttural sounds were full of anguish. Scott thought it was some kind of an act; yet the old man seemed to be carried away with his own words.

Scott said, "What does he say? Is he the chief, or is your father the chief?"

"My father is the chief." The young Indian spoke in a low voice as if not to interrupt something sacred. "But the old man knows many things. My father listens to him. The old man prays now and speaks about the time before we lost the corn. He knows more about those times than any other man, for he was told long ago by other old men. He is sad that we lost the corn."

The white-haired Indian had stared at the sun until tears ran down his cheeks. He lowered his hands and untied a bulky burlap covering behind his saddle. Then he slipped to the ground with the grace of a young man and jerked the object from under the burlap and threw it viciously down on the ground in front of the trail drivers. It was a buffalo skull. The black curved horns contrasted with the broad bleached white of the bone. The big eye sockets and the broken nose where the cartilage had rotted away gave it the eerie appearance, representing death, which the old man evidently appreciated. He was yelling shrill, short demands.

"He wants to know where the cattle of the Cheyenne are," the young man said. "He says you should give us all your cattle, for the white man has killed the buffalo and even picks up the bones off the land."

The old man put his moccasined foot on the buffalo skull and again spoke straight at the sun. He moved nimbly back and swung his arms in grand motions at the bare prairie and at the sky. He seized green grass from the ground, pressed it to his chest, and flung it ceremoniously into the air.

Blackie scowled at the old man and the buffalo skull.

Martinez' dark eyes flicked between the three Indians. Scott studied the young one and the chief, trying to see how much they were affected by the actions and words of the old one. He believed that the two must have seen the same demonstration many times, but they seemed respectful.

The young man translated in a low voice. "He says this land was given to us by the god in the sun, and after that it was given to us by the Great White Father. The land and the water and the grass and the air—they are all ours. The white man has killed our cattle, which the god in the sun gave to us, and now he brings cattle with long horns and long legs. He ought to give us many more than ten beeves. Our women and children are starving."

"You say there are no beggar Indians here," Scott said. "Why does the old man tell us all his troubles? We have troubles too, but we don't tell them when we make a peaceful trade."

The young man talked about it with the chief and then translated some more of the old man's harangue. "He says the white man cuts down our trees and muddies our water."

Then Scott raised his voice and said forcefully to the chief, "Trees? What trees? Is the old man trying to be funny?" He made some sweeping gestures of his own. "We burn buffalo chips and cow chips as you do. As for the water, you saw us cross the Canadian River. Did we make it muddy? No, it was already muddy. Maybe your sun god made it muddy."

The chief seemed calm as he talked it over with the young man. Then the young one said, "My father says you are right about the trees and water. The old man is wrong.

But the white man did kill the buffalo."

Martinez said to Scott, "Tell them they ought to brand their cows."

"Hell yes," Blackie said. "Tell them to brand their cows like we do. Then won't nobody kill them."

"That's right," Scott said to the young one. He drew the I-D Connected brand in the dirt with his finger and pointed to the bunched herd below them. "If the Cheyenne will brand his cows, the Great White Father and the Colonel at Fort Reno will protect them."

The chief talked with his son a minute and then the young man said, "My father says you will give us ten beeves and we will eat some and brand some. He will not ask for all your cows. If you don't wish to do this, you can pay ten cents for each cow; it is what the Cherokee charges. If you don't wish to do this, you can turn around and go back the way you came, and do not make any camps on Cheyenne land."

Scott was thinking of an offer which might be acceptable, but he wanted to make the chief realize that he must be willing to compromise. "The Cherokee did charge ten cents a head. But this was too much. So now we drive cattle here and pay the Cherokee nothing. If the Cheyenne charge too much, we will drive farther west and pay nothing."

The old white-haired Indian, now ignored, was making yelping sounds and beating his chest. He began to scoop up dust from the ground and throw it straight into the air over his head. It was a kind of sign of defiance.

Blackie scrambled backward on his bootheels and said, "Scott, you better tell that damned old man to stop throwing that dirt. By God! I'll throw some dirt on him. Tell them we got plenty of six-guns and rifles too, and we ain't going to put up with nothing like that."

The chief spoke a few short words, and the old man suddenly became calm and started tying his buffalo skull behind his saddle again.

Scott started making his offer without further answer from the chief. "We want to pay what is right for grazing on Cheyenne land. We will pay three paint horses. *Pinto* horses. Spotted horses, like the chief's. They are skinny now, from the winter and from traveling a long distance, but they will soon get fat. Three beautiful horses. What do you say?"

The chief proved to be interested. If they were good spotted horses, ones that were not crippled, he would accept the three horses and two beeves.

"No beeves," Scott said. "Horses are much better than cows, especially spotted horses. You can ride a horse, and if you need food you can eat him. Three good horses. What do you say?"

After some more consultation, the young man said, "My father wants you to know that there has been a bad stampede of some cow herds south of the Canadian. We think you must have very tame cows, or they would have run away with the rest. But because of the stampede we are afraid the *Tejanos* will not come back into Cheyenne land for a week or more. So we would like to have two beeves besides the three spotted horses."

The words "we would like to have two beeves" were music to Scott's ears. "Since you are great chief, Seven Killer, I will make a good trade with you. Three spotted horses and one beef. One big beef. But you must guarantee that we will not be bothered in Indian Territory. Not here and not in the Cherokee outlet. Do you agree?"

When the chief understood, he agreed. He held up three fingers on one hand and one on the other. The old Indian, now mounted on his horse, began talking hurriedly, probably trying to enter a claim to one of the spotted horses.

"One of the horses will pitch," Scott said.

"A Cheyenne can ride any horse," the young man said.

"All right, you all stay here. We'll bring them to you."

The three trail drivers rose and mounted and rode back to the outfit. Scott was well pleased. They had a contract to meet for a thousand head of she-stuff and two thousand steers, and they were getting through the Nation for only one beef, that a cripple. The remuda would be sold in Nebraska, but there was no contract for it. And the funny thing was that paint markings, precious to the Indian, were objects of suspicion to a cattleman. The three horses he had in mind, two from Shorty's string and one from Murphy's old string, would not have been worth as much as three steers at trail's end.

They caught out the horses and drove out the blinded steer with the horn missing. The three paints, which had been named after their rider's opinions of them—Outlaw and Puddin' Foot and Goathead—they led out to the three Indians with ten-foot sections of well rope.

Two braves came forward to drive away the big steer, with much whooping and kicking of their heels into their horses' sides. The three Indians who had taken part in the powwow took the ropes of the three horses. To the chief, Scott held up his two index fingers, exactly side by side.

The chief returned the sign. They were even.

As the outfit went northwest along the North Canadian, the talk in camp was about the slick bargain with the Indians which had been made by Blackie, Scott, and Martinez. Scott could see that Blackie actually believed that he had been in charge of the bargaining, and that he, Scott, had been the interpreter. But Martinez knew the truth, though he said nothing. And Scott had respect for the Mexican's opinion.

Scott had been looking ahead to Camp Supply, because of the slender hope that he would receive the letter giving him undisputed authority. If he got the letter, he would do whatever he needed to do to take charge, and he believed he had enough of the men behind him to make it easy. If he got the letter . . . But what kind of hope was that?

Out of the confusion of his disgust toward the owners and Kittredge and Blackie and his sometime fierce desire to take the herd to the trail end, Camp Supply stood as a point. It was a point in a logical story such as might be believed by a civilized man who was ignorant of trailing cattle long distances. The story said that the foreman was killed; the segundo took over; the outfit pushed on north; the segundo notified the owners at the first point of civilization, Doan's. The owners wrote naming a new trail boss and the letter was received at Camp Supply. It was a neat story; it passed lightly over such things as hands quitting, the running of a spooky herd, the bargaining with a savage who called himself Seven Killer, the back-breaking work of bringing a herd across a swollen river. And sometimes the neat, logical story broke down. It had broken down for several trail bosses behind them—in the big stampede where they lost big portions of their herds. And this little story about the authorized leadership of the I-D Connected outfit would break down at Camp Supply. He wouldn't get any damned letter. He alternated between cursing Greer and hoping for the letter, if not at Camp Supply, then ahead at Dodge City.

The land was slowly changing as they went northwest through the rolling hills. More and more the country was like the high plains rather than the fertile prairie plains. The bluestem grass grew in bunches rather than a solid mat, and the short grass of the higher western country had begun to appear. In some areas sage and shinnery were scattered through the broad expanses of grass.

The grass, long developed in a country where the spring months were temperate and rainy and the summer months hot and dry, had already matured its seeds. Now in early June the seeds were golden yellow. The herd, in spite of being spooky, was gaining weight. The hollows under the points of their hips were disappearing.

They ran again two days south of Camp Supply—west into the sand hills. They scattered badly but were slowed by the hard labor of running in the sandy soil. The outfit lost one day, but the tally was holding. Martinez counted three thousand and eight, and Scott's surreptitious tally agreed with him.

On June 7, they crossed Wolf Creek, trailed past Camp Supply, and made early night camp. As soon as the herd was grazing quietly in a bunch Blackie headed back to the military post, where Ostler had gone with the wagon. Scott, without asking permission, ran his horse to catch up with the big segundo and rode along with him in silence.

In the little sutler's store, which was also the civilian post office, the cook had already bought two or three items of grub. Scott stood by Blackie's elbow while the big man asked for the mail and told the storekeeper the names of the men in the outfit. There was only one letter and that in a feminine hand, for Dandy.

Out by the hitch rail, Scott said, "You didn't write at Doan's, did you, Blackie?"

"By God, you fixing to start that again?"

"Did you write at Doan's, like we agreed?"

Blackie swung into the saddle. "Trouble with you, Scott, you can't seem to get it into your head that it ain't none of your business to check up on me. I thought I showed you who was bossing this outfit."

"We're going to get this straightened out at Dodge, Blackie."

"By God! we can get it straightened out right now if you never had enough before. But if you hit me in the nose again, I'm going to kill you."

"I don't intend to fight you with my fists. But I mean to see this thing straightened out before we leave Dodge."

They rode back together in silence. Scott didn't know what his threat meant himself. But he knew that the trail beyond Dodge, out through western Kansas and Nebraska, was less well marked and less traveled than this one and would require a boss who knew what he was doing; he knew that at the rate they had been going since Kittredge's death, they could never meet the delivery date of July 1; he knew that the conflict in himself, between the strong desire to quit and the strong desire to see the drive to a successful end, must be resolved.

The next day they made a good drive, across the North Canadian early in the morning and due north to Buffalo Springs for a late night camp. The following day, without anyone realizing it except Scott, they came out of Indian Territory into the state of Kansas; thence, to the Cimarron River.

The Cimarron had been up but was now in a more reasonable state. It was another of the broad, winding, muddy rivers. Most of them remembered it as the worst on the Chisholm Trail, but this far west it was not so broad or troublesome as the South Canadian. They crossed it in one day and left in its turbid currents one animal, a lean, sore-footed steer which had lagged in the rear all the way from south Texas. When they left this river behind, no obstacles lay between them and the famous shipping center of Dodge City.

On June 12, they pushed across Bluff Creek and camped on Mulberry Creek, one easy drive south of Dodge. They had caught Kid with his French harp that day, and now they ganged up on him to make him play for his supper. He told them that he had thrown the harp away, that he had lost it, that he couldn't play anything anyway, and that his lips were too chapped. But they would not be denied. Blushing deeply, he began to play. "Louder, Kid," they said. "Play that thing!"

He got into the swing of it, and he played it. He played "Oh, Susanna" and "Turkey in the Straw" and "Way down Yonder" and "Buffalo Gals." They tapped their boots in the dirt. After more than two hard months on the trail, the music was nothing less than magic to them. It was possible that the Kid was not really much of a musician, but they could hear in his little harp with ten holes in it all the violins and sweet voices they had ever heard. He played "When You and I Were Young, Maggie," and they all became motionless and silent. Ostler stopped puttering over the cow-chip fire. Then the Kid tried to play "Home, Sweet Home." He got halfway through the chorus before he started having trouble; he played a little farther, roughly, and gave up. He pounded the contrary harp on his leg to get the saliva out of it.

At his age, Kid might have been justified in falsely believing that he had a good home and in remembering that he was a long way away from it. But they all, even Ostler, four times his age, were thinking about things far away, and hardly a word was spoken during the evening meal.

Baldy would not be subdued for long. As he scraped out his plate and threw it in the tub, he said, "You all smell that funny smell in the air?" Some of them fell for it and began sniffing the air.

"I'll tell you what that is," Baldy went on. "You know how a buzzard can smell a dead cow about ten miles away. Well, that's how far a Texas man can smell them sporting gals in Dodge."

"You got a good nose on you," Dandy said, "seeing as how we're upwind."

"Hell, I can smell them gals ten miles away upwind."

"Say, Blackie," Dandy said, "how much money we going to get to go into Dodge on?"

Blackie thought about it. "I ain't decided yet." It was obvious that he had done no planning about it.

"Ain't decided? This is the damnedest outfit I ever worked for. I never worked so hard in my life and we ain't had a chance to go to town once. Listen, I want some damned money tomorrow night! How much money you got?"

"Yeah," Baldy said, "how much money did you inherit from Kittredge?"

"I know one thing," Blackie finally said. "Colonel Kittredge never liked for his hands to be running into town all the time and drinking and raising hell."

"By God!" Dandy said. "If you think we're going to pass right on by Dodge and not have a little fun, you got another think coming. We got a right to draw some money and have some time off."

There was a chorus of "Yeah," and "Hell yes."

"I know one thing," Ostler said. "We're out of grub and we got a long ways to go, and I got to have another collar to fit that crazy horse I'm trying to work. They better be some things like that bought before all the money is squandered on liquor."

Scott listened in silence. The best thing for a trail boss to do was to decide exactly what he was able to do and what was best for the drive and then tell the men and stick by his decision. He knew that Blackie must have a wad of cash and probably a letter of credit besides. Likely the big man didn't even realize that he had a letter of credit, and if he knew it wouldn't know how to get money on it now with Kittredge dead. It was unthinkable for an outfit to sweep past Dodge City without a night on the town. But it happened to be Blackie's problem.

Art and Booger Red had been talking in low voices

together. Booger Red said to Blackie, "I think we ought to get two months' wages all around. We got it coming."

"I ain't got that kind of money, even if I want to pay out that much."

"You could sell a few head of cows or something. You running this drive, ain't you? How come you can't get the money to pay us what we got coming?"

Dandy put in, "Yeah, we're going to have some money, Blackie, and some time off; you may as well get used to the idea."

Scott thought the conversation was taking a dangerous turn. Art and Booger Red bunked together, and they might have decided that the outfit would never make it to Ogallala successfully. They might be planning desertion. "I think we ought to have some money, Blackie," he said. "I think you ought to get together with Ostler and figure out what it will take for about three weeks' provisions and divide the rest up among us. And lay over one day, so everybody can go to town when he's not on guard."

All of them except Art and Booger Red seemed to agree to the idea.

Blackie finally said that he had decided to do it. He had three hundred and forty dollars. Ostler did some figuring, and it was decided that each man could be paid slightly over twenty dollars.

The prospects of twenty dollars and Dodge City was enough to relieve the tension and raise the spirits. Baldy got started again. "Kid, I might ought to give you a little warning about these damned Kansas towns. Those women cover theirselves all over with that perfume and it lowers your resistance."

Someone asked, "Was that what you were smelling a while ago, Baldy?"

"Sure, that's what I was smelling. What did you think I was smelling? Anyway, Kid, they wear you down with that perfume and with that coffin varnish they give you to drink . . ."

"Do they *give* it to you, Baldy? They always charge me for it."

"Here I am trying to give this young feller some advice, and you all keep on messing me up. Don't pay no attention to him, Kid. Anyway, my point is, these gals is after your money. You see one of them cutting her eyes around at you, you run for the door. Savvy? And watch that redeye. I always carry a pocketful of rocks myself, and when I get me a drink I drop a rock in it. If it eats the rock up, it ain't fit to drink. They's one kind called 'sheepherder's delight' that will make you go plum stone blind."

After Baldy had been shouted down, they entered into a discussion, of Dodge and her sister Kansas towns. Mixed with their appreciation was resentment that the Kansans seemed to want the cattle business but didn't want the cattle drivers.

"I guess what they'd like," Dandy said, "is for us to just *send* the cows up here. That way they could make money on the railroads and the stockyards and commissions, and they wouldn't have to put up with any wild cowboys."

"I've seen some that didn't even want the cows," Scott said. "Those farmers in the eastern part of the state start foaming at the mouth when they see a longhorn steer."

Professor said, "That's the trouble. They don't know what they want. One of these big augurs in one of these towns will be making plenty of money out of cattle. He dresses his wife up like a queen. She doesn't have enough sense to know she would be scrubbing floors for a living if it wasn't for the cattle business, so she joins one of these civic improvement leagues. And the league does its best to drive the old dirty cattle business away."

"Some of them wants the cowboys, all right," Baldy said. "Or anyway his wages. Maybe what we ought to do is not send the cows and not any cowpunchers go either; just send them money."

"What hurts my feelings," Dandy said, "is them talking about cowboys being wild. They hire these gamblers and outlaws for city marshals. The streets are crowded up with broken-down buffalo hunters and drunk soldiers and pimps and whores. But you just let one trail hand try to ride his horse into a store, when he wants to buy something, and they say all Texas cowboys are wild."

A Settling in Dodge

14

So round up your foreman and hit him for your roll;
You're going into town to get taller on your pole.
Come-a ti yi yippi, yippi yea, yippi yea,
Come-a ti yi yippi, yippi yea.

They had found the Arkansas River in an easy crossing stage at Point of Rocks four miles upstream from Dodge. Ostler had taken the wagon straight through by the toll bridge, gaining enough time to load up with provisions before he went to meet them northwest of town. They skirted several waiting herds and camped out between Duck Creek and Sawlog.

They divided into three guards of four men each: one to hold the herd that night, one to hold them the next day, one to hold them the next night. The men off guard would have as much as twenty-four hours to see the town. They traded back and forth, each trying to get what seemed to him the best schedule. Scott, Shorty, Cory, and Kid wound up with the third guard. These four, along with the four of the second guard, pounded for town at dusk.

They were dressed in their best clothes, the worst of which were quite sorry and the best of which were wrinkled from a long trip in warbag or bedroll. But none of them worried much about appearance. They were full of zest and expectancy.

Scott was not immune to the spirit of gaiety as they rode toward town, even though he still felt strongly that "something" must be settled. He rode up beside Blackie and asked, "What time do you mean to pick up the mail?"

"I ain't worried about no mail. If you're worried about it, pick it up yourself. I don't give a damn."

They came out of the rounded bare hills to the town, a sprawling, garish, dusty town, lying between the high ground and the Arkansas River bottoms. They turned east along the Santa Fe Railroad tracks and, coming even with the first plank houses, kicked their horses into a hard run. Broad Front Street lay astride the tracks like a carnival, alive with people and music and horses and yoked oxen, sparkling with lights from hotels and false-front stores. They went in with style, yelling, waving hats. Here and there yells came from the plank sidewalks in answer, but not many were impressed. They turned down south to the livery stable.

Scott, Cory, and Shorty had discussed in mock-seriousness the question of what was the very first thing that should be done in town—whether get a drink, get a haircut and shave, eat a good restaurant meal of ham and scrambled eggs, or do the brief search that Scott had in mind. Cory won out and they had a quick drink first.

Scott left them at the barbershop. He had a faint hope that Greer, or perhaps Brown, had planned to meet the drive here. Why they might do it, he did not know. It was a slim hope that he couldn't put out of his mind. He was feeling good from the drink as he searched the main establishments where owners hung out, the Dodge House, the Long Branch Saloon, the fancy places on the north side of the Plaza. Twice he met acquaintances and asked them; he asked bartenders and hotel clerks. Some of them knew Greer or knew of him as Lawson's partner, but no one had seen him. In half an hour Scott was satisfied that neither Greer nor Brown was in Dodge. He thought that he dismissed it all from his mind. Why worry about a trail herd on your only night off in two months?

They got an agreement out of Cory that they would stay south of the tracks. Almost anything went on the Texas side of town; on the north side you could easily get a lawman's gun barrel across your head and find yourself in jail. They were making a tour of places that sold liquor, looking for old friends. When they would come out on the street, Cory would point his nose up like a wolf and yell, "Yah . . . hoo . . . oo . . . ee . . . ee! The Lawson outfit's in town!" After three drinks, Scott and Shorty joined his chorus.

As they came up to a low-roofed dance hall made of adobe, Cory said, "Don't you all tell these floozies we're going on north. They'll treat you nicer if they think you're at the end of the drive and got two or three months' wages in your pockets."

At every excuse, Scott's mind flicked back to the ideas he had dismissed. Don't tell them we're going on north. Don't consider the days and distance to Ogallala—that if we took the straightest route and trailed them a steady fifteen miles a day we would get there on the evening of delivery day, that it could be done if we don't have a single hitch, not a single day lost from those spooky critters running and scattering in those wastelands of western Kansas and Nebraska, that it could be done if we don't get lost ourselves out there where the trail is not a trail at all because the grass cannot stand concentrated grazing and where all the land looks alike and all the streams run the same way and you cannot tell whether you are on the south fork or the middle fork or the north fork of a sluggish red river, that we have only eight extra head and have lost seventeen since south Texas, that we have wasted so much time since Kittredge died that we have averaged less than eight miles a day. But it could be done; we could make fifteen miles a day going on north and have a successful drive—if a miracle would come along.

The dance hall was one of the old buildings from pre-railroad days. The four by ten adobe bricks made up the inside walls, carelessly mortared. Around the wall, head high, ran a plank with nails for hats and gunbelts. Lamps with wide reflectors and glass oil containers swung low overhead. Liquor and women were flowing freely. There was a bar and tables scattered around the walls, the tables surrounded by wooden chairs and boxes for seats.

They danced. Dancing required no particular skill. If you had the spirit, you could dance, and if you appeared to have money to buy drinks, you could have a partner. The sawdust on the floor was swirled by boots and slippers; the lamps swayed, making even the shadows of the room move to the fiddle and banjo music. Scott found himself with a girl who said her name was Nellie. She smelled of the perfume Baldy had warned against and her cheeks were painted to a high tint. She was attractive and lively; her inclination to giggle and squeal didn't bother a man after he had downed several drinks.

"Drink up, gals," Cory said. "There's plenty more where that come from. Ain't there, my old podner Shorty?"

"Hell yes. Ain't there, my old podner Billy?"

"Hell yes. My old podners, there's plenty for all."

As they sat there assuring themselves and the girls that they were all fine people, the salt of the earth, Scott lost them for a moment, the girls, the lights, the music, everything. It was a sound he heard. He sprang to his feet and cocked his head, straining to hear it. He said, "What's that?" then sat down grinning. "There's a good one for you. For a second I thought that was cattle running."

"Why, honey, that's a choo-choo train," Nellie said. "Didn't you ever hear a choo-choo train?"

"Who's on the herd tonight?" Scott asked.

They decided it was Martinez, Professor, Booger Red, and Art. "Them fellers won't let our cows run off, old podners," Cory said.

"No sir, they won't, old podners," Shorty agreed. "Gals, we got the best outfit, the ornyest and cow-drivingest cowboys ever hit this town. Good men, one and all. Salts of the earth."

They drank to the outfit, the best trail outfit ever put together; they drank to several of the cows and horses; they drank to Blackjack; they drank to Dodge and its pretty girls. One of the girls proposed, "Here's to your trail boss, the best that ever hit town," and they drank to him.

"Who is our trail boss?" Cory said.

"I ain't sure," Shorty said. "But he's a good man. Salt of the earth."

"That reminds me of a man I hit in the nose one time," Scott said. "I hit him a good lick and it nearly killed me." They laughed. Such was the tenor of their jokes.

"Trouble was, it was the wrong man I hit in the nose in the first place. I hit a dumb cowboy, and I ought to been swinging at a fancy-dressed drover named Greer. I could whip him."

"I used to know a freighter at Wichita named Green," Nellie volunteered.

"Not Green. Greer. Greer."

"Well, there's a soldier out at the fort named Greer right now, honey."

Shorty said, "You better stay away from them soldiers, honey. They're not salts of the earth like we are. Have a drink."

Through the haze of drink Scott viewed the town and it looked exactly like a dozen other cowtowns he had known,

San Antonio, Fort Griffin, Abilene. The idea of staying south of the tracks got tangled up with the idea of having only one night in town after two months on the trail. When it was that way you had to cram a lot into that one night. And people who lived another kind of life looked at you and said you were wild.

You didn't have time to court a decent girl, and if you found time, you had nothing to offer her. So you took a girl who wasn't decent. She looked pretty good through the haze; at least she was friendly.

What had he got from his long years of cow work outside of infrequent nights like this? Well, there was the satisfaction of doing well at a hard job that not everyone could do. Then, too, there were men like Shorty and Cory you worked with, who actually were, as they drunkenly said, salt of the earth. And there was the big black horse he had saved for and bought. Still, he had dreamed of staying in cow work and getting more out of it some way, getting a home of his own on another man's ranch or getting a small spread of his own. The trail boss job, next year, Greer had promised him; the year-around foreman job— that would do it, or be a step in the right direction.

Promises, promises. Cowboy, you're a fool to trust in the promise of a man like Greer, the man who was afraid of Kittredge and sent you along in case he didn't make it and didn't give you one jot of authority to back up the responsibility he expected you to accept. Or, did he really? There's a new idea. Maybe all Greer and his half-wit partner Brown really thought about was that they needed three more hands and, knowing that he would be sore because of the broken promise, had buttered him up with flattery and more worthless promises.

Cowboy, you really are a fool. Take hold of this town, whatever its name is, and enjoy it. That one night, that long-awaited one night with money in your pockets among the bright lights, is right now; and you moon around arguing with yourself.

What in God's name did he expect from Greer? A letter? He knew that Blackie had not written at Doan's. It was plain that Blackie could not write, further that the big segundo was too proud to admit it and get Doan to write for him, further that the big segundo didn't want to notify the owners anyway, because he had the idea that he could boss the herd through.

Then wild speculation passed through his mind. Suppose Greer wrote and gave Blackie authority? Suppose Greer said: "I hereby give you authority to boss the herd and they won't run any more, and you will be able to take them straight through the wilderness of western Kansas and Nebraska." Much like the authority he had given Kittredge. "Colonel Kittredge, I hereby give you authority to take this herd north. Get them road broke and when you cross the Brazos you will see a place where there is a red clay bank—pass by there. There is a lone scraggly oak on the rise above the bank and it's only three feet under the dirt to solid rock you can't dig through. But pass by there and go on north; I give you authority."

There was sure enough a joker in the deck. He could see himself with a paper, written authority, holding it up, saying to the quicksand in the South Canadian, "Turn the cows loose. I've got authority from Greer, and he's a big augur, a big medicine man, an owner."

It was funny and he told the painted girl. She wasn't Nellie and she resented being called Nellie. Nellie was gone somewhere, or maybe he had gone away from her. But he said to this girl, "You know there's no law west of Hays City and no God west of Dodge. And I'll tell you some more: there's no Greer north of the Frio River country."

You could see she didn't understand it, but she thought it must be funny and she laughed and slapped herself on the hip. She wasn't quite as pretty as Nellie, but she was friendly. She was the one who offered to carry his money for him since he was drinking so much and he might get rolled. Some people around Dodge were not honest and didn't know how hard a cowboy worked for his money.

The front door glass of one building was brilliant red; bright lights inside streamed through the colored pane, beckoning in the darkness. The one scarlet door glass gave a name to its part of town and was to give a new word to the world: red light district.

But the gay women were all over town, as was the drinking and gambling. Dodge City was a center of transportation because of its railroad and wagon freight lines and stagecoach lines. Considerable business of all kinds was transacted, but its most apparent business this time of year was entertainment, all day and all night. Scott, Shorty, and Cory avoided the faro, monte, hazard, and poker, and found themselves with money left even in the small hours of the morning.

The night was so different from the lonely nights on the trail that they forgot they had not slept after a hard day's work. As dawn drew near, Scott began to feel weariness and a headache. Cory had become lost from them somewhere. They had a cup of coffee, and Shorty went back to search for their younger friend, while Scott headed for the post office.

The town looked different in the early daylight. The dirt of the broad streets was ground to fine powder by wagon tires and the hoofs of animals. Horse droppings and trash of every kind littered the streets. The porch roofs below the false fronts carried a film of dust, as did the boardwalks and every other place where dust could settle. The long signs, heavy lettered—GRAND OPERA HOUSE, PEACOCK SALOON, LADY GAY DANCE HALL, PROVISIONS, LEATHER GOODS, CATTLEMEN WELCOME—they were garish and desolate over the nearly empty street. Even the fancy hotels with gingerbread trimmings around their upper galleries had lost some of their magic when they put out their lights and the light of day came on them. Here and there a tied horse slept at a hitch rail with his head down, his rump cocked to one side then the other. The laughter of a single voice from a dance hall, the song of a drunk somewhere, the creak of one freight wagon toward the bridge—these contrasted with the bustle of the night before.

He was trying to figure out what he had meant when he told Blackie they would get it settled in Dodge. He could send a telegram to the lawyer in San Antonio who handled the Lawson-Greer business; Greer would get it in three or four days, and he, Scott, could receive one in return five or six days from now. And those five or six days were precious; lost, they would certainly ruin the drive.

Maybe they should just stay in Dodge and forget the contract. Let Greer and Brown straighten it out as best they could. After all, the outfit had accomplished no less than a miracle already in bringing the spooky herd this far. He could justify himself. Any fool who wanted to look could see that every last bit of the blame lay at the door of Greer and Kittredge and Blackie.

But, God, the shame of it! The filthy, stinking shame. Was it possible that they could do it without any kind of miracle, just with more of the same?

He was waiting when the postal clerk opened the door; the post office was one of the few establishments that did not stay open all night. He gave the clerk the names one by one. There were letters for Shorty, Professor, and Dandy.

He turned at the door and came back. "Anything for Mr. Horace Kittredge?"

"Colonel Horace Kittredge?"

"That's him."

"You sure he's in your outfit? Got to be careful handing out mail, you know."

"I'm sure."

Greer's name and address were in the upper left-hand corner. He waited until he got outside to open it. It read:

Colonel Horace Kittredge
My Dear Sir,
    You will recall that I was uncertain as to whether I would see you in Dodge City and as it has turned out I have been so much occupied with the business affairs of the Lawson estate and the new partnership with Mr. Brown that it has become impossible to meet you there. However, I am sure any problems that may have arisen

you will solve according to your own best judgment.

I am happy to inform you the business problems incident to Lawson's death have been straightened out, and I will surely meet you in Ogallala by July 1. Mrs. Lawson has moved to San Antonio. She sends her regards.

I will not arrive in Ogallala before June 29 or 30. Will stop at the Drover's House. If you arrive before me, I am sure you will find good grazing somewhere south of the river for a camp.

Please excuse me for reminding you again of the importance of meeting the contract with the 3,000 head of animals and in time to make the transfer by July 1. This has become of such importance to Mr. Brown and myself that I feel obliged to mention it again.

Give my regards to William Scott. We have conjectured as to why he returned and took his personal saddle horse, since we believed we had provided enough horses in quantity and quality for the drive. However, it is of no importance; we realize there is some good explanation. As you have found out by now, Scott is an excellent cowhand and a man of reliable judgment. He will justify any trust you put in him.

We wish you the best of luck.

Very Sincerely Yours,
Cecil E. Greer

Scott folded the letter and started toward the telegraph office. He was in the process of realizing a decision that would amount to a "settling." The decision maybe had its seeds back as far as the time when as a kid he had cried at the loss of the cows in the Pecos and had seen into the mind of Mr. Loving; surely the decision was growing that day when, holding the slight broken body of Kittredge in his arms, he had stared at the vast prairie and seen all the world in a new light. The decision had been made as he took this letter.

Back in the bunkhouse at Lawson's he had not known quite all the secret of trailing cattle. The final part of the secret was that some of the obstacles were not fair. Not fair at all. Pride and authority and jealousy and justification crowded for the attention of a man, but he, one man alone, still had the right to ask the simple question—do I intend to do what Lawson and I planned ages ago, even before the broken promise?

Who had he been fighting? Lawson was dust, and Kittredge too. There was no Greer north of the Frio River country. And Blackie. The big man was a lot like that old gal, the South Canadian River.

On the telegraph blank he addressed Greer in care of the lawyer and wrote:

"Kittredge died May 6 in stampede north of Brazos. I will take charge . . ."

He wadded up the blank and started over on another.

"Kittredge died May 6 in stampede north of Brazos. I have taken charge of herd. Will meet delivery July 1.
William Scott"

Shorty had found Cory semiconscious, draped over a

table in a saloon. They got their horses, poured a cup of coffee down their young comrade, and loaded him into his saddle. He alternated between complaining that he wasn't ready to leave, singing the ballad of Captain Kidd, and making sudden grabs at his jolting saddle, as they rode back to camp.

Lost

15

Oh, we drove them dogies on, and we made a bee-line,
But where the hell we really went—your guess is good as mine.
Come-a ti yi yippi, yippi yea, yippi yea,
Come-a ti yi yippi, yippi yea.

They pushed the herd out north-northwest into the heart of the country that was called on school maps "The Great American Desert." It was the kind of country that had killed or turned back Spanish explorers such as Coronado, and it was the kind of country that men still thought of as a wilderness to be crossed, first with wagons, later with rails, and not a country to be lived in.

They had started their long drive something over two months before in the upper portion of the coastal plains, in a land of springs and clear streams. They had flirted briefly with the arid desert-like country as they came across the tip of Edwards Plateau. Most of their trek north had been along an uncertain dividing line between the prairie plains and the high plains. The land had slowly changed as they came through the northwestern part of Indian Territory and into Kansas. It was flattening out and there was less timber, even along the streams. They had not noticed the change much, because Dodge had been like an oasis in their expectations, but as they left the town behind they were strongly aware of the barren distance, the treeless expanse of plain.

It was a country so flat that in places the streams went nowhere, but evaporated or seeped down into the soil of their own beds, or collected in shallow, stagnant lakes to evaporate. The short grasses and other plants native to the region had already finished their growing season now in mid-June, in preparation for the heat and drought of summer and fall.

Spring rains had been good. At intervals about the length of a day's drive sluggish streams wandered eastward across the plains, between shallow banks, almost invisible from a distance because of their lack of timber. These streams would be nearly all dry in two months, but now they furnished satisfactory, though muddy and mineral-filled, drink for man and beast.

The first day out of Dodge, they crossed Buckner Creek. The second day they crossed Pawnee River and went on five miles to a night camp on a small stream tributary to it. It was clouding up and the cattle bedded nervously. When they had finished supper, all the men went on guard.

Too many of the steers were standing up, watching the clouds. Scott studied them; they were on the verge of running. He believed that there is a key to the running of cattle, a key usually hidden by darkness and confusion. He believed that there is a sequence of events that can be seen in the herd, that most of the animals are entirely followers, that sometimes the leadership is taken from the regular leaders, and that one animal or a few animals make themselves sentinels and impart their fear to the herd.

Two of the standing steers were snorting back and forth across the bedded animals as if in conversation. Scott could see that the one on his side of the herd was the one with red around his eyes that they called Blinders. He couldn't identify the other one in the half light. Other grunting and snorting was hard to locate because of the singing of the full guard.

He could feel that they were about to run for sure, and he wanted to see what happened in the exact instant before they were all on their feet. He passed Cory and later Shorty and told both of them the same thing: "If they run northwest, let's let them run a while."

The movement started on the other side of the herd. With a clatter of hoofs, they were up and gone, northwest into the wind. The rumble and clacking the men had already heard so many times surged up again. The songs of the riders ceased or gained suddenly in tempo to match the running of their horses.

Scott wheeled Blackjack and circled the rear of the herd, yelling at the dark form of each rider. "Let 'em run! Keep 'em together! Let 'em run!"

But before long he was aware, because of the jogging course of the run and an occasional yell over the thunder of the herd, that some effort was being made to turn them. Dust billowed around him. He could feel it more than see it, feel it stinging his face and its grittiness in his mouth. He pulled his bandanna up under his eyes. They were running almost exactly into the wind, somewhat west of the true direction of the trail. He let Blackjack have his head as much as possible, thinking of gopher holes in this soft soil, but guided his path left around the flank of the running cattle and out to the side to be free of the dust. He had to see what was going on.

A pistol shot cracked toward the front of the herd. Scott pulled still farther out to the left, racing along toward the highest portion of the nearly level terrain. More shots pierced through the rumble. Scott could see the flashes stab the darkness. He counted five in all, enough to empty a side gun which had been carried with the hammer down on an empty chamber.

He had gained a position far enough to the side and high enough that he could see, by moonlight filtering through scattered clouds, the herd moving as a dark flood, raising a heavy curtain of dust. They had already split once, and he saw them divide again. The three bunches fanned out like fingers, all going northwest. He kept to the high ground, generally following the bunch which went most westerly but noting as well as possible the course of the other two. He kept his sense of direction as clear as he could by constant reference to such stars as he could see.

The Great Dipper had swung low, so that it would hold almost a full load of water, when he caught up to one of the bunches. It was about the time when they regularly changed to the last guard. These cattle had run themselves out and were under control. He found Shorty and Cory singing to them in weary voices.

The three dismounted and talked it over. Scott and Shorty did the talking; Cory had little to say. Shorty asked, "What do you figure we ought to do? Backtrack?"

"We can't afford to backtrack," Scott said. "The other two bunches are east of here. If you two will drive straight north, I'll try to see that the rest of the outfit meets you before noon tomorrow."

"How far straight north?" Shorty asked.

"To the first creek with water in it. It'll be a branch of Walnut Creek. Say six, eight miles from here."

"We'll have trouble holding straight north."

"You'll have to get your bearings real good before the North Star disappears at daylight. I'd stretch out a lariat rope on the ground or something. How's your belly holding up?"

"I can feel it, but it ain't no worse than it's been before. Cory's the one that's down tonight."

"What the hell's the matter with you, old drinking podner?"

"I'm so sleepy and so sick of this goddam drive that I don't give a hoot any more."

Scott slapped him on the back. "I know what's the matter with you; you still haven't got over that last drink we had in Dodge."

"Naw, it's worse than that, Billy. This drive is getting more screwed up all the time. It was Blackie done that shooting last night. I seen him kill at least one steer."

They kidded Cory a few minutes until they had coaxed a grin onto his face. Then Scott left them and rode east.

He knew the general course the next bunch had taken but had not seen them stop. He rode, peering at the ground. The moon had gone down. Occasionally he dismounted to look more clearly. Finally he cut the sign of trampled grass and followed up it, coming to the middle bunch of cattle half an hour before dawn. Martinez and Professor were with them.

Scott had been evaluating his own position in the outfit. He knew he had Shorty and Cory with him. From what he had been told, Kid must have tried to help him in the fight with Blackie. For some unexplainable reason and for whatever it was worth, Kid was with him. He, Scott, respected the work of Martinez and believed the feeling was mutual. At least Martinez had been in the parley with the Cheyenne bucks and knew who had really done the dickering. Probably in any trouble with Blackie he could count on the Mexican. As for the others, even Ostler, he didn't know. They generally seemed to accept Blackie as the boss, and the outcome of the fist fight had not helped. But they were an experienced bunch of cowhands and had a good stake in the drive by this time. They would probably go along with rebellion against Blackie if it made good sense.

Martinez and Professor had the bunch bedded and were circling slowly as if nothing had happened. Scott stopped Martinez and told him of the plan to rendezvous north on the first water. "You'll have to hold just a little west of north," he said. The Mexican seemed to agree to it.

When Professor rode up to them, Scott fished the letter from Greer to Kittredge from his pocket and handed it to the man. "I got this in Dodge. I didn't give it to Blackie, because the last letter I handed to him he threw in the fire. It's to Kittredge from Greer. Blackie has never notified the owners about Kittredge's death. Why don't you fellers read it when you get time and pass it on to someone else?"

Professor took the letter and shrugged. "Well, Blackie *is* segundo. Does it change that?" He had guessed the sense of Scott's intentions.

Scott eyed him in the dim dawn light and made the sharpest thrust he could based on his understanding of the book-reading man. "You don't seem to me like a man that would follow a big dumb bastard through foul-up after foul-up, just because he has a weak claim to leadership. I figure you've got more spine than that."

The Mexican was smiling.

"I don't know about spine, Scott. I stopped worrying about things like that away back in the war. Tell me, what is it to me if this drive's not successful? The owners made Kittredge boss and he made the big dumb bastard—and that's a pretty good description—made him second in command. Now, my insignificant life's complicated enough without worrying about wealthy cattle barons' troubles." Professor laughed. "Let them reap the fruits of the anarchy they have sown. Do they worry that I lose sleep chasing their damn spooky cows?"

"I doubt it," Scott said, "but you wouldn't have to lose so much sleep if the herd was handled with any sense."

"We don't need to scatter them all the time," Martinez put in.

"That's right," Scott said. "And I'll tell you what it is to you besides the sleep. If we lose this herd you won't get paid a cent for your work. And if we get there short or late, you won't get any bonus. And I don't care what you say, you don't want to take a job this far and then mess it up; you're a better cowhand than that."

Professor laughed. "What does the letter say?"

"It mentions me, but that's not the reason I want you to read it. It reminds Kittredge of how important it is to meet the July first delivery."

"Well, what form is this revolt against constituted authority to take?"

"I don't know. As Martinez says, we don't have to scatter the herd all over hell this way every time they run. And we've got to stop them from running some way. It can be done, maybe if we pull out the right steers and hobble them. We haven't got time for any more mistakes."

"All right. All right. I'll read the letter. That's the way it goes; here I was riding along peacefully, trying to make up a couple of new verses to 'The Old Chisholm Trail,' and my only worry was trying to find a rhyme for 'dry plains.' And you come along and tell me I've got spine and that I'm a good cowhand."

"Will you give it to somebody else, after you read it?"

"Yeah, I guess so. You're not going to fight 'the big dumb bastard' again, are you?"

Scott laughed. "No, I learned my lesson."

He rode east again. Probably both of them were with him, but you could never tell how the mind of a man like Professor would work. Counting them, Shorty, Cory, Kid, and himself, that made six—half the outfit.

It was getting light enough to see across the distances. Three miles farther on he found the third bunch, up and grazing, held by three riders whom he could identify as Blackie, Baldy, and Dandy. Blackie came out three hundred yards from the cattle and waited for him. The big man's form was slumped in the saddle but had a kind of determined immobility about it.

"Hello, Blackie."

"I ought to drag you right off of that damned horse and

stomp your ass right into the dirt!"

Scott didn't answer him for a moment, and then he kept his voice calm. "Did you load up that pistol after you got through killing a steer and scattering the herd all over the country with it?"

"What the hell's that got to do with it?"

"You better load up your pistol before you start to drag me off of a horse. I don't mean to fight you with my fists again, and I don't mean to worry about your threats. Do you think any man in this outfit is going to work just because he thinks you'll whip him? If you lay a hand on me, one of us is going to stay out here on this bald prairie from now on. You better get used to that idea."

"By God! if you don't aim to fight me again how come you act a fool like you done last night? You just asked for it."

Scott didn't answer his question.

"I want to know what the hell you thought you was doing? There I am killing myself trying to turn a stampede. And I ain't got a lick of help. Why? By God, because you're yelling to all the men, 'Let 'em go! Let 'em run!' That's why. I'd like to know what the hell you thought you was doing."

"All right, I'll explain it and then I'd like you to explain something to me. I thought we ought to let them run because they were heading toward Ogallala and because a herd will stay together when they're scared if you leave them alone. We made only eight miles a day from the Brazos to Dodge, and we've got fifteen miles a day to make from here on. Most of the time we lost because the herd scattered. Do you know where the rest of the herd is right now?"

"Hell no! How could I? I never had any help."

"You had more help than you know about. Now, explain to me why you fired off that gun last night. You say that Kittredge was a great man, and you know that was one of his strict rules: no guns are to be fired around the herd. Why in the hell do you think he had such a rule?"

Blackie shifted his heavy bulk in the saddle. "I don't have to explain nothing to you."

"We only had two thousand and five steers at the last tally. You killed at least one of them last night, maybe more. How in the hell do you expect to meet the contract?"

"I never killed but one last night. And I don't have to explain nothing to you."

"Did you buy a compass in Dodge?"

Blackie was surprised and at a loss for a moment.

"Kittredge needed a compass, but you don't. Is that the way it is? We haven't seen another trail herd since we left Dodge, and we're off the trail anyway. On top of that it's clouding up. How in the hell do you expect to find your way?"

"Dammit, I don't have to explain nothing to you."

"Why not, Blackie? Are you such a big auger that you can't talk to another member of the outfit about the problems of the drive?"

"Because, by God, all you want to do is get smart and show off how much you know in front of the other boys!"

"All right, there's none of the boys here right now. I'll make you a deal, Blackie. Away down yonder in Texas you wanted Professor to read the Bible in the morning, and he wouldn't do it. Well, we're in a worse fix now than we were then. I'll start reading the Bible every morning, just like Kittredge did, and I'll read anything else you want me to. We'll go over the maps together, and we'll try to work out some way to stop the cows from running all the time. And I'll ride on one of the points. We can take these damn cows up there on time. What do you say?"

Blackie stared all around himself at the distant horizon with a frown cutting the heavy features of his face. "I guess you can read the Bible in the mornings if you want to. The rest of that sounds like some more of that smart-aleck advice I done whupped you over once. I'm bossing this god-damned outfit."

"No, the whole deal goes together, Blackie. No help; no Bible reading. I don't see why you shouldn't accept suggestions and talk things over, without jumping all over me when I open my mouth."

But Blackie was adamant. He would cede nothing. Scott knew that it would be no better, in fact would be worse, in front of the rest of the men. The only hope was that most of the outfit would back him, Scott, when the chips were down, or that the big man would somehow realize his need of help before it was too late.

Scott told him where the other two bunches of cattle would come together, on the fork of Walnut Creek, and pointed definitely in the direction this bunch would need to take to meet them. He asked, "Do you want me to go back after Ostler?"

"I'll tell you if I want you to go after Ostler."

"Well?"

"I guess you can, and tell that damn sorry Kid to bring some horses up here fast as he can. We got to have fresh horses. I got a hundred things on my mind, and on top of that a sorry bunch of hands that don't know a thing to do till I tell them."

As Scott rode south he had a new worry. During his talk with Blackie, it had slowly sunk into his mind that he had almost certainly seen the bulk of the cattle of their herd but not all of the men who should have been with them. It indicated something he had been vaguely suspicious of, but he had thought the danger was over when they passed Dodge.

His one pleasant thought was this: that if they all came together ahead on the creek as he intended, they would have completed a good long drive for this day, with nothing lost from the stampede but one steer. He patted the tired Blackjack on the neck and urged him into a trot south over the flat, seemingly endless plain.

Details of the monotonous land stood out clearly in the morning light. He saw the bows of the wagon, then all of the camp of the night before. The remuda had not run; Kid was riding beside them as they grazed. Ostler had already harnessed his team and broken camp, and now sat on the ground leaning against a wagon wheel.

"They's hell to pay now, Billy," the old cook said as Scott went to the water keg.

"That's what I figured. We lost Art and Booger Red, didn't we?"

"I don't see how you knowed about it, but we did. They said they was fed up."

"When did they leave?"

"They come in right after the cows started running. Booger Red said this screwed-up outfit won't never get to Ogallala, and they was fed up. Wasn't a thing I could do; it was two against one."

Scott caught his grullo, took Blackjack down to the muddy stream to drink, and turned him loose. He was pondering the probable actions of the two deserters, gone now nearly twelve hours. They would head south to the Arkansas River and follow down it to Dodge, probably planning to get work in the stockyards or with some cattle outfit there. He had a small chance to bring them back and catch up with the herd, if Blackie didn't make some idiotic mistake while he was gone; and, of course, even then they would still be unwilling hands. The plain truth was that there was no way to hold men to their work contract when they lost all their faith in the outfit.

He came back to the wagon and told Ostler, "Those two men have had their heads together ever since Kittredge died, and they hardly ever said anything to anybody else. I've been afraid of them all along."

"I knowed they wasn't up to any good, myself," the old cook said.

"You been around a lot of cowhands, Ostler. Do you think there's anybody else that would quit?"

The cook rubbed his cheek and spat. "Not as I can make out."

"Well, let's go north then." He tied the saddled grullo behind the wagon and climbed up with the cook.

They talked about the difficulty of handling the herd with only eight hands plus the cook and wrangler, about the impossibility of making Art and Booger Red return to work, about the days and distance to trail's end, about Blackie's mistakes. Ostler freely admitted that several men in the outfit knew more about bossing a trail drive than did Blackie, but he couldn't forget that the big man had been appointed segundo and had successfully defended his position with his fists. The cook slowly realized that he was not merely engaged in a discussion, but that Scott was asking for something. Finally the cook said, "I know it's a mess, but what the hell can I do about it?"

"Well, who in the outfit knows anything about running a trail drive, in your opinion?"

"I'd say they was all pretty good hands. As far as handling the drive, I'd say . . . you . . . Shorty . . . Martinez. That Greaser don't say much but he knows cattle. I know plenty about it myself, Billy, but I ain't got time. . . ."

"You can back us up. The men respect you."

The cook studied his laboring team and the monotonous horizon a minute. "I'll back you up, on anything that makes good sense."

"That's all I want. Pull up a minute; I better help Kid get those horses moving faster. Everybody wants a fresh mount."

"They's some biscuits in the box back there. I reckon you can . . ."

"I'll wait if you'll whip that damn lazy team up a little and get to where the herd is by dinnertime."

"You worry about the saddle horses, and I'll worry about the team and wagon. Ain't nobody missed no dinner yet on account of me that I know of." He drove on north grumbling, but flailing the lines against the rumps of the team.

The outfit came back together again on the bank of the shallow, muddy stream in the middle of the day. They had finished the tally before Ostler had the noon meal ready. The count was two thousand and four steers, one thousand and three cows. All of the tired men, except two with the herd, had come to the wagon before Blackie noticed any-thing wrong. "Where in the hell's Art and Booger Red?"

Then ensued a repetition of the scene when Murphy had quit. Blackie ranted with all the energy that never seemed to diminish in his big body. "It's all your fault!" he screamed at Scott. "If we'd of went after that god-damned Murph and hung him, like I said, this wouldn't never of happened." The men responded to the wild outburst with silence. The two on the herd were Dandy and Baldy. All of them at the wagon were either men Scott felt sure he could count on or men he had talked to and found reasonably agreeable during the preceding night and morning. Blackie ended his tirade with, "Mount up, by God! We're going after those sons-a-bitches! Ostler, get the rifles out!"

No one moved. They were more serious now than they had been about Murphy. Murph had been sick, probably. Also, they were in worse straits now as far as being short-handed. But no one moved.

"Dammit! Mount up! Right now! Can't you hear me when I talk plain English?"

Then they began to produce objections. They were the objections Scott would have offered had he been doing the talking, and some of them, indeed, he had planted in their minds. Scott let them talk, but put in, during every lull in the argument, "We can make it without them." "We can take these damn cows up there on time." "This is the best outfit I ever worked with, and I know we can do it."

Blackie lost the argument, ungracefully, but he told them in a loud, positive voice that he was still bossing the outfit and he would personally kill the next man that looked like he wanted to quit.

They went on to another branch of Walnut Creek for night camp. The clouds were thickening, building up around them in the distance into thunderheads. Some of the men went to sleep with their heads on the saddles they had thrown on the ground while Ostler prepared supper. The men looked at the clouds and shook their heads and studied the cattle. But they were tired enough to sleep, for all of their fear of another stampede. And the cattle slept too, that night.

Next morning clouds had completely covered the sky. Blackie swore that he had pointed the wagon tongue at the North Star the night before and that someone had moved it. He wheeled, looking all around savagely at the sky and the far horizon, and said, "This don't even look like the same goddamned place we camped last night!" He was completely lost, but took his bearings from the wagon tongue, as everyone denied having moved it.

Scott knew they were going generally in the right direction and that they were somewhere west of the trail. They pushed on with uncertainty that day and half of the next. Then they struck a river that could be none other than the Smoky Hill. It was no barrier, but a good landmark, the largest stream in the area.

That afternoon as they trailed on north, Scott searched the terrain for the wheel tracks of Butterfield's Overland Dispatch Line, which followed along the Smoky Hill River, but he saw nothing. Once, ahead, he saw what might have been a dim road, but the blowing sand and the sparseness of the grass made it difficult to tell what it was; when he came even with it, he could see nothing. He thought they must be near to Monument Station on the Line. Surely they were west of the trail, yet had they been very far west they would have struck more of the Smoky Hill's tributaries: Twin Butte, Chalk, and Ladder Creeks. He knew the stage station *must* be there somewhere but could see nothing other than the broad empty plain.

He figured that a scouting trip five miles to the east or five miles to the west would reveal the station and pinpoint their location, but there was no one to take his place pushing the herd. He searched the cloudy sky again, noting the lightest part, which must be the location of the sun, and satisfied himself that they were traveling in the right general direction—and accepted the fact that he had to be satisfied with that.

Strange Sights

16

So I headed up the trail the funny sights to see,
And the things I seen made a believer out of me.
Come-a ti yi yippi, yippi yea, yippi yea,
Come-a ti yi yippi, yippi yea.

They had camped on the north side of another muddy stream, which Scott believed was either Big Creek or the Saline River. The cloud cover had thickened and darkened and now was stirred into streaks and curls by winds in the sky. Gusts of wind came down from above and struck dust from the ground. The herd would not bed, and the men all caught night horses and went on full guard after supper.

Again Scott was studying the cattle. He knew they were going to run. But they were nearly all still on their feet, nervous, and he could pick out no unusual individual action. For some reason there was no lightning from the dark mat of clouds that hung low over them in the twilight sky. The air was heavy and oppressive. Scott could feel the moisture and the grit mixed in his clothes, and when he wiped his forehead it was as if he had smeared mud across it.

The strong animal smell of the herd came to him in the changeable wind. The thick, dank air seemed to mound over the cattle and charge itself with the smell, then stream outward with the gusts. Sometimes Blackjack snorted nervously, perhaps calling to the other horses.

The men were singing. It had become too dark to see anything but the nearest cattle, but Scott could hear Blackie's unmistakable voice as the big man came around the herd. "Sing church songs! God dammit! Sing church songs!"

The big man was about a hundred feet from Scott when he yelled, "Everybody sing church . . ." and did not finish his admonition.

The mysterious St. Elmo's fire, called "fox fire" by cattlemen, had come down upon the herd. It began in balls on the upstretched horns, pallid, white-green fire. The growths of phosphorescence quivered in their places, then danced to horns that were held lower, and to ears. The lights spread to mark every beast and seemed, in the darkness across the expanse of the herd, like the night fires of some ancient army horde encamped in a rough plain.

All the singing had stopped. The cattle stood still and made no sound. The wind had ceased. The fox fire seemed to impose an eerie stillness over everything around it. Scott was aware of a plunging horse no more than fifty feet from him, and Blackie's voice broke the silence with a hoarse whisper. "God Almighty! Have mercy on us! We're done for!"

For some interminable period of time the cattle stood in silence, somewhere moving their heads, causing the weird lights to weave. They were as if hypnotized into a slow rite of nature. The seconds stretched into minutes. Time seemed to stand still while the fox fire spread and ran down into snakes of pale light that writhed along the animals' backs.

Scott saw the light jump from nowhere onto his horse's ears, so near that he could have touched it. Then it appeared on the ears and mane of the horse he had been aware of nearby. The other rider slid off his horse at the nearness of the fire, making a gasping noise. Scott half saw, half heard the horse plunge and rear against jerked reins. Blackie was whispering violent curses and prayers together.

Big drops of rain began to spatter on Scott's hat. He realized that lightning flashes and thunder had finally begun. The fox fire disappeared as suddenly and mysteriously as it had come. Then the herd, as if released from a spell, ran. They went west. The smell of the rain in the hot dust was sweet and fresh.

They ran for an hour. Scott began singing and in a minute he could hear other voices sometimes break through the thunder of hoofs. No one tried to turn them and they held together until they ran out their fear and came under the calming influence of the singing. By the time Blackie caught up, the herd had already stopped.

Some of the men got a little sleep in their saddles that night. Ostler and Kid joined them two hours after daybreak. They had lost nothing but sleep; however, sleep was becoming a precious thing to the shorthanded outfit.

The clouds stayed with them the following day, low-hanging clouds that made a ceiling over the flat country and oppressed them. By midday the ground had already dried following the rain of the night before. By midafternoon the gusty wind was again sending up starts of dust. The clouds turned streaky and curly in their lower reaches.

They had grazed some two miles during the two hours since noon camp; then, coming into a region where the grass was spotty, strung them out. Blackie and Martinez were on the points; Professor, Cory, Dandy, and Baldy served as outriders; Scott and Shorty had the hard labor of pushing the drags. The land was generally flat, with shallow draws leading away to the east, but in places where the grass was sparse the fine sand of the soil was blown into mounds and ridges, etched by the wind. Under the dark cloud ceiling, the light-colored sand seemed to be the source of lighting.

Scattered along the shallow draws, whose stream beds were hardly noticeable because of the little slope in the land, the yucca plants were blooming. The tall cream-colored spikes of blossoms stood like sentinels, incongruous, even ridiculous in the barren terrain.

Scott knew that they must be in the country of the Solomon River, but its tributaries, this far west, represented no certain landmarks. He had to be satisfied with the uncertain determination that the land sloped, almost indiscernibly, away to the right of their course and that they were making reasonable progress. He was involved with the work at hand, pushing the stubborn, footsore drags, when he heard Shorty yell "Hey!" in a voice that was unlike the one he used with the cattle. Shorty had pulled up and was pointing west.

Out of a dark spot on the horizon, where the clouds shadowed the hazy distance, a funnel-shaped cloud had emerged. It was a tornado.

"Cyclone!" Shorty yelled. Scott rode up beside him.

From the bottom of the dark cloud mass a twisted streamer of cloud moved lazily in the air. It was impossible to judge the distance to it—it might have been two miles or ten miles. The end of the cloud swung slowly, even gently, down to earth and touched. Then its lazy appearance was revealed as sham. The shadowed ground exploded in the place where it was touched and showered yellow-brown dust upward. The dust hung in the air after the dark tail had curved back up.

"You think it's coming this way?" Shorty asked.

"Can't tell," Scott said. "Too far away. Let's move these damn cows. If they start running, maybe they'll keep on going north."

Up ahead, at either side of the long string of cattle, they could see the other riders, stopped, all staring west at the tornado. The cows were stopping, knotting up. Scott and Shorty took their quirts from their saddle horse and tore into the drags, yelling. The movement they introduced passed up the string of cattle to Dandy and Baldy ahead of them, thence to the others, and the herd was moving north again.

The tail of the tornado touched ground again and again, and each time it raised the earth as if a giant gun had been fired into the ground. The funnel's distance and course could not be judged, but the scattered explosions of yellow-brown dust drew a jagged line toward the herd. And then its muffled roar grew audible. The herd ran. Blackie left his point and raced back screaming at the men. Martinez took the lead and did not try to head them but fled due north, the cattle following.

They heard the roar of the storm for fifteen minutes. It swung down and touched earth once directly behind them, a mile away, and moved on east. The riders ran their lathered horses at the sides of the frightened cattle, keeping out the gaps. They ran more than an hour; then Martinez turned left up a shallow, muddy stream. The cattle slowed and stopped at the water.

Baldy pulled up to water his horse where several other of the riders were watering. "Say, that moved them damned cows, didn't it!" he said. "Ain't nothing like a good cyclone to make cows get a move on."

Blackie fixed him with a harsh stare. "It ain't a thing to joke about, Baldy. It's a wonder we ain't dead."

That night Scott was awakened by a touch on his shoulder. He jerked back and grabbed for his gun under his warbag pillow. Then he heard Shorty's whispered voice. "It's me, Billy. It's me."

"Don't tell me it's time to go on guard and I slept right through it."

"Naw, it ain't that. Be quiet and get your britches on."

Scott put on his pants and boots and followed Shorty into the darkness. He was waking up slowly. When they were out of the area of spread "soogins" he asked, "What's the matter?"

"It's Cory; I think he's gone crazy."

"What do you mean? Is he out here?"

"If he ain't already gone. He's cussing you, Billy, and he ain't making any sense. He promised me he'd wait five minutes."

"Five minutes? I don't see what you mean."

"Hell, he's packed and ready to take off. I tell you, he's gone plum crazy."

Some little moonlight seemed to be filtering through the clouds. They were two hundred yards from camp when Scott could see the still horse and rider. It was the slender form of Cory, but with an unusual stiffness to his bearing.

"Why didn't you bring Blackie? I figure he'd like to be in on this." Cory's voice was dry, almost like that of a stranger.

Scott asked, "What's the trouble, boy? Get down and let's talk about it."

"Don't call me 'boy'! Shorty, you brought the wrong man to talk me out of anything. Why didn't you just bring the whole outfit and try to hang me for a horse thief?"

Scott said, "You know why he brought me, Cory, as well as he does. We've been friends a long time. Whatever's eating you, get down and let's talk about it." Cory didn't move, and Scott went on, "We've had it kind of rough lately, missing sleep and everything, but we've had it that rough before. You just don't seem to me like the same kind of man as Murphy and Scratchy and Art and Booger Red. Hell, get down and let's talk. We'll laugh about this two weeks from now."

"You all may laugh about it, but I won't be around. Get

your god-damned hand off of my horse, if you don't want a pistol barrel over your head!"

Shorty said, "Have you gone crazy? This is Billy and Shorty you're talking to. You act like we was a couple of strangers. Get down!"

"I can say what I aim to say setting right here. I told you I got nothing against you, Shorty, long as you don't try to stop me."

"Then it's me you're sore at?" Scott asked.

"You damned right, it's you I'm sore at! Don't give me that old bull: 'We've had it kind of rough lately'! I can take anything as rough as you can. But I'm so damn sick of this outfit and you, it makes me want to puke!"

"Well, that's what we're trying to find out—what's eating you. I guess you've got a reason for being sick of me, haven't you?"

"I've got plenty of reason. Here we are lost out in this Godforsaken country, and don't tell me we ain't lost, not only Blackie, but you and everybody else. We may be in Colorado, for all you know. We're lost. And there's that damned Blackie still yelling and throwing his stupid weight around and screwing up worse every day. If you had a bit of guts about you, you'd of called him out and shot the son-of-a-bitch a long time ago. You're the only man that knows enough about maps and everything to boss this drive, and you was near to being boss in the first place. Why in God's name ain't you took charge of it? There ain't but one reason: you just ain't got the guts!"

"So that's why you're sore. I haven't killed Blackie, so you're sore."

"You damn right I'm sore, and I'm through. I used to

have a lot of respect for you, even if I didn't understand you. But I ain't no more. You're short one thing to make a good boss and that's guts. Shorty, if you don't turn loose of that bridle, I'm going to hit you with this quirt."

Scott said, "Don't you figure we three have been friends long enough that you ought to listen to my side of it?"

"You ain't got no side that I see. You all ain't talking me out of leaving."

"Well, because you don't see it doesn't mean I've got no side. Don't you realize I've been thinking about this business for a month and a half? Suppose you were working for me, Cory. Would I have to run the outfit just the way you think I should, or could I run it according to my own judgment?"

"If you'd of took charge of the outfit like a man, I'd of followed you to hell! I told you I used to respect you."

"You *are* working for me, Cory. And you'll still be tomorrow and the next day, if you decide to stick around. I've been in charge of this outfit a long time; only thing is, I'm not running it just the way you think I should."

Cory was silent a moment; then he said, "That's a good laugh."

"It is kind of funny, but I'm as serious as I've ever been in my life. Get down; I want to talk to you about killing Blackie."

"About what?"

"You heard me. About killing Blackie. I want to tell you my ideas, and I'd like to hear yours; you know so damn much about what ought to be done. Maybe when we get through talking, Shorty and I will decide to go with you."

Cory slowly raised his right leg up over the saddle horn

and slid to the ground. "You all ain't talking me out of going. All of that's just words; it don't mean a thing to me."

"Well, I'm trying to understand your idea of killing Blackie. How far up the trail will it move us? I mean if I call him out in the morning and shoot him, will that move the herd fifty miles more north?"

"That's just talk," Cory insisted. "You know damned well Blackie has kept on screwing up and making us lose time, till now we ain't got a prayer of making the contract. You're running the outfit! You been in charge a long time! That kind of talk ain't going to make me change my mind."

Shorty put in, "Cory, that kind of talk ain't as wrong as you think. You know when this drive would have blowed up, without Billy? The day after Kittredge died. Me and Kid was out there by ourselves trying to hold about eighteen hundred head. By ourselves, mind you, and plenty sleepy, and Kid wasn't much of a hand. What the hell could I do with eighteen hundred head of cows? They'd done run once, and they would again whenever they got ready. I couldn't drive them; I couldn't keep them from scattering; I couldn't even watch all of them. I said to myself, I said, 'If that damned Colonel wants these cows, he better get me some help out here.' I didn't know the old man was dead. Well, who come along? Billy, here, with some boys to drive the bunch back. But it wasn't Blackie's idea; he'd of left me and Kid out there another day and night by ourselves."

"I ain't denying that," Cory said.

"Well, let's get back to shooting Blackie," Scott said. "Suppose I'd shot him back there when we had that fight.

It might have split the outfit up, right there in the Nation. Who knows? Or suppose I call him out tomorrow. It might be me that gets shot instead of him; I'm no more of a gun-fighter than he is. But regardless of who gets shot, the outfit has either got a dead man to bury or a wounded man to take care of, and then the outfit has still got the same job ahead of it, only it's one more man short. The plain fact is that we can't make the contract now without Blackie. Or maybe you've got it figured where we can; you seem to know just what I ought to do."

"You damn sure can't make it *with* him!"

"Yes, we can."

"Yes we can. Yes we can. Yes we can. How? It's getting worse all the time."

"No, it's getting better all the time. You know we're only about a week and a half from the end of the trail? That's all. You know the men are more behind me than they are Blackie? That's a fact. Some of them don't know it, but they are. Even Blackie's closer to taking my orders than he knows.

"I'm taking the herd away from him—the hard way, Cory. But there just isn't any easy way to do it. And I'll tell you one thing: I never expected to have any trouble with you, maybe Professor or somebody, but not you. You say you once thought you'd follow me through hell. Well, we're just about through hell right now; we've got just a week and a half to go."

"That's just talk! Talk's all it is!" Cory's voice was still dry, almost like that of a stranger. "We're lost and you know it. How the hell can you say it's getting better?"

"You may be lost. I'm not."

"You ain't seen the sun or a star in days, and the herd has run all over everwhere, and all this Godforsaken country looks alike. You expect me to believe you ain't lost?"

"I'm not. I know within twenty miles of where we are. I know which direction the herd has run and about how far. I know about how far we trail in a day. Every little draw in this country right here runs east by a little north, and if you hold square across them, you're going in the right direction. Martinez knows that, if Blackie doesn't. We're not over fifteen miles west of the trail. Don't tell me I'm lost, Cory, just because you are."

"Look at the sky right now," Shorty said. "It's fixing to clear up."

Cory said nothing for a minute. He gathered up his horse's reins. Then he said, "Well, I'd better get to riding. I knew you fellers would try to talk me out of it; you think you can talk me out of anything."

Scott asked, "Which way are you going? North or south?"

"I ain't saying. And the first bastard that tries to stop me is liable to get shot."

Shorty said, "I guess he's just too soft to make a trail hand, Billy."

"I guess so. He was a damn good drinking pardner, though. I might mention one more thing, Cory. I'm kind of short on hands. If you were to decide to stay, I'd guarantee your wages."

"There's another good laugh! How could you guarantee my wages? You ain't got no more money than I've got. That's just some more talk."

"No, it's not talk. I'll sell my horse and pay you every

cent of wages you've got coming, if you don't get it from the owners. I've had some good offers for him."

"Blackjack?"

"That's right."

Cory stared a minute, then began making a cigarette deliberately. His shoulders slumped. He looked around at his horse and at the warbag tied down behind the cantle. Evidently his cigarette spilled. He jerked his hat from his head and threw it against the ground with a loud slap. "You dirty bastards!" he said in a muffled voice. His horse had shied back and he scrambled for the reins. "Whoa!" Then he repeated, "You dirty bastards!"

Scott and Shorty began laughing at him.

"You dirty bastards!" Finally he laughed in a strained manner and said, "I swore you all wasn't going to talk me out of it, but I ought to of known you would. You don't have to sell your horse, Billy. I don't want no damn pay if you have to sell your horse to get it."

Cory belonged on guard. Shorty had taken his bag to carry it back to the wagon, and Cory had mounted his horse. "I've got it out of my system, I guess," the younger man said. "And I ain't going to quit no matter what you answer me, Billy, but do you really think we've got a chance to make the contract?"

Scott laughed at him. Something in Cory, almost completely concealed, reminded him of Kid. "When we get that bonus," Scott said, "you're going to buy me a bottle of liquor. You've cost me a whole hour's sleep tonight."

But he couldn't sleep when he was back on his bedroll. He wished that he was as certain in his own mind as he had tried to sound with Cory. The clouds were actually breaking up. He could see enough of the stars to make out the familiar patterns and it was a comfort. In the southern sky the great Scorpion lay on his side, ready to crawl down below the horizon. In the north the Big Dipper had swung low and its handle curved out across the western sky. He got up and tugged the wagon tongue around and pointed it at the North Star.

They knew things about the heavenly bodies and their apparent motions, such things as are learned from familiarity, from watching the night sky as hours pass and as months pass, from watching it as they moved north on the surface of the earth. The kinds of things they knew were such as have been known for thousands of years by sailors standing watch at night or by nomadic herders standing watch at night, and such as are rarely known among people who live among artificial lights under a roof. They knew that the stars seem to rotate in fixed patterns and that one point about which they rotate is the North Star, that the moon and planets wander across the face of the fixed patterns, that as one trails north the southern constellations sink but the North Star rises until at last the Big Dipper swings clear of the ground and is like a giant clock in the sky, that the moon falls behind almost an hour each night, that the fixed stars gain on the days so that during a three-month drive a star which comes up as darkness falls will rise so that it is overhead when darkness falls. And a trail driver who had been north with cattle every year for the past ten years might have been able, awakening suddenly like Rip Van Winkle and gazing at the night sky, to tell about how far north he was and the month of the year, or, if he were a shrewd guesser, he might have been able to say, "We're a few days' drive south of the Nebraska line and it's a little past the middle of June."

The next morning there were no clouds. When the sun was up in it, the sky was like polished brass. It appeared as if it had never been softened by any clouds. By midmorning the ground in the distance jumped with heat waves, then sheets of water appeared to lie on the ground at the horizon. It was the day they saw their first mirages.

Scott and Shorty had their hands full on the drag. One cow, which they had called "Nellie Sue" ever since she fell back to the drag with sore feet, would stop at every opportunity. A younger heifer and two steers walked with her and circled back to stand behind her each time she stopped. It required most of one man's time to keep her going.

They were quartering into a slight wind. The air on one flank of the drag was not only full of dust and pungent animal odor, but hot from the heat of the many bodies, searing hot. Scott and Shorty took turns going into the downwind flank to urge on laggard beasts and would come out panting. They could sometimes see Baldy and Dandy up ahead; the rest of the riders and the strung-out herd were hidden by dust and shimmering heat.

Then the pall of dust became like a broad screen above them and upon the screen appeared, magnified, the leaders of the herd plodding north. The giant horns and heads swayed rhythmically from side to side, deliberately. The point riders were there, also like giants out of a legend, their hats as broad as a wagon tarp. The illusion appeared near, yet dreamlike, hazed about with points of light.

Scott and Shorty watched it and finally pulled up side by

side to comment on it. Scott asked, "Did you ever see any thing like that before?"

"Not exactly, did you?"

"No, I saw a bunch of wild mustangs one time, big and up in the air that way."

"Do you reckon they can see us the same way from up toward the front?" Shorty asked.

"Hard telling. I think the sun's got to be just right."

"You know, Billy, reckon it was that kind of stuff—you know that fox fire and that cyclone was kind of the same eerie stuff—reckon that was what was eating old Cory?"

"I figure that had something to do with it. Good thing he got it out of his system last night."

"Yeah. Ho, Nellie Sue! Damn your sore feet! Get moving."

They fell back into the hot labor. At noon camp they found that all the other riders had seen a different mirage, a snowcapped mountain. They talked about it excitedly and swore that it was as clear as anything they had ever seen.

The two outriders who had been on the downwind side that morning, Baldy and Cory, complained about the heat and demanded that they take the other side of the herd during the afternoon. Blackie agreed to the change and also, without explanation, changed the night guards, moving Scott from the last guard to the first. The big man was moody. Scott thought that Blackie started to say something to him several times but acted as if he couldn't find the words.

Dominion Over Cattle

17

Oh, we couldn't find a tree for to save our soul,
So the cusi had to cook the grub with plain old prairie coal.
Come-a ti yi yippi, yippi yea, yippi yea,
Come-a ti yi yippi, yippi yea.

The next morning about 2 A.M. Scott awoke as usual, though he had already served his guard and had gotten no more than three hours' sleep. He had thought the evening before that the herd was about to run again; they seemed to run, then rest a day or two, then run again. If they scattered again . . . If anything happened again to make the outfit lose time or lose sleep . . . If they were farther off the trail than he had estimated . . .

He was half asleep during those early morning hours when he usually served on guard, and then was halfway aware that Ostler and Kid had risen and were starting their work for the day. He snapped wide awake with the realization that Blackie was up and saw the big man disappear behind the wagon with something in his hand.

Scott hurriedly dressed and followed him, not knowing exactly what he intended saying to the big man. Blackie was holding Kittredge's brown leather-covered Bible in both hands. He held it close to his face as if trying to read it in the dim light. They faced each other a full minute; then Blackie thrust the Bible out toward him at arm's length.

Scott let him hold it there for the time being. "Did you

274

decide to take me up on my deal?"

"I guess you can ride on the left point. I . . . uh . . . got to go all around the herd and watch everything like Colonel Kittredge used to do."

"We've got a new calf out there, maybe two by now. I think we ought to carry it in the wagon and put it with the cow at night. A calf will calm down a spooky herd sometimes."

"I guess we can do that. I don't like to kill no calves no more than anybody else does. Here."

Scott took the Bible. Ostler had just started banging against a tin plate and yelling at the sleeping men.

The men were usually silent until they had drunk some morning coffee. None of them noticed Scott and Blackie. Scott suddenly realized that the Colonel must have had passages picked out for reading, but he had no idea where they might be. Maybe it didn't matter; he could start at the beginning. He felt ridiculous standing there beside Blackie, but he read in a voice as clear and firm as he could make it:

"In the beginning God created the heaven and the earth . . ."

There was a jerking movement among the slowly dressing men, maybe a faint gasp. Scott looked up. They were staring at him as if he were a ghost. They were frozen in their positions.

He went on:

"And the earth was without form, and void; and

darkness was upon the face of the deep. And the Spirit of God moved upon the face of the waters.

"And God said, Let there be light: And there was light.

And God saw the light, that it was good: and God divided the light from the darkness.

"And God called the light Day, and the darkness he called Night. And the evening and the morning were the first day."

The men said nothing about the reading. No doubt they thought about it; they were altogether less boisterous and more moody and thoughtful than they had been two months before. During breakfast Scott felt their puzzled surreptitious glances.

Two calves had been dropped during the night. They hazed the cows out to the vicinity of the wagon, then caught the calves by hand. Ostler swore that there was no room on the wagon and he was not going to put up with any such nonsense. Scott climbed on the wagon and began restacking the bedrolls, leaving a space immediately in front of the chuck box.

"Billy, I tell you I ain't going to have it," Ostler said. "I'm in charge of this wagon, and I got plenty to do without playing nursemaid to a couple of filthy calves. Get out of there!"

Scott went ahead making room.

"I tell you I ain't going to put up with it! I told you I'd go along with anything with you, if it made sense. Well, this don't make sense. I'll throw them out."

"I don't think you will." Scott took the long-legged, new

born calves as they were handed up by Shorty and Martinez.

"What makes you so blamed sure I won't? I'm running this wagon."

"Because you know as well as I do that we have to try everything. We're getting too short on time and too short on hands. I've seen this work."

"I don't care. It ain't my place to nursemaid no calves."

Scott laughed. "If it doesn't work, you may have to start standing guard. We're losing too much sleep on account of these stampedes."

"That ain't my fault. I'll throw them out soon as you all leave."

"I don't think you will."

Ostler didn't throw them out, though he told the calves with every jolt of the wagon that morning that he was going to, and he swore mightily at the two cows that followed the wagon on the prod.

At the noon camp they had to drive the two cows off a few hundred yards and carry the calves out, leaving them to suck, so that the dismounted men around the wagon would have a degree of safety. The cook continued to bang pots around and swear that he was not going to pick up any more cow chips for fuel—he sure couldn't be getting off the wagon with two proddy cows around it all the time; somebody else could gather the chips or they could eat their blamed grub raw.

That night they put the calves with their mothers and bedded the two cows on opposite sides of the herd. This was accomplished with a peculiar kind of leadership. The men quietly cooperated with Scott, but Blackie, seeing what was being done, shouted detailed directions for its doing.

On the first guard that night Scott found the animal which had been snorting back and forth with Blinders. It was a big line-back steer they called Yeller Belly. The snorts and grunts across the herd between the two steers was almost like a conversation.

They ran for no apparent reason. Perhaps it was a faint sound picked up by their hairy ears; more likely it was an unusual smell that came on the wind. Whatever it was, they had all been ready, and they sprang up together and thundered west. Only the men of the first guard were with them, Scott, Professor, and Blackie. These three witnessed an amazing phenomenon. The effect of the calves was beyond Scott's wildest hopes.

Somewhere hidden under the rushing rumble of twelve thousand hoofs and the clacking of six thousand horns was the weak "Ba . . . aa . . ." of the calves and the anxious bawling of the two cows. Always before the herd had run without voice. Now, before they had been going a minute, other cows began stopping and bawling, for calves long weaned or dead back along the trail or never born. Steers began stopping, answering long-forgotten mothers. The mournful calling became as loud as the sound of the hoofs. It moved forward in the flood of cattle to the leaders, and the leaders stopped and bawled and turned back, searching.

The herd had not moved a mile, and they did not begin milling when they stopped. Instead the individual animals walked about at random, complaining. Finally the two cows found their calves, and every other animal seemed to find some familiar companion in the horde. They began to lie down of their own volition.

Professor rode up to Scott. "Is that you, Scott?"

"Yeah. It looks like our calves helped, doesn't it?"

"Helped? It's absolutely the damnedest thing I ever saw! Did you think of that yourself?"

"No, I've seen it done before. I knew it would calm them some, but I didn't expect it to work so well."

"You've well-nigh made a believer out of me," Professor said. "I let Baldy and Dandy read that letter you gave me. Who else shall I give it to?"

"I guess that's enough." Scott laughed. "Blackie has started to bend a little."

By the time the others of the outfit had raced up to help, the herd had all lain down on a new bed ground. All but the first guard returned to camp. The cattle ran twice more that night; they still had the energy. The men got no more than three hours' sleep apiece, but in the morning, after three stampedes, the herd was only two miles away from the chuck wagon and in clear sight.

They pushed the herd north-northwest through a land that had no green in it. The scattered bunch grass was golden brown, and the land in the distance was yellow from the grass and sand and sunlight. It was the kind of arid and monotonous land that wandering herdsmen and camel drivers and Arabian horsemen had traveled during long thousands of years between ancient centers of civilization. The trail drivers squinted through narrowed eyes at the haze where the pale sky met the sun-shimmering land, as had the ancient travelers. Their faces were burned almost as brown. They felt the same heat and dust. They smelled the same animal sweat and animal dung.

They had seen no other trail herds at all, and Scott was concerned. It might mean that they were too far off of the direct trail, and it might simply mean that no other herd was near them on the trail. It was an advantage to graze virgin grass, a disadvantage to find so few cow chips for fuel. They were using some chips, years old, that must have been buffalo chips. But the real disadvantage in not knowing their exact position lay in the lack of time for scouting.

They made camp that night at what Scott thought must be about the Kansas-Nebraska line. Besides putting the two calves with the herd, they cut out Blinders and Yeller Belly. They threw these two steers and hobbled and side-lined them, so that they could do no more than barely walk; then they left them a quarter of a mile from the main herd. But the herd ran again, a short mile. It cost more sleep. Scott had not found the key or had found only part of it. Shorty was sure that it was one of the black Spanish heifers, but he couldn't tell which one.

The next morning Scott read from the Bible. Always the reading had been impressive to him, but this day it seemed more meaningful, and he was wondering as he read whether it had the same meaning for the other weary men that it had for him.

"And God made the beast of the earth after his kind, and cattle after their kind, and every thing that creepeth upon the earth after his kind: and God saw that it was good.

"And God said, Let us make man in our image, after our likeness: and let them have dominion over the fish of the sea, and over the fowl of the air, and over the cattle, and over all the earth, and over every creeping thing that creepeth upon the earth.

"So God created man in his own image, in the image of God created he him; male and female created he them.

"And God blessed them, and God said unto them, Be fruitful, and multiply, and replenish the earth, and subdue it: and have dominion over the fish of the sea, and over the fowl of the air, and over every living thing that moveth upon the earth."

That afternoon they crossed what he knew must be the Republican River. It was smaller than he remembered it, but larger than the branches of Sappa Creek and Beaver Creek, which they had been crossing the last three days. By his estimation of the distances they had made, it could be nothing but the Republican.

That evening, after they had put the calves with the bedding herd and cut out the two steers, Martinez cut out one more, a black Spanish heifer with short keen horns. "That's her," Shorty said. "That's the one I was talking about." They hobbled and sidelined her along with the steers. All the men had come to cooperate in the matter of the key to the stampedes. Blackie still gave orders, but no leader seemed to exist.

That night the herd did not run. And the cattle did not seem tired. They rose here and there about midnight, stretched, relieved themselves, and lay back down. At day-light they lay on the same ground. When they threw the black Spanish heifer to remove the ropes, they cut both of her ears in a broad swallow fork; they would have no trouble picking her out again. That same morning they added another tiny calf to the wagon, and Ostler bounced north that day complaining louder than ever.

On the evening of the 29th of June, they camped beside the stream they had been following all day. Scott was in a dilemma. He knew they had crossed Frenchman Creek. If they were on the trail, this stream would be the Stinking Water, but he had been afraid all afternoon that it was bearing too much westerly. He could not tell exact enough directions by the sun. While it was still light he pulled the wagon tongue around and pointed it up the long stretch of creek that he could see.

Blackie walked over, frowning. "What you doing, Scott? That's my job to do that. You can't see no North Star no way."

"We can turn it north after dark," Scott told him. "I'm afraid this isn't the Stinking Water. It may be Spring Creek. Why don't you get Kittredge's map and I'll get mine and we can tell what creek this is when the North Star comes out."

Blackie stared at him, not understanding at all. But after dark Scott got him to bring the other map, and they bent over them under the lantern light. "Both maps show the same thing," Scott said. "The Stinking Water bears north-northwest, but Spring Creek bears northwest." He pointed at the North Star and along the wagon tongue. "This creek we're on bears too much west to be anything but Spring

Creek. That's for sure."

Blackie was frowning. In the dim lantern light his eyebrows seemed to be one black mass across his forehead. He looked around at the stars and at the maps and at the wagon tongue. It was clear that he didn't understand and that he was troubled. He even forgot that it was "his job" to point the wagon tongue north. Scott did it and followed the big man out to serve the first guard.

Scott got only two hours' sleep that night. He awoke when it was time to go on last guard and then could not get back to sleep, even though he was sleepy. It seemed clear that he was going to have to ride ahead and scout out the exact route for the herd. If they struck the South Platte and the little town of Ogallala was not there, they wouldn't know whether to turn east or west. He arose and went out and checked the hobbled animals, then came back and lay down, but could not sleep. As Ostler rose in the dim morning, Scott was thinking: When Mr. Lawson and I planned this drive, today was the day we were supposed to end it. And tomorrow was the . . . tomorrow is the delivery day.

After he had read from the Bible as usual, Scott saw Blackie motioning from the other side of the wagon. Scott walked around to him. The big man had something to say and had trouble putting it into words. Finally he said, "Scott, me and you get along pretty good, is the reason I wanted to talk to you. I been having a hard time trying to make up my mind."

Scott waited.

"We got to do something, Scott. You're lost too, ain't you?"

"No, I'm not lost. That's Spring Creek, right down there."

"Well, they's so many creeks out here—seems like we've come across a hundred. All this country just keeps on looking the same every day, and I'm just about to make up my mind . . . I think we better turn around and go back to Dodge. I mean, we know where Dodge is; we was there not long ago, and we could find it pretty easy."

Scott was torn with two ideas. He felt sorry for the man in front of him. And, too, he understood what Cory had felt in wanting to kill the big man. It was incomprehensible. The fool did not understand at all that it was two long weeks back to Dodge, that it was probably no more than thirty miles to Ogallala, that they didn't have supplies to go back south even if they wanted to, that it would be better to go ahead even though they arrived a day or two late. How could he have come up with the ridiculous idea of turning back to Dodge?

Scott was thinking that he could kill him now, if it came to a showdown. He had thought that, if it came to gunplay, they would each have an even chance, but he knew it wasn't true now. He could leave this big man here in a shallow grave—and would if that was what it took. But even as these ideas were crossing his mind, he saw something in the man's eyes, beneath the beetling black brows. How fantastically difficult it must have been to push farther and farther out into this country, pretending that you are boss and having such little idea of where you are going! He thought of Blackie's oft-repeated statement: "I got so much on my mind."

Scott did not talk about the proposal of going back to

Dodge. He said, "Blackie, Ogallala is thirty miles north of here, one hard day's drive, straight north. I'm going to ride up there today, until I see it, so I can guide us straight in. You take the herd on up this creek today, not more than ten miles, and water them twice. Bed them on the water. They won't run any more."

Blackie was staring, uncertain, trying to find something to say.

Scott went on, "We'll have a long drive tomorrow, but if any outfit can push cows this one can."

"I know how to push a bunch of cows," Blackie said.

"Let them get plenty of water today and don't go over ten miles up this creek."

"Yeah," Blackie said. "We got to get ready for a hard drive tomorrow."

After breakfast, Scott made sure that Shorty and Martinez understood about the day's drive and the water. Then he saddled Blackjack and rode north. He held the horse to a walk where it was rough, but urged him into a ground-eating pace on the level.

Sometimes on the lonely ride he spoke to the horse. "Just because you work at night, you expect to run free in the daytime, do you? You black devil, thought you would have an easy spring when I left you at Lawson's, didn't you?" One time he leaned forward and patted the sturdy shoulder. "You're going back on the cars, and you'll have oats to eat." "Here I am talking to myself like a sheepherder; it's because there's no trees for company. Horse, do you remember what a tree looks like?"

They went through fields of rounded stones, across vast bars of pebbles and sand. Here in a barren wilderness that became a desert every summer was the unmistakable evidence of the action of water upon rock. The soil was made of the washings of ages, where ancient streams had sluggishly flowed east, writhing, shifting, weaving through countless centuries.

He was sleepy and dismounted to walk a few hundred yards. The sun was at its zenith and cast his short shadow straight in front of him. When he remounted, he realized that the land ahead of him generally fell away, but far beyond he could see it rising again. He had come far enough; he was looking at the broad, shallow valley of a river. But where in the hundreds of square miles of hazy shimmering distance?

He squinted and shielded his eyes above and below with thumbs and forefingers. He swept the terrain slowly. There, almost due east, a brown dust cloud lay on the ground, close, maybe six miles. A man never saw that many buffalo in one herd these days. Cavalry soldiers never rode that many together. The source of the dust was too compact to be Indians from the Red Cloud Agency. He had seen it too many times to be mistaken; it was another trail herd. The dust thinned and drifted away behind them. He could tell the direction they were going.

It required several minutes of scanning before he saw the other cloud, far out to the northeast. It was as black as a heavy pencil mark. His eyes returned to it again and again, and he was satisfied that it moved. It could be nothing but a Union Pacific engine coming up the valley of the South Platte.

He sat on the horse half an hour watching the two clouds creeping along the terrain, studying the place where their courses would cross. He saw neither river nor town but was satisfied as he turned the black horse to retrace his morning's ride. Relief was flooding over him in a slow tide. They were going to cut it close, but they were going to make it. With the relief the drowsiness returned.

Twice he jerked with the sudden knowledge that he had gone to sleep. It was the regular motion of the horse. He dismounted and walked a few paces but found himself stumbling, asleep on his feet. He took out his tobacco sack, made a little mound of tobacco flakes in the palm of his hand, and ground them into dust. Quickly and cruelly he rubbed the dust into both his eyes. Tears welled up to wash out the stinging foreign matter, but the sleep had been pushed back. Twice more that afternoon he used the tobacco; the landmarks he used to maintain his course south he saw through heat waves and also through waves of burning tears.

At dark he was back on Spring Creek. He watered Black-jack and turned up it. At midnight he saw the lantern. Someone had shown the good sense to hang it from a bow of the chuck wagon.

The Reckoning

They say there will be a great roundup,
Where cowboys like cattle will stand
To be cut by the riders of judgment,
Who are posted and know every brand.

They had crossed several trails during the past three months, some of them not a trail at all that you could see, but rather a way or a route, and most of the men were unaware that they had been crossed:

The Goodnight-Loving Trail to New Mexico; the Southern Overland Mail Route; the California Trail south of the Canadian; the Santa Fe Trail at the Arkansas River; Butterfield's Overland Dispatch Line along the Smoky Hill River; the Pony Express Road near the Republican River. Now they were pushing toward the end of their northern trek—seven miles south of the Oregon Trail.

They were surprised, most of them. The lights were there to see when they came over the last divide, twinkling gas lights and kerosene lights in the distance, dim because of the moonlight. "What is that?" they would say as they came near one another in their work. "Is that a town?" "Where? I don't see anything." "Right down in yonder." "You must be seeing things." They didn't all believe it until the cattle, even the drags, began to sniff the air and walk faster, finally breaking into a trot.

And then as they spread the herd out down toward the

water and the sparkling river lay in clear view, they began to say, "Hey, it ain't midnight yet! See where the Dipper is!" "You know it ain't midnight!" "Hell no! it ain't midnight!" "That's Ogallala too; this here's the little old South Platte River!"

Scott had been watching the stars and his pocket watch. As soon as he saw most of the herd on the water and under control he pulled out and rode hell-for-leather through the shallow river and into the town.

He did not have to waste any time hunting. In the light that streamed from the doorway of Drover's House stood two men talking. One of them was the most worried-looking cattleman Scott had ever seen.

Greer glanced at him as he slid Blackjack to a halt, then stared at him as if he were a ghost. Scott had not realized how dirty he had become during the day and that his dash through the river had further disturbed his appearance.

"Scott! is that you? My God, man! I'm glad to see you."

Scott grinned and shook hands.

"Where's the herd?"

"Mr. Greer, they're out there bedded down south of the river, where they're supposed to be. This is July the first. I wonder why the buyer isn't out there to receive the herd?"

Greer jerked out his watch, looked at it, and showed it to the other man. Greer started laughing and the other man joined in, shaking his head and looking at his own watch. "Well, it is still July the first," he said.

"Shake hands with Mr. Fleming, Scott. Charles Fleming. He's the buyer you were looking for. Do you have the thousand head of cows and two thousand steers?"

"Yes, sir."

"Did you have any trouble?"

"Some, Mr. Greer. Of course, Colonel Kittredge was killed, as I told you in the telegram."

"How did it happen?"

"Well, nobody saw it. It was storming kind of bad. Hailing. They ran and went down over this low bank. I guess he was trying to turn them. Quite a few cows ran over him."

"I wrote his brother and told him I was sure you had given him a decent burial."

"Yes, sir. We did the best you can do out that way."

"I don't mind telling you, Scott, that we've had a few anxious days. I wrote the Colonel at Dodge . . ."

"Yes, sir, I got that letter."

"Well, the day after I wrote, I found out about the big stampede south of the Canadian. Some drovers lost pretty heavily. We couldn't find out the exact date it happened, but we finally convinced ourselves that you must have been past that point. Of course we were relieved, about the herd, that is, when we got your wire. But that date on it. We could see you were very short on time." Greer laughed. "Brown doesn't worry like I do. He kept saying, 'If Scott says he'll meet the delivery on July the first, he'll meet the delivery on July the first.' You must have crossed the Canadian late; how did you miss the big stampede?"

"I guess we were lucky. We thought they were crowding a little too much, and we pulled back the day before it happened."

"What was Kittredge doing on the Brazos May the sixth? He was already running late, wasn't he?"

"Well, yes, sir. I believe he said he would have them road broke by the time he hit Mason. He never did get them road broke, and I never did either. The fact is, we've got a spooky herd out there, Mr. Greer."

"How many times have they run?"

Scott laughed. "I guess I lost count. Mr. Fleming, I'll talk to your foreman when we turn the cattle over to you. We've got it worked out where we can handle them pretty good."

Greer asked, "What kind of shape are they in?"

"Well, that's funny; I'd say they're in fair to good condition. We had good grass all the way."

They wanted Scott to come in and have some kind of refreshment, but he thought he had better return to camp. He said that he would be in early the following day to guide them to the herd south of the river. Greer thought they would not need a guide, but Scott said, "Well, I've got a couple of things I want to ask you about. I'd like to get them straightened out first thing in the morning."

He rode back in with Blackie in the early dawn. They went up to Greer's room. The rancher, with a towel around his neck and shaving soap on his face, opened the door. He looked questioningly at Blackie.

"Hello there, Blackburn. Come in. If you boys will excuse me, I was sprucing up a little." The room was not well lighted so early in the morning by the one window, and the rancher held his face near the lamp on the washstand, moving this way and that as he started to shave to get a good view in the mirror.

"You said you wanted to get a couple of things straightened out, Scott. What kind of things?"

"I guess you'd call them requests, Mr. Greer. Fact is, I've got three."

"Fire away."

"I want trail-boss pay since Kittredge died May the sixth." As he said it, Scott was watching Blackie. The big segundo was surprised, not ready for any such move. His heavy black brows were drawn together in wrinkles, in anger or in thought. He was about to say something for a second, but nothing came out, and he stared at Greer and Scott.

"That's understood," Greer said. "What else?"

Blackie rubbed his forehead and looked out the window at the empty street.

"I'd like to have freight back home for my horse. I needed him."

Greer laughed. "Did you need him or did you just get lonesome for him?"

"I needed him."

"All right. What else?"

"I think the men ought to have a bonus of a month's pay. It's been a hard drive."

Greer washed the soap from his face and stood patting it dry with the towel. "That's pretty stiff. I was thinking about ten dollars per man and maybe a few boxes of cigars."

"We've been shorthanded, Mr. Greer. There's only ten of us left."

"You mean ten besides you and the cook and the wrangler."

"No, sir. I mean ten counting me and the cook and the

wrangler. And they're a real good bunch of men. Best outfit I ever worked with."

Greer kept patting himself with the towel. "Did you say the herd is in fair to good condition just for Fleming's benefit? Have they actually put on weight?"

"They've put on weight. They're in fair to good condition."

"All right. You're the foreman. If you're convinced they deserve such a bonus, I'll pay it. Is that all your requests? I hope to the devil it is. It gets rougher on my pocketbook every time you open your mouth."

They laughed. Greer wanted them to have breakfast with him, but they said they had already eaten. The rancher looked at them both with a faint quizzical smile. "Here it is about sunrise, and you two stood guard last night, I suppose, and you've already eaten breakfast, saddled up, and ridden to town. You know, I trailed herds to Abilene two years, but a man forgets how it is out there. Did you lose much sleep?"

"Some," Scott said.

Greer laughed. "I bet these shorthorn cowboys we are going to turn the herd over to are not even out of bed yet. We won't need a guide, unless you two just want to stick around."

They decided to go back to the herd. Scott was satisfied with the interview. Blackie followed him downstairs and they mounted in silence. The big man followed him out of town, across the river, and on to camp, never saying a word.

The "shorthorn" outfit that received the herd consisted of

thirty-two men, fifteen cavalry soldiers, and seventeen cattle workers. They laughed at the "rawhides" who had driven the herd north, but were also amazed at them. These trail drivers were the dirtiest, raggedest, wildest crew of men imaginable. They were burned dark brown; you could tell that one of them was a Mexican, but you weren't sure about the others. Besides the bushy beards and mustaches, they all had an inch growth of beard stubble—except for the kid with them; he didn't look over sixteen but cursed vilely and was a good rider.

There were only ten of them in all but they seemed fifty when they lined the herd out for the tally. Most of them rode scrawny little ponies that could turn on a dime and seemed to love chasing cows. The one who was their boss rode a beautiful big black horse that seemed to know enough about the work to make a hand by himself. The whole bunch screamed and whistled and cursed interminably and called the wild longhorns by individual names—Highboy, Spot, Lonesome, Pussyfoot, Spud, Blinders, Slewfoot, Nellie Sue. One of them was a big man with black hair; he could tail down a twelve-hundred-pound steer as if it were a week-old calf.

Greer had sold the horse band, the chuck wagon, and everything. About half of the outfit went along on the short drive to deliver the horses, as much for a lark as anything. Greer had rented a wagon to bring back their saddles and to carry a small amount of camping gear.

Scott and Blackie were saddling up side by side. Scott was watching the big man as he threw on the stiff saddle blanket.

Scott said, "He's got a little dirt on his back you better clean off, Blackie."

"Aw, it's all right." He was reaching for the saddle.

"No, it's not all right. Take the blanket off."

Blackie took the blanket off. "I don't see anything much."

"What the hell do you call that dried mud there? That'll make a sore."

"Well, I ain't got no currycomb or anything."

"Use your fingernails. Don't ever saddle up a horse with dirt on his back. And the first chance you get, wash out that filthy blanket. It's stiff as a piece of rawhide."

Blackie laborously worked at the horse's back with his hands. Scott mounted and rode on.

The Professor was driving the wagon, Kid on the spring seat beside him. The mules loved it; the two that felt like pulling pulled at their own pace; the other two loafed. The singletree on the off side dragged and bounced against the front wheel. The lines in the Professor's hands drooped down onto the tongue and neck yoke.

"Professor," Kid said, "ain't you glad me and you are cowboys instead of mule drivers? It would worry a man to death to look at the back end of a mule all the time."

The older man grunted and said, "Look out yonder, Kid," pointing to where Scott rode, followed closely by Blackie, behind the remuda. "Did you ever see anything like that?"

"Like what? You mean old Blackie being so big?"

"I mean old Blackie following right behind Scott like a big dumb dog. You know something, Kid. That damned Blackie never did really want to boss the drive. Only he's slow about figuring things out."

The Kid seemed to chew the idea over a minute and find it indigestible and drop it. Then he advanced one of his own. "Boy, that Scott is a man that's really going places, ain't he? Boy, would I ever like to go on a drive and him the top dog!"

Professor chuckled. "And Blackie segundo?"

"Hell's fire, I wouldn't care who was segundo if I could ride for Scott and me a regular hand, you know, instead of horse wrangler. Do you reckon he would hire me on for a regular hand? I'll be seventeen come next spring."

"Yes, Kid," the Professor said slowly, "I expect he would. I'm sure he will." He was letting the mules pick their way while he watched the two riders of whom they spoke. He could feel that the youngster was wishing that he had come along horseback so he could be riding with Scott and Blackie.

When Professor had first noticed the two riders he had felt a ridiculous pang of pity for the big dumb man. Now, musing, placing the Kid out there behind them in his mind, he felt the pathos hanging over them all, even Scott, the man "who's really going places." The fool would boss cattle drives, was probably dreaming right now what big things he would do, what places he would go, now that he had gained his deserved status through work and stubborn ability. Would. In the future. Never understanding that he could hardly match for grandeur the events he had already been part of, the things he had already done in his young life. Would! They had just got through taking three thousand big wild animals out of the brush in south Texas and, wanting these animals to be at a certain place some nine hundred miles distant, had proceeded to make the wild brutes walk it, to the exact place they wished them to be.

So now, having done this little thing, they were really going places.

They were somewhat like the longhorns, men on a trail, with eyes trying to see over the horizon, confident, expecting, moving, poignantly capable, never seeing the trail itself as they trod it. And Scott was like a good lead steer, one who will move out, one who will plunge into a river or take in stride any obstacle that stands in his way of going. But to what Dodge or Ogallala? To what iron trail east?

He thought he could read the signs, the Professor did. The trail end had been pushed ever westward until there was little place for it to go. Decent women walked down the main street of old Abilene, talking about when it used to be a wild town. Tick inspectors in central Kansas were themselves as thick as ticks. The last of the free Indians were asking for, and sometimes getting, their rights. The northern ranges were becoming stocked. Blooded cattle, Hereford and even Angus, grazing where buffalo had grazed. Railheads pushing west in Texas.

Scott would boss drives, but he probably never dreamed how few. And it wasn't that he would have no place to go then. A good man is a good man. There are always places for a good man to go, but a trail that's gone is gone forever. God, the pity was that they couldn't appreciate the trail they were traveling. Old, as old as Kittredge or older, they would look back and then from the distance they would say something small: "Those were the days." Dandy was the only one who would tell it with vigor, but his account would be false, with too much gunsmoke, chasing outlaws, wild times. The others, without the vision of Moses to say, "In those days there were giants in the earth," would say something small and maybe make up harmless lies, trying to recall the faded trail.

The Professor imagined that he was far above them, so that he could see men and their unknown ends as men can see longhorns and the ends they cannot see. He saw the remuda and the cowboys; then he saw a wagon jolting along and himself holding drooping lines, sitting looking at the back ends of four mules. He was one of them and for a brief moment he pitied himself, but was suddenly graced with the tendency to laugh, which he did, having forgotten that the Kid sat on the spring seat beside him.

He laughed before he knew what the laugh was about— that he was there of his own free will, with the others on the trail because he wanted to be. Then a quite practical idea occurred to him: what if he learned to cook? A cook ought to be able to sneak along a spring seat like this one, and a few books under it, and maybe he would get a little more sleep than a regular trail hand. It would be a good deal with a man like Scott for trail boss.

"Kid," he said, "if I were to learn to cook, do you reckon Scott would hire me on as a wagon man? I'll be old enough and cranky enough by next spring."

Kid puzzled over it a while and dismissed it with a laugh. He took his French harp out of his pocket, beat the dust out of it against his leg, and began to play.

T*he Trail to Ogallala,* published in 1964, was Benjamin Capps's breakthrough book. His first novel, *Hanging at Comanche Wells,* had appeared two years earlier, an uneven work owing more to the formula Western than to the kind of novel that Capps truly aspired to write. *The Trail to Ogallala* achieved what the first novel did not: it mediated between the claims of the formula and the claims of historical fiction. It also won its author two awards: the Spur Award of the Western Writers of America and the Levi Strauss Golden Saddleman Award.

The Trail to Ogallala went through several ephemeral paperback printings and was invariably marketed as a formula shoot-'em-up. One edition shrilly announced on its cover: "NINE HUNDRED MILES OF TERROR—STAMPEDE." The sort of reader at whom this was aimed—I see him on a Greyhound from Lordsburg to Yuma—would look for stampedes and he would find them, all right, but he would also find a much quieter, more thoughtful book than he might have reckoned on. It is here, in the transformation of the predictable materials of pulp fiction, that Capps excels. The result is a serious and authentic (and yes, entertaining) novel.

Capps's careful mediation between formulaic expectations and realistic portrayal is evident in all phases of the novel. We receive both a sense of the cowboys' immediacy, their unanalytical involvement in a heroic undertaking, and at the same time a perspective above and superior to the cowboys' limited field of vision. By means of interior monologue Capps dramatizes this double perspective. One of the cowboys, the Professor, is a man of books. He has read, for example, *Moby Dick,* and in a wonderful passage near the beginning of the novel, as the cattle graze before him, the Professor works out correspondences between driving cattle and hunting whales. He concludes that Ishmael had it easy: "And note, Ishmael, no blubber. It's all horn and rawhide, lean muscle, sinew, bone. No, you soft fellows can go whaling, Ishmael, but we who are tough, who love hard work and hard life. . . ." Near the end of the drive the Professor muses upon the grand adventure and compares the cowboys to the longhorns: ". . . with eyes trying to see over the horizon, confident, expecting, moving, poignantly capable, never seeing the trail itself as they trod it." Even the best of the cowboys, the trail boss Billy Scott, does not understand that "he could hardly snatch for grandeur the events he had already been part of, the things he had already done in his young life." By giving us the long view, Capps provides a convincing sense of historical depth missing from the formula powderburners.

In another sense, too, Capps's novel displays an ironic awareness of the requirements of pulp Westerns. After the drive is over, the cowboys remember their epic experience, but none can accurately tell of the meaning of those days. Only one cowboy, Dandy, a flamboyant dresser and ladies' man, is capable of telling the story "with vigor," but "his account would be false, with too much gunsmoke, chasing outlaws, wild times." Dandy's lurid version is the stuff of the formula Western, a version of the West that Capps explicitly rejects.

Instead Capps focuses the scattered energies of the typical trail-drive narrative into a serious inquiry into a major issue—the nature of leadership. He thereby makes central to his novel the question of the kind of leadership required to move three thousand head of cattle under the most trying conditions to a place nine hundred or more miles away, and by a prescribed date. In most trail narratives the conflict is invariably external: the group versus a series of threats from natural forces such as waterless expanses, swollen rivers, extreme weather conditions, or from external "savage" forces such as Indians or outlaws. Each of these except outlaws appears in Capps's novel, but the real conflict shifts from the group versus external difficulties to internal difficulties within the group (rival leaders) to, finally and most interestingly, psychological and ethical conflicts in the mind of the hero.

Unfairly deprived of his first job as trail boss, Billy Scott spends over half of the journey aggrieved by a sense of injured merit. The ongoing conflict appears to be between him and the usurper, Colonel Kittredge, appointed by the dead owner's widow to command the drive. Silently Scott measures the Colonel's performance against what he himself would have done, and comes in time to appreciate the Colonel's knowledge if not the austerity of his manner. Then in the first stampede the old man is killed, and the leadership falls to the segundo, Blackie, a useful cowboy if governed properly but a completely incompetent leader. Scott and the other cowboys chafe under the mistakes made by Blackie and fear his constant physical threats, which are the only source of his power. Blackie is simply too stupid to meet even the minimum requirements, such as keeping to a northerly direction, and is totally unequipped to plan strategies or provide authority for the cowboys. So Scott thinks that now the conflict is with Blackie, and in a fistfight with the giant segundo, Scott, abandoning reason and coolness for the first time in the journey, knows instantly that he has been foolish. The beating he receives confirms this impression.

Scott's problem is difficult, but in a formula Western the answer would be simple: Shoot the villain! Cory, one of Scott's friends on the drive and a hot-tempered man, urges Scott to do exactly that. But Scott must perform a more difficult task; he must deliver the herd on time while letting Blackie preside as nominal leader; he must use Blackie's physical skills because he can't afford to lose another cowboy, no matter how troublesome. Challenged by Cory as to why he won't deal with Blackie with force, Scott carefully explains his reasons:

> . . . I'm no more of a gunfighter than he is. But regardless of who gets shot, the outfit has either got a dead man to bury or a wounded man to take care of, and then the outfit has still got the same job ahead of it, only it's one more man short. The plain fact is that we can't make the contract now without Blackie.

He goes on to add that he's "taking the herd away from him—the hard way. . . ." Such a way, by reason, by the use of the intellect, is rarely what we find in pulp fiction; there the solution is nearly always the gun, the duel.

Scott's way prevails, the herd gets to Ogallala on time,

and Blackie, like the owners, recognizes Scott's quiet, irresistible authority. Yet Capps is still working clearly within the mold of traditional conceptions of the Western hero, even though Scott does not resort to the gun as the final arbiter of his and the nation's destiny. For Scott, like the traditional Western hero, is "one man alone." Only with a difference: he relies upon his brains and a consciousness able to plumb the ethical considerations of the original promise he made to Lawson, the late owner, to deliver the herd to Ogallala. Nothing that happens afterward—the unfair decision by Lawson's widow to appoint Colonel Kittredge trail boss instead of Scott, the indignity of having to serve as an anonymous cowboy under the incompetent segundo Blackie—cancels the pledge to Lawson. So Scott, coming to terms with that responsibility, acts heroically but without resorting to blazing sixguns.

The Trail to Ogallala, then, is a triumph of quiet artistry over the predictable demands of trail-drive formula fiction, demands so predictable that from Emerson Hough's *North of 36* (1923) to Borden Chase's *Red River* (1948), writers and moviemakers felt obliged to introduce a romantic heroine when the audience grew restive in the face of one more flood, one more stampede. Like Andy Adams before him, Capps sticks to the task at hand, getting the herd to trail's end without benefit of a cooked-up romance.

One famous reader who appreciated Capps's accomplishment was J. Frank Dobie. Dobie annotated his copy of the novel with care and spotted Capps's indebtedness to Adams's *The Log of a Cowboy* and to his own *The Longhorns.* Dobie especially liked the air of authenticity created in *The Trail to Ogallala,* a quality he usually found lacking in most popular Western fiction. Dobie was right—Capps passes the test of authenticity—but as I have suggested, he also passes a higher test—that of the imaginative requirements of good fiction.

Don Graham
University of Texas at Austin

Center Point Publishing
600 Brooks Road • PO Box 1
Thorndike ME 04986-0001 USA

(207) 568-3717

US & Canada:
1 800 929-9108